THE MONTANA STORIES

Persephone Book N° 25
Published by Persephone Books Ltd 2001

Reprinted 2007 and 2014

The Montana Stories are taken from *The Sphere* for 1921; and from *The Garden Party* (1922), *The Doves' Nest* (1923), *Journal of Katherine Mansfield* (1927), *The Letters of Katherine Mansfield* (1928) all published by Constable

Notes and Commentary © Persephone Books
Drawings © The Estate of W. Smithson Broadhead

Endpapers taken from 'Stems and looping tendrils with harebells' –
roller-printed cotton designed by Constance Irving for William Foxton
in 1921, reproduced by courtesy of the Trustees of the Victoria and
Albert Museum, London

Typeset in ITC Baskerville by Keystroke,
Wolverhampton

Colour by Banbury Litho

Printed and bound in Germany by
GGP Media GmbH, Pöessneck

ISBN: 978-1-903155-15-8

Persephone Books Ltd
59 Lamb's Conduit Street
London WCIN 3NB
020 7242 9292

www. persephonebooks.co.uk

THE MONTANA STORIES

by

KATHERINE MANSFIELD

PERSEPHONE BOOKS
LONDON

Montana-Vermala en hiver — Chalet des Sapins (alt. 1500 m)

2070 Edit. H. Ruedi, Phot. Montana

Photograph 1913 © T & H Deprez, Crans-Montana

PUBLISHER'S NOTE

At the end of May 1921 Katherine Mansfield, aged 32 and seriously ill with tuberculosis, left the south of France for Switzerland. With her companion Ida Baker she stayed first at Montreux and then went up the Rhône valley to a hotel in Sierre, in order to consult an English doctor. She refused to enter a sanatorium, preferring his offer of a chalet that belonged to his mother, high up above Sierre at a village known as Montana-sur-Sierre (and nowadays as Montana-Crans); set among pine trees, the chalet looked south down to Sierre and across over the valley to the snow-capped peaks beyond. She moved to the Chalet des Sapins towards the end of June, once her husband, John Middleton Murry, had arrived from England. Katherine's room, which had a large square balcony, was on the top floor, and it was here she spent the next seven months, the most fruitful period of her life. After she left Montana she wrote three more short stories; then nothing. She died a year later.

In this new collection everything Katherine Mansfield wrote in Montana, both completed stories and uncompleted fragments, together with quotations from her letters, has been gathered in one volume. It presents her work chronologically, so that the reader is able to see, month by month, how a writer of genius who knew, in her heart, that she had little time to live, forced herself on during these extraordinarily creative and productive few months. 'The surface of these stories is calm and even bright,' wrote her biographer, Claire Tomalin, 'but their theme is mortality, and even the joy in them is like Keats' joy, "whose hand is ever at his lips / Bidding adieu"; and it is this precariousness which gives them their stinging clarity.' Apart from Keats, the closest parallel is in music – the last pieces for piano written by Schubert.

Katherine Mansfield was born in 1888 in New Zealand, the daughter of a banker, but was sent to board in England at Queen's College, Harley Street, from the age of fourteen to seventeen. After a brief stay back in New Zealand she returned to London in 1908, became part of a progressive and liberated literary and artistic set and soon began to write poems and short stories, principally for small literary magazines such as *New Age* and *Rhythm*. She had an eventful and difficult personal life, involving an affair and pregnancy, a face-saving marriage to another man, a miscarriage, another affair with a Polish writer (who may have given her gonorrhea at the age of 21), and then a decade of penurious *de facto* marriage to the writer and editor, John Middleton Murry.

She and Murry became two of D.H.Lawrence's closest friends, at one point sharing a cottage with him and Frieda Lawrence in Cornwall. Katherine was a more distant friend of Virginia Woolf's, whom she influenced and who wrote on hearing of her death in 1923: 'When I began to write, it seemed to me there was no point in writing. Katherine won't read it, Katherine's my rival no longer.'

In 1918 she was diagnosed as having tuberculosis (possibly caught from Lawrence), and was finally divorced from her first husband and able to marry Middleton Murry. Initially she sought a cure in the warmth of the French and Italian Rivieras. And then, like so many famous consumptives, she chose to go to Switzerland for the clear, dry air and the beauty of the mountains.

Here 'M. and I live like two small timetables. We work all the morning and from tea to supper. After supper we read aloud and smoke; in the afternoon he goes walking and I crawling.' The chalet was 'so high up (5000 feet above the sea) that a cool breeze filters through from Heaven, and the forests are always airy. . . . the windows look over the tree tops across a valley to snowy peaks the other side.' By mid-September she had completed 'At the Bay' and in October 'The Garden-Party'. She wrote in her journal in November: 'I consider this enforced confinement here as God-given. But, on the other hand, I must make the most of it quickly.'

Yet as winter approached her period of remission gave way to fevers and new pain. Some of her stories were unfinished because she felt she had to turn to magazine stories to pay for more medical treatment. On 30 January 1922 she left the Chalet des Sapins for Paris, where she was to have X-ray treatment. Here she wrote her last major story, 'The Fly'. She was to die in France nearly a year later, on 9 January 1923.

For several reasons publishing her work as 'the Montana stories' is unlikely to have been how Katherine Mansfield herself would have wanted it to be read. Few short story writers arrange their work chronologically, preferring to intersperse moods and themes. Six of the first stories, written for the rather middlebrow *Sphere* magazine in order to pay for medical treatment, were accompanied by drawings she disliked – but their idiom must have accompanied her imaginatively, and the illustrator's versions of the story been to some extent anticipated by her, making it interesting for us to see them for the first time since their publication in 1921. Nor would Katherine have wanted fragments included – yet these unfinished pages can give just as much insight into her mind as a fully completed and polished story (rather as a block of stone left unfinished by a sculptor can convey something of what he might have achieved). Finally, she would certainly have done some editing, both of her prose and to take into account the ordering: to take one tiny example, she would have been mortified that the second and third stories both begin with the words 'of course'.

However, this method of setting out Katherine Mansfield's work gives a true and touching insight into her mind, especially when accompanied by the extracts from her letters and journal reprinted at the end of this volume. She berates herself often for her laziness and is critical of what she writes; yet she produced some of the greatest literature of the twentieth century and her output was large – these stories total about 80,000 words, the length of a novel, a great achievement for someone feverish and in pain. Overall, Katherine Mansfield might have liked the human, frightened, heartfelt person who emerges from the letters, from the journal – and from the stories themselves.

THE MONTANA STORIES

THE MONTANA STORIES

THE SPHERE

August 6, 1921

"...Dicky had suddenly seized the bread plate, but it upside down on his head, and clutched the bread knife."

Drawn by W. Smithson Broadhead

The Sphere 6 August 1921 p144

SIXPENCE

Children are unaccountable little creatures. Why should a small boy like Dicky, good as gold as a rule, sensitive, affectionate, obedient, and marvellously sensible for his age, have moods when, without the slightest warning, he suddenly went 'mad dog', as his sisters called it, and there was no doing anything with him?

'Dicky, come here! Come here, sir, at once! Do you hear your mother calling you? Dicky!'

But Dicky wouldn't come. Oh, he heard right enough. A clear, ringing little laugh was his only reply. And away he flew; hiding, running through the uncut hay on the lawn, dashing past the woodshed, making a rush for the kitchen garden, and there dodging, peering at his mother from behind the mossy apple trunks, and leaping up and down like a wild Indian.

It had begun at tea-time. While Dicky's mother and Mrs. Spears, who was spending the afternoon with her, were quietly sitting over their sewing in the drawing-room, this, according to the servant girl, was what had happened at the children's tea. They were eating their first bread and butter as nicely and quietly as you please, and the servant girl had just poured out the milk and water, when Dicky had suddenly seized the bread plate, put it upside down on his head, and clutched the bread knife.

'Look at me!' he shouted.

His startled sisters looked, and before the servant girl could get there, the bread plate wobbled, slid, flew to the floor, and broke into shivers. At this awful point the little girls lifted up their voices and shrieked their loudest.

'Mother, come and look what he's done!'

'Dicky's broke a great big plate!'

'Come and stop him, mother!'

You can imagine how mother came flying. But she was too late. Dicky had leapt out of his chair, run through the french windows on to the verandah, and, well – there she stood – popping her thimble on and off, helpless. What could she do? She couldn't chase after the child. She couldn't stalk Dicky among the apples and damsons. That would be too undignified. It was more than annoying, it was exasperating. Especially as Mrs. Spears, Mrs. Spears of all people, whose two boys were so exemplary, was waiting for her in the drawing-room.

'Very well, Dicky,' she cried, 'I shall have to think of some way of punishing you.'

'I don't care,' sounded the high little voice, and again there came that ringing laugh. The child was quite beside himself. . . .

'Oh, Mrs. Spears, I don't know how to apologise for leaving you by yourself like this.'

'It's quite all right, Mrs. Bendall,' said Mrs. Spears, in her soft, sugary voice, and raising her eyebrows in the way she had. She seemed to smile to herself as she stroked the gathers. 'These little things will happen from time to time. I only hope it was nothing serious.'

'It was Dicky,' said Mrs. Bendall, looking rather helplessly for her only fine needle. And she explained the whole affair to Mrs. Spears. 'And the worst of it is, I don't know how to cure him. Nothing when he's in that mood seems to have the slightest effect on him.'

Mrs. Spears opened her pale eyes. 'Not even a whipping?' said she.

But Mrs. Bendall, threading her needle, pursed up her lips. 'We never have whipped the children,' she said. 'The girls never seem to have needed it. And Dicky is such a baby, and the only boy. Somehow . . .'

'Oh, my dear,' said Mrs. Spears, and she laid her sewing down. 'I don't wonder Dicky has these little outbreaks. You don't mind my saying so? But I'm sure you make a great mistake in trying to bring up children without whipping them. Nothing really takes its place. And I speak from experience, my dear. I used to try gentler measures' – Mrs. Spears drew in her breath with a little hissing sound – 'soaping the boys' tongues, for instance, with yellow soap, or making them stand on the table for the whole of Saturday afternoon. But no, believe me,' said Mrs. Spears, 'there is nothing, there is nothing like handing them over to their father.'

Mrs. Bendall in her heart of hearts was dreadfully shocked to hear of that yellow soap. But Mrs. Spears seemed to take it so much for granted, that she did too.

'Their father,' she said. 'Then you don't whip them yourself?'

'Never.' Mrs. Spears seemed quite shocked at the idea. 'I don't think it's the mother's place to whip the children. It's the duty of the father. And, besides, he impresses them so much more.'

'Yes, I can imagine that,' said Mrs. Bendall faintly.

'Now my two boys,' Mrs. Spears smiled kindly, encouragingly, at Mrs. Bendall, 'would behave just like Dicky if they were not afraid to. As it is. . . .'

'Oh, your boys are perfect little models,' cried Mrs. Bendall.

They were. Quieter, better-behaved little boys, in the presence of grown-ups, could not be found. In fact, Mrs. Spears' callers often made the remark that you never would have known that there was a child in the house. There wasn't – very often.

In the front hall, under a large picture of fat, cheery old monks fishing by the riverside, there was a thick, dark horsewhip that had belonged to Mr. Spears' father. And for some reason the boys preferred to play out of sight of this, behind the dog-kennel or in the tool-house, or round about the dustbin.

'It's such a mistake,' sighed Mrs. Spears, breathing softly, as she folded her work, 'to be weak with children when they are little. It's such a sad mistake, and one so easy to make. It's so unfair to the child. That is what one has to remember. Now Dicky's little escapade this afternoon seemed to me as though he'd done it on purpose. It was the child's way of showing you that he needed a whipping.'

'Do you really think so?' Mrs. Bendall was a weak little thing, and this impressed her very much.

'I do; I feel sure of it. And a sharp reminder now and then,' cried Mrs. Spears in quite a professional manner, 'administered by the father, will save you so much trouble in the future. Believe me, my dear.' She put her dry, cold hand over Mrs. Bendall's.

'I shall speak to Edward the moment he comes in,' said Dicky's mother firmly.

The children had gone to bed before the garden gate banged, and Dicky's father staggered up the steep concrete steps carrying his bicycle. It had been a bad day at the office. He was hot, dusty, tired out.

But by this time Mrs. Bendall had become quite excited over the new plan, and she opened the door to him herself.

'Oh, Edward, I'm so thankful you have come home,' she cried.

'Why, what's happened?' Edward lowered the bicycle and took off his hat. A red angry pucker showed where the brim had pressed. 'What's up?'

'Come – come into the drawing-room,' said Mrs. Bendall, speaking very fast. 'I simply can't tell you how naughty Dicky has been. You have no idea – you can't have at the office all day – how a child of that age can behave. He's been simply dreadful. I have no control over him – none. I've tried everything, Edward, but it's all no use. The only thing to do,' she finished breathlessly, 'is to whip him – is for you to whip him, Edward.'

In the corner of the drawing-room there was a what-not, and on the top shelf stood a brown china bear with a painted tongue. It seemed in the shadow to be grinning at Dicky's father, to be saying, 'Hooray, this is what you've come home to!'

'But why on earth should I start whipping him?' said Edward, staring at the bear. 'We've never done it before.'

'Because,' said his wife, 'don't you see, it's the only thing to do. I can't control the child. . . .' Her words flew from her lips. They beat round him, beat round his tired head. 'We can't possibly afford a nurse. The servant girl has more than enough to do. And his naughtiness is beyond words. You don't understand, Edward; you can't, you're at the office all day.'

The bear poked out his tongue. The scolding voice went on. Edward sank into a chair.

'What am I to beat him with?' he said weakly.

'Your slipper, of course,' said his wife. And she knelt down to untie his dusty shoes.

'Oh, Edward,' she wailed, 'you've still got your cycling clips on in the drawing-room. No, really –'

'Here, that's enough.' Edward nearly pushed her away. 'Give me that slipper.' He went up the stairs. He felt like a man in a dark net. And now he wanted to beat Dicky. Yes, damn it, he wanted to beat something. My God, what a life! The dust was still in his hot eyes, his arms felt heavy.

He pushed open the door of Dicky's slip of a room. Dicky was standing in the middle of the floor in his night-shirt. At the sight of him Edward's heart gave a warm throb of rage.

'Well, Dicky, you know what I've come for,' said Edward.

Dicky made no reply.

'I've come to give you a whipping.'

No answer.

'Lift up your night-shirt.'

At that Dicky looked up. He flushed a deep pink. 'Must I?' he whispered.

'Come on, now. Be quick about it,' said Edward, and, grasping the slipper, he gave Dicky three hard slaps.

'There, that'll teach you to behave properly to your mother.'

Dicky stood there, hanging his head.

'Look sharp and get into bed,' said his father.

Still he did not move. But a shaking voice said, 'I've not done my teeth yet, Daddy.'

'Eh, what's that?'

Dicky looked up. His lips were quivering, but his eyes were dry. He hadn't made a sound or shed a tear. Only he swallowed and said, huskily, 'I haven't done my teeth, Daddy.'

But at the sight of that little face Edward turned, and, not knowing what he was doing, he bolted from the room, down the stairs, and out into the garden. Good God! What had he done? He strode along and hid in the shadow of the pear tree by the hedge. Whipped Dicky – whipped his little man with a slipper – and what the devil for? He didn't even know. Suddenly he barged into his room – and there was the little chap in his night-shirt. Dicky's father groaned and held on to the hedge. And he didn't cry. Never a tear. If only he'd cried or got angry. But that 'Daddy'! And again he heard the quivering whisper. Forgiving like that without a word. But he'd never forgive himself – never. Coward! Fool! Brute! And suddenly he remembered the time when Dicky had fallen off his knee and sprained his wrist while they were playing together. He hadn't cried then, either. And that was the little hero he had just whipped.

Something's got to be done about this, thought Edward. He strode back to the house, up the stairs, into Dicky's room. The little boy was lying in bed. In the half light his dark head, with the square fringe, showed plain against the pale pillow. He was lying quite still, and even now he wasn't crying. Edward shut the door and leaned against it. What he wanted to do was to kneel down by Dicky's bed and cry himself and beg to be forgiven. But, of course, one can't do that sort of thing. He felt awkward, and his heart was wrung.

'Not asleep yet, Dicky?' he said lightly.

'No, Daddy.'

Edward came over and sat on his boy's bed, and Dicky looked at him through his long lashes.

'Nothing the matter, little chap, is there?' said Edward, half whispering.

'No-o, Daddy,' came from Dicky.

Edward put out his hand, and carefully he took Dicky's hot little paw.

'You – you mustn't think any more of what happened just now, little man,' he said huskily. 'See? That's all over now. That's forgotten. That's never going to happen again. See?'

'Yes, Daddy.'

'So the thing to do now is to buck up, little chap,' said Edward, 'and to smile.' And he tried himself an extraordinary trembling apology for a smile. 'To forget all about it – to – eh? Little man. . . . Old boy. . . .'

Drawn by W. Smithson Broadhead

"*Edward came over and sat down on his boy's bed, and Dicky looked at him through his long lashes*"

The Sphere 6 August 1921 pii (supp.)

Dicky lay as before. This was terrible. Dicky's father sprang up and went over to the window. It was nearly dark in the garden. The servant girl had run out, and she was snatching, twitching some white cloths off the bushes and piling them over her arm. But in the boundless sky the evening star shone, and a big gum tree, black against the pale glow, moved its long leaves softly. All this he saw, while he felt in his trouser pocket for his money. Bringing it out, he chose a new sixpence and went back to Dicky.

'Here you are, little chap. Buy yourself something,' said Edward softly, laying the sixpence on Dicky's pillow.

But could even that – could even a whole sixpence – blot out what had been?

MR. AND MRS. DOVE

Of course he knew – no man better – that he hadn't a ghost
of a chance, he hadn't an earthly. The very idea of such a
thing was preposterous. So preposterous that he'd perfectly
understand it if her father – well, whatever her father chose
to do he'd perfectly understand. In fact, nothing short of
desperation, nothing short of the fact that this was positively
his last day in England for God knows how long, would have
screwed him up to it. And even now. . . . He chose a tie out
of the chest of drawers, a blue and cream check tie, and sat
on the side of his bed. Supposing she replied, 'What imper-
tinence!' would he be surprised? Not in the least, he decided,
turning up his soft collar and turning it down over the tie.
He expected her to say something like that. He didn't see,
if he looked at the affair dead soberly, what else she could
say.

Here he was! And nervously he tied a bow in front of the
mirror, jammed his hair down with both hands, pulled out
the flaps of his jacket pockets. Making between £500 and
£600 a year on a fruit farm in – of all places – Rhodesia. No
capital. Not a penny coming to him. No chance of his income
increasing for at least four years. As for looks and all that sort

of thing, he was completely out of the running. He couldn't even boast of top-hole health, for the East Africa business had knocked him out so thoroughly that he'd had to take six months' leave. He was still fearfully pale – worse even than usual this afternoon, he thought, bending forward and peering into the mirror. Good heavens! What had happened? His hair looked almost bright green. Dash it all, he hadn't green hair at all events. That was a bit too steep. And then the green light trembled in the glass; it was the shadow from the tree outside. Reggie turned away, took out his cigarette case, but remembering how the mater hated him to smoke in his bedroom, put it back again and drifted over to the chest of drawers. No, he was dashed if he could think of one blessed thing in his favour, while she. . . . Ah! . . . He stopped dead, folded his arms, and leaned hard against the chest of drawers.

And in spite of her position, her father's wealth, the fact that she was an only child and far and away the most popular girl in the neighbourhood; in spite of her beauty and her cleverness – cleverness! – it was a great deal more than that, there was really nothing she couldn't do; he fully believed, had it been necessary, she would have been a genius at anything – in spite of the fact that her parents adored her, and she them, and they'd as soon let her go all that way as . . . . In spite of every single thing you could think of, so terrific was his love that he couldn't help hoping. Well, was it hope? Or was this queer, timid longing to have the chance of looking after her, of making it his job to see that she had everything she wanted, and that nothing came near her that wasn't perfect – just love? How he loved her! He squeezed hard against the chest of drawers and murmured to it, 'I love her, I love her!' And just for the moment he was with her on the way to Umtali. It was night. She sat in a corner asleep. Her soft chin was tucked into her soft collar, her gold-brown lashes lay on her cheeks. He doted on her delicate little nose, her perfect lips, her ear like a baby's, and the gold-brown curl that half covered it. They were passing through the jungle. It was warm and dark and far away. Then she woke up and said, 'Have I been asleep?' and he answered, 'Yes. Are you all right? Here, let me –' And he leaned forward to. . . . He bent over her. This was such bliss that he could dream no further. But it gave him the courage to bound downstairs, to snatch his straw hat from the hall, and to say as he closed the front door, 'Well, I can only try my luck, that's all.'

But his luck gave him a nasty jar, to say the least, almost immediately. Promenading up and down the garden path with Chinny and Biddy, the ancient Pekes, was the mater. Of course Reginald was fond of the mater and all that. She – she meant well, she had no end of grit, and so on. But there was no denying it, she was rather a grim parent. And there had been moments, many of them, in Reggie's life, before Uncle Alick died and left him the fruit farm, when he was convinced that to be a widow's only son was about the worst punishment a chap could have. And what made it rougher than ever was that she was positively all that he had. She wasn't only a combined parent, as it were, but she had quarrelled with all her own and the governor's relations before Reggie had won his first trouser pockets. So that whenever Reggie was homesick out there, sitting on his dark verandah by starlight, while the gramophone cried, 'Dear, what is Life but Love?' his only vision was of the mater, tall and stout, rustling down the garden path, with Chinny and Biddy at her heels. . . .

The mater, with her scissors outspread to snap the head of a dead something or other, stopped at the sight of Reggie.

'You are not going out, Reginald?' she asked, seeing that he was.

'I'll be back for tea, mater,' said Reggie weakly, plunging his hands into his jacket pockets.

Snip. Off came a head. Reggie almost jumped.

'I should have thought you could have spared your mother your last afternoon,' said she.

Silence. The Pekes stared. They understood every word of the mater's. Biddy lay down with her tongue poked out; she was so fat and glossy she looked like a lump of half-melted toffee. But Chinny's porcelain eyes gloomed at Reginald, and he sniffed faintly, as though the whole world were one unpleasant smell. Snip, went the scissors again. Poor little beggars; they were getting it!

'And where are you going, if your mother may ask?' asked the mater.

It was over at last, but Reggie did not slow down until he was out of sight of the house and half-way to Colonel Proctor's. Then only he noticed what a top-hole afternoon it was. It had been raining all the morning, late summer rain, warm, heavy, quick, and now the sky was clear, except for a long tail of little clouds, like duckings, sailing over the forest. There was just enough wind to shake the last drops off the trees; one warm star splashed on his hand. Ping! – another drummed on his hat. The empty road gleamed, the hedges smelled of briar, and how big and bright the hollyhocks glowed in the cottage gardens. And here was Colonel Proctor's – here it was already. His hand was on the gate, his elbow jogged the syringa bushes, and petals and pollen scattered over his coat sleeve. But wait a bit. This was too quick altogether. He'd meant to think the whole thing out again. Here, steady. But he was walking up the path, with the huge rose bushes on either side. It can't be done like this. But his hand had grasped the bell, given it a pull, and started it pealing wildly, as if he'd come to say the house was on fire. The housemaid must have been in the hall, too, for the front door flashed open, and Reggie was shut in the empty drawing-room before that confounded bell had stopped ringing. Strangely enough, when it did, the big room, shadowy, with some one's parasol lying on top of the grand piano, bucked him up – or rather, excited him. It was so quiet, and yet in one moment the door would open, and his fate be decided. The feeling was not unlike that of being at the dentist's; he was almost reckless. But at the same time, to his immense surprise, Reggie heard himself saying, 'Lord, Thou knowest, Thou hast not done *much* for me. . . .' That pulled him up; that made him realise again how dead serious it was. Too late. The door handle turned. Anne came in, crossed the shadowy space between them, gave him her hand, and said, in her small, soft voice, 'I'm so sorry, father is out. And mother is having a day in town, hat-hunting. There's only me to entertain you, Reggie.'

Reggie gasped, pressed his own hat to his jacket buttons, and stammered out, 'As a matter of fact, I've only come . . . to say good-bye.'

'Oh!' cried Anne softly – she stepped back from him and her grey eyes danced – 'what a *very* short visit!'

Then, watching him, her chin tilted, she laughed outright, a long, soft peal, and walked away from him over to the piano, and leaned against it, playing with the tassel of the parasol.

'I'm so sorry,' she said, 'to be laughing like this. I don't know why I do. It's just a bad ha-habit.' And suddenly she stamped her grey shoe, and took a pocket-handkerchief out of her white woolly jacket. 'I really must conquer it, it's too absurd,' said she.

'Good heavens, Anne,' cried Reggie, 'I love to hear you laughing! I can't imagine anything more –'

But the truth was, and they both knew it, she wasn't always laughing; it wasn't really a habit. Only ever since the day they'd met, ever since that very first moment, for some strange reason that Reggie wished to God he understood, Anne had laughed at him. Why? It didn't matter where they were or what they were talking about. They might begin by being as serious as possible, dead serious – at any rate, as far as he was concerned – but then suddenly, in the middle of a sentence, Anne would glance at him, and a little quick quiver passed over her face. Her lips parted, her eyes danced, and she began laughing.

Another queer thing about it was, Reggie had an idea she didn't herself know why she laughed. He had seen her turn away, frown, suck in her cheeks, press her hands together.

But it was no use. The long, soft peal sounded, even while she cried, 'I don't know why I'm laughing.' It was a mystery. . . .

Now she tucked the handkerchief away. 'Do sit down,' said she. 'And smoke, won't you? There are cigarettes in that little box beside you. I'll have one too.' He lighted a match for her, and as she bent forward he saw the tiny flame glow in the pearl ring she wore. 'It is to-morrow that you're going, isn't it?' said Anne.

'Yes, to-morrow as ever was,' said Reggie, and he blew a little fan of smoke. Why on earth was he so nervous? Nervous wasn't the word for it.

'It's – it's frightfully hard to believe,' he added.

'Yes – isn't it?' said Anne softly, and she leaned forward and rolled the point of her cigarette round the green-ashtray. How beautiful she looked like that! – simply beautiful – and she was so small in that immense chair. Reginald's heart swelled with tenderness, but it was her voice, her soft voice, that made him tremble. 'I feel you've been here for years,' she said.

Reginald took a deep breath of his cigarette. 'It's ghastly, this idea of going back,' he said.

'*Coo-roo-coo-coo-coo*,' sounded from the quiet.

'But you're fond of being out there, aren't you?' said Anne. She hooked her finger through her pearl necklace. 'Father was saying only the other night how lucky he thought you were to have a life of your own.' And she looked up at him. Reginald's smile was rather wan. 'I don't feel fearfully lucky,' he said lightly.

'*Roo-coo-coo-coo*,' came again. And Anne murmured, 'You mean it's lonely.'

'Oh, it isn't the loneliness I care about,' said Reginald, and he stumped his cigarette savagely on the green ash-tray. 'I could stand any amount of it, used to like it even. It's the idea of –' Suddenly, to his horror, he felt himself blushing.

'*Roo-coo-coo-coo! Roo-coo-coo-coo!*'

Anne jumped up. 'Come and say good-bye to my doves,' she said. 'They've been moved to the side verandah. You do like doves, don't you, Reggie?'

'Awfully,' said Reggie, so fervently that as he opened the french window for her and stood to one side, Anne ran forward and laughed at the doves instead.

To and fro, to and fro over the fine red sand on the floor of the dove house, walked the two doves. One was always in front of the other. One ran forward, uttering a little cry, and the other followed, solemnly bowing and bowing. 'You see,' explained Anne, 'the one in front, she's Mrs. Dove. She looks at Mr. Dove and gives that little laugh and runs forward, and he follows her, bowing and bowing. And that makes her laugh again. Away she runs, and after her,' cried Anne, and she sat back on her heels, 'comes poor Mr. Dove, bowing and bowing . . . and that's their whole life. They never do anything else, you know.' She got up and took some yellow grains out of a bag on the roof of the dove house. 'When you think of them, out in Rhodesia, Reggie, you can be sure that is what they will be doing. . . .'

Reggie gave no sign of having seen the doves or of having heard a word. For the moment he was conscious only of the immense effort it took to tear his secret out of himself and offer it to Anne. 'Anne, do you think you could ever care for

THE SPHERE

" To and fro over the fine red sand on the floor of the dove house walked the two doves "

Drawn by W. Smithson Broadhead

The Sphere 13 August 1921 p172

me?' It was done. It was over. And in the little pause that followed Reginald saw the garden open to the light, the blue quivering sky, the flutter of leaves on the veranda poles, and Anne turning over the grains of maize on her palm with one finger. Then slowly she shut her hand, and the new world faded as she murmured slowly, 'No, never in that way.' But he had scarcely time to feel anything before she walked quickly away, and he followed her down the steps, along the garden path, under the pink rose arches, across the lawn. There, with the gay herbaceous border behind her, Anne faced Reginald. 'It isn't that I'm not awfully fond of you,' she said. 'I am. But' – her eyes widened – 'not in the way' – a quiver passed over her face – 'one ought to be fond of –' Her lips parted, and she couldn't stop herself. She began laughing. 'There, you see, you see,' she cried, 'it's your check t-tie. Even at this moment, when one would think one really would be solemn, your tie reminds me fearfully of the bow-tie that cats wear in pictures! Oh, please forgive me for being so horrid, please!'

Reggie caught hold of her little warm hand. 'There's no question of forgiving you,' he said quickly. 'How could there be? And I do believe I know why I make you laugh. It's because you're so far above me in every way that I am somehow ridiculous. I see that, Anne. But if I were to –'

'No, no.' Anne squeezed his hand hard. 'It's not that. That's all wrong. I'm not far above you at all. You're much better than I am. You're marvellously unselfish and . . . and kind and simple. I'm none of those things. You don't know me. I'm the most awful character,' said Anne. 'Please don't interrupt. And besides, that's not the point. The point is' – she shook her head – 'I couldn't possibly marry a man I laughed at. Surely you see that. The man I marry –' breathed Anne softly. She broke off. She drew her hand away, and looking at Reggie she smiled strangely, dreamily. 'The man I marry –'

And it seemed to Reggie that a tall, handsome, brilliant stranger stepped in front of him and took his place – the kind of man that Anne and he had seen often at the theatre, walking on to the stage from nowhere, without a word catching the heroine in his arms, and after one long, tremendous look, carrying her off to anywhere. . . .

Reggie bowed to his vision. 'Yes, I see,' he said huskily.

'Do you?' said Anne. 'Oh, I do hope you do. Because I feel so horrid about it. It's so hard to explain. You know I've never –' She stopped. Reggie looked at her. She was smiling. 'Isn't it funny?' she said. 'I can say anything to you. I always have been able to from the very beginning.'

He tried to smile, to say 'I'm glad.' She went on. 'I've never known any one I like as much as I like you. I've never felt so happy with any one. But I'm sure it's not what people and what books mean when they talk about love. Do you understand? Oh, if you only knew how horrid I feel. But we'd be like . . . like Mr. and Mrs. Dove.'

That did it. That seemed to Reginald final, and so terribly true that he could hardly bear it. 'Don't drive it home,' he said, and he turned away from Anne and looked across the lawn. There was the gardener's cottage, with the dark ilex-tree beside it. A wet, blue thumb of transparent smoke hung above the chimney. It didn't look real. How his throat ached!

Could he speak? He had a shot. 'I must be getting along home,' he croaked, and he began walking across the lawn. But Anne ran after him. 'No, don't. You can't go yet,' she said imploringly. 'You can't possibly go away feeling like that.' And she stared up at him frowning, biting her lip.

'Oh, that's all right,' said Reggie, giving himself a shake. 'I'll . . . I'll –' And he waved his hand as much as to say 'get over it'.

'But this is awful,' said Anne. She clasped her hands and stood in front of him. 'Surely you do see how fatal it would be for us to marry, don't you?'

'Oh, quite, quite,' said Reggie, looking at her with haggard eyes.

'How wrong, how wicked, feeling as I do. I mean, it's all very well for Mr. and Mrs. Dove. But imagine that in real life – imagine it!'

'Oh, absolutely,' said Reggie, and he started to walk on. But again Anne stopped him. She tugged at his sleeve, and to his astonishment, this time, instead of laughing, she looked like a little girl who was going to cry.

'Then why, if you understand, are you so un-unhappy?' she wailed. 'Why do you mind so fearfully? Why do you look so aw-awful?'

Reggie gulped, and again he waved something away. 'I can't help it,' he said, 'I've had a blow. If I cut off now, I'll be able to –'

'How can you talk of cutting off now?' said Anne scornfully. She stamped her foot at Reggie; she was crimson. 'How can you be so cruel? I can't let you go until I know for certain

Drawn by W. Smithson Broadhead
" She clasped her hands and stood in front of him "

The Sphere 13 August 1921 p173

that you are just as happy as you were before you asked me to marry you. Surely you must see that, it's so simple.'

But it did not seem at all simple to Reginald. It seemed impossibly difficult.

'Even if I can't marry you, how can I know that you're all that way away, with only that awful mother to write to, and that you're miserable, and that it's all my fault?'

'It's not your fault. Don't think that. It's just fate.' Reggie took her hand off his sleeve and kissed it. 'Don't pity me, dear little Anne,' he said gently. And this time he nearly ran, under the pink arches, along the garden path.

'*Roo-coo-coo-coo! Roo-coo-coo-coo!*' sounded from the verandah. 'Reggie, Reggie,' from the garden.

He stopped, he turned. But when she saw his timid, puzzled look, she gave a little laugh.

'Come back, Mr. Dove,' said Anne. And Reginald came slowly across the lawn.

SUSANNAH

Of course there would have been no question of their going to the exhibition if Father had not had the tickets given to him. Little girls cannot expect to be given treats that cost extra money when only to feed them, buy them clothes, pay for their lessons and the house they live in takes their kind generous Father all day and every day working hard from morning till night – 'except Saturday afternoons and Sundays,' said Susannah.

'Susannah!' Mother was very shocked. 'But do you know what would happen to your poor Father if he didn't have a holiday on Saturday afternoons and Sundays?'

'No,' said Susannah. She looked interested. 'What?'

'He would die,' said their Mother impressively.

'Would he?' said Susannah, opening her eyes. She seemed astounded, and Sylvia and Phyllis, who were four and five years older than she, chimed in with 'Of course,' in a very superior tone. What a little silly-billy she was not to know that! They sounded so convinced and cheerful that their Mother felt a little shaken and hastened to change the subject. . . .

'So that is why,' she said a little vaguely, 'you must each thank Father separately before you go.'

'And then will he give us the money?' asked Phyllis.

'And then I shall ask him for whatever is necessary,' said their mother firmly. She sighed suddenly and got up. 'Run along, children, and ask Miss Wade to dress you and get ready herself and then to come down to the dining-room. And now, Susannah, you are not to let go Miss Wade's hand from the moment you are through the gates until you are out again.'

'Well – what if I go on a horse ?' inquired Susannah.

'Go on a horse – nonsense, child! You're much too young for horses! Only big girls and boys can ride.'

'There're roosters for small children,' said Susannah undaunted. 'I know, because Irene Heywood went on one and when she got off she fell over.'

'All the more reason why you shouldn't go on,' said her mother.

But Susannah looked as though falling over had no terrors for her. On the contrary.

About the exhibition, however, Sylvia and Phyllis knew as little as Susannah. It was the first that had ever come to their town. One morning, as Miss Wade, their lady help, rushed them along to the Heywoods', whose governess they shared, they had seen carts piled with great long planks of wood, sacks, what looked like whole doors, and white flagstaffs, passing through the wide gate of the Recreation Ground. And by the time they were bowled home to their dinners, there were the beginnings of a high, thin fence, dotted with flagstaffs, built all round the railings. From inside came a tremendous noise of hammering, shouting, clanging; a little engine, hidden away, went *Chuff-chuff-chuff. Chuff!* And round, woolly balls of smoke were tossed over the palings.

First it was the day after the day after to-morrow, then plain day after to-morrow, then to-morrow, and at last, the day itself. When Susannah woke up in the morning there was a little gold spot of sunlight watching her from the wall; it looked as though it had been there for a long time, waiting to remind her: 'It's to-day – you're going to-day – this afternoon. Here she is!'

(Second Version)

That afternoon they were allowed to cut jugs and basins out of a draper's catalogue, and at tea-time they had real tea in the doll's tea-set on the table. This was a very nice treat indeed, except that the doll's teapot wouldn't pour out even after you'd poked a pin down the spout and blown into it.

But the next afternoon, which was Saturday, Father came home in high feather. The front door banged so hard that the whole house shook, and he shouted to Mother from the hall.

'Oh, how more than good of you, darling!' cried Mother, 'but how unnecessary too. Of course, they'll simply love it. But to have spent all that money! You shouldn't have done it, Daddy dear! They've totally forgotten all about it. And what is this! Half-a-crown?' cried Mother. 'No! Two shillings, I see,' she corrected quickly, 'to spend as well. Children! Children! Come down, downstairs!'

Down they came, Phyllis and Sylvia leading, Susannah holding on. 'Do you know what Father's done?' And Mother held up her hand. What was she holding? Three cherry tickets and a green one. 'He's bought you tickets. You're to go to the circus, this very afternoon, all of you, with Miss Wade. What do you say to that?'

'Oh, Mummy! Lovely! Lovely!' cried Phyllis and Sylvia.

'Isn't it?' said Mother. 'Run upstairs. Run and ask Miss Wade to get you ready. Don't dawdle. Up you go! All of you.'

Away flew Phyllis and Sylvia, but still Susannah stayed where she was at the bottom of the stairs, hanging her head.

'Go along,' said Mother. And Father said sharply, 'What the devil's the matter with the child?'

Susannah's face quivered. 'I don't want to go,' she whispered.

'What! Don't want to go to the Exhibition! After Father's – You naughty, ungrateful child! Either you go to the Exhibition, Susannah, or you will be packed off to bed at once.'

Susannah's head bent low, lower still. All her little body bent forward. She looked as though she was going to bow down, to bow down to the ground, before her kind generous Father and beg for his forgiveness. . . .

unfinished

AN IDEAL FAMILY

That evening for the first time in his life, as he pressed through the swing door and descended the three broad steps to the pavement, old Mr. Neave felt he was too old for the spring. Spring – warm, eager, restless – was there, waiting for him in the golden light, ready in front of everybody to run up, to blow in his white beard, to drag sweetly on his arm. And he couldn't meet her, no; he couldn't square up once more and stride off, jaunty as a young man. He was tired and, although the late sun was still shining, curiously cold, with a numbed feeling all over. Quite suddenly he hadn't the energy, he hadn't the heart to stand this gaiety and bright movement any longer; it confused him. He wanted to stand still, to wave it away with his stick, to say, 'Be off with you!' Suddenly it was a terrible effort to greet as usual – tipping his wide-awake with his stick – all the people whom he knew, the friends, acquaintances, shopkeepers, postmen, drivers. But the gay glance that went with the gesture, the kindly twinkle that seemed to say, 'I'm a match and more for any of you' – that old Mr. Neave could not manage at all. He stumped along, lifting his knees high as if he were walking through air that had somehow grown heavy and solid like water. And the homeward-going crowd hurried by, the trams clanked, the light carts clattered, the big swinging cabs bowled along with that reckless, defiant indifference that one knows only in dreams. . . .

It had been a day like other days at the office. Nothing special had happened. Harold hadn't come back from lunch until close on four. Where had he been? What had he been up to? He wasn't going to let his father know. Old Mr. Neave had happened to be in the vestibule, saying good-bye to a caller, when Harold sauntered in, perfectly turned out as usual, cool, suave, smiling that peculiar little half-smile that women found so fascinating.

Ah, Harold was too handsome, too handsome by far; that had been the trouble all along. No man had a right to such eyes, such lashes, and such lips; it was uncanny. As for his mother, his sisters, and the servants, it was not too much to say they made a young god of him; they worshipped Harold, they forgave him everything; and he had needed some forgiving ever since the time when he was thirteen and he had stolen his mother's purse, taken the money, and hidden the purse in the cook's bedroom. Old Mr. Neave struck sharply with his stick upon the pavement edge. But it wasn't only his family who spoiled Harold, he reflected, it was everybody; he had only to look and to smile, and down they went before him. So perhaps it wasn't to be wondered at that he expected the office to carry on the tradition. H'm, h'm! But it couldn't be done. No business – not even a successful, established, big paying concern – could be played with. A man had either to put his whole heart and soul into it, or it went all to pieces before his eyes . . . .

And then Charlotte and the girls were always at him to make the whole thing over to Harold, to retire, and to spend his time enjoying himself. Enjoying himself! Old Mr. Neave stopped dead under a group of ancient cabbage palms outside the Government buildings. Enjoying himself! The wind of evening shook the dark leaves to a thin airy cackle. Sitting at home, twiddling his thumbs, conscious all the while that his life's work was slipping away, dissolving, disappearing through Harold's fine fingers, while Harold smiled. . . .

'Why will you be so unreasonable, father? There's absolutely no need for you to go to the office. It only makes it very awkward for us when people persist in saying how tired you're looking. Here's this huge house and garden. Surely you could be happy in – in – appreciating it for a change. Or you could take up some hobby.'

And Lola the baby had chimed in loftily, 'All men ought to have hobbies. It makes life impossible if they haven't.'

Well, well! He couldn't help a grim smile as painfully he began to climb the hill that led into Harcourt Avenue. Where would Lola and her sisters and Charlotte be if he'd gone in for hobbies, he'd like to know? Hobbies couldn't pay for the town house and the seaside bungalow, and their horses, and their golf, and the sixty-guinea gramophone in the music-room for them to dance to. Not that he grudged them these things. No, they were smart, good-looking girls, and Charlotte was a remarkable woman; it was natural for them to be in the swim. As a matter of fact, no other house in the town was as popular as theirs; no other family entertained so much. And how many times old Mr. Neave, pushing the cigar box across the smoking-room table, had listened to praises of his wife, his girls, of himself even.

'You're an ideal family, sir, an ideal family. It's like something one reads about or sees on the stage.'

'That's all right, my boy,' old Mr. Neave would reply. 'Try one of those; I think you'll like them. And if you care to smoke in the garden, you'll find the girls on the lawn, I dare say.'

That was why the girls had never married, so people said. They could have married anybody. But they had too good a time at home. They were too happy together, the girls and Charlotte. H'm, h'm! Well, well! Perhaps so. . . .

By this time he had walked the length of fashionable Harcourt Avenue; he had reached the corner house, their house. The carriage gates were pushed back; there were fresh marks of wheels on the drive. And then he faced the big white-painted house, with its wide-open windows, its tulle curtains floating outwards, its blue jars of hyacinths on the broad sills. On either side of the carriage porch their hydrangeas – famous in the town – were coming into flower; the pinkish, bluish masses of flower lay like light among the spreading leaves. And somehow, it seemed to old Mr. Neave that the house and the flowers, and even the fresh marks on the drive, were saying, 'There is young life here. There are girls –'

The hall, as always, was dusky with wraps, parasols, gloves, piled on the oak chests. From the music-room sounded the piano, quick, loud and impatient. Through the drawing-room door that was ajar voices floated.

'And were there ices?' came out from Charlotte. Then the creak, creak of her rocker.

'Ices!' cried Ethel. 'My dear mother, you never saw such ices. Only two kinds. And one a common little strawberry shop ice, in a sopping wet frill.'

'The food altogether was too appalling,' came from Marion.

'Still, it's rather early for ices,' said Charlotte easily.

'But why, if one has them at all . . .' began Ethel.

'Oh, quite so, darling,' crooned Charlotte.

Suddenly the music-room door opened and Lola dashed out. She started, she nearly screamed, at the sight of old Mr. Neave.

'Gracious, father! What a fright you gave me! Have you just come home? Why isn't Charles here to help you off with your coat?'

Her cheeks were crimson from playing, her eyes glittered, the hair fell over her forehead. And she breathed as though she had come running through the dark and was frightened. Old Mr. Neave stared at his youngest daughter; he felt he had never seen her before. So that was Lola, was it? But she seemed to have forgotten her father; it was not for him that she was waiting there. Now she put the tip of her crumpled handkerchief between her teeth and tugged at it angrily. The telephone rang. A-ah! Lola gave a cry like a sob and dashed past him. The door of the telephone-room slammed, and at the same moment Charlotte called, 'Is that you, father?'

'You're tired again,' said Charlotte reproachfully, and she

stopped the rocker and offered him her warm plum-like cheek. Bright-haired Ethel pecked his beard; Marion's lips brushed his ear.

'Did you walk back, father?' asked Charlotte.

'Yes, I walked home,' said old Mr. Neave, and he sank into one of the immense drawing-room chairs.

'But why didn't you take a cab?' said Ethel. 'There are hundreds of cabs about at that time.'

'My dear Ethel,' cried Marion, 'if father prefers to tire himself out, I really don't see what business of ours it is to interfere.'

'Children, children!' coaxed Charlotte.

But Marion wouldn't be stopped. 'No, mother, you spoil father, and it's not right. You ought to be stricter with him. He's very naughty.' She laughed her hard, bright laugh and patted her hair in a mirror. Strange! When she was a little girl she had such a soft, hesitating voice; she had even stuttered, and now, whatever she said – even if it was only 'Jam, please, father' – it rang out as though she were on the stage.

'Did Harold leave the office before you, dear?' asked Charlotte, beginning to rock again.

'I'm not sure,' said old Mr. Neave. 'I'm not sure. I didn't see him after four o'clock.'

'He said –' began Charlotte.

But at that moment Ethel, who was twitching over the leaves of some paper or other, ran to her mother and sank down beside her chair.

'There, you see,' she cried. 'That's what I mean, mummy. Yellow, with touches of silver. Don't you agree?'

" She laughed her hard, bright laugh and
patted her hair in a mirror."

Drawn by W. Smithson Broadhead

The Sphere 20 August 1921 p196

'Give it to me, love,' said Charlotte. She fumbled for her tortoise-shell spectacles and put them on, gave the page a little dab with her plump small fingers, and pursed up her lips. 'Very sweet!' she crooned vaguely; she looked at Ethel over her spectacles. 'But I shouldn't have the train.'

'Not the train!' wailed Ethel tragically. 'But the train's the whole point.'

'Here, mother, let me decide.' Marion snatched the paper playfully from Charlotte. 'I agree with mother,' she cried triumphantly. 'The train overweights it.'

Old Mr. Neave, forgotten, sank into the broad lap of his chair, and, dozing, heard them as though he dreamed. There was no doubt about it, he was tired out; he had lost his hold. Even Charlotte and the girls were too much for him to-night. They were too . . . too. . . But all his drowsing brain could think of was – too *rich* for him. And somewhere at the back of everything he was watching a little withered ancient man climbing up endless flights of stairs. Who was he?

'I shan't dress to-night,' he muttered.

'What do you say, father?'

'Eh, what, what?' Old Mr. Neave woke with a start and stared across at them. 'I shan't dress to-night,' he repeated.

'But, father, we've got Lucile coming, and Henry Davenport, and Mrs. Teddie Walker.'

'It will look so *very* out of the picture.'

'Don't you feel well, dear?'

'You needn't make any effort. What is Charles *for*?'

'But if you're really not up to it,' Charlotte wavered.

'Very well! Very well!' Old Mr. Neave got up and went to

join that little old climbing fellow just as far as his dressing-room. . . .

There young Charles was waiting for him. Carefully, as though everything depended on it, he was tucking a towel round the hot-water can. Young Charles had been a favourite of his ever since as a little red-faced boy he had come into the house to look after the fires. Old Mr. Neave lowered himself into the cane lounge by the window, stretched out his legs, and made his little evening joke, 'Dress him up, Charles!' And Charles, breathing intensely and frowning, bent forward to take the pin out of his tie.

H'm, h'm! Well, well! It was pleasant by the open window, very pleasant – a fine mild evening. They were cutting the grass on the tennis court below; he heard the soft churr of the mower. Soon the girls would begin their tennis parties again. And at the thought he seemed to hear Marion's voice ring out, 'Good for you, partner. . . . Oh, *played*, partner. . . . Oh, *very* nice indeed.' Then Charlotte calling from the verandah, 'Where is Harold?' And Ethel, 'He's certainly not here, mother.' And Charlotte's vague, 'He said –'

Old Mr. Neave sighed, got up, and putting one hand under his beard, he took the comb from young Charles, and carefully combed the white beard over. Charles gave him a folded handkerchief, his watch and seals, and spectacle case.

'That will do, my lad.' The door shut, he sank back, he was alone. . . .

And now that little ancient fellow was climbing down endless flights that led to a glittering, gay dining-room. What legs he had! They were like a spider's – thin, withered.

'You're an ideal family, sir, an ideal family.'

But if that were true, why didn't Charlotte or the girls stop him? Why was he all alone, climbing up and down? Where was Harold? Ah, it was no good expecting anything from Harold. Down, down went the little old spider, and then, to his horror, old Mr. Neave saw him slip past the dining-room and make for the porch, the dark drive, the carriage gates, the office. Stop him, stop him, somebody!

Old Mr. Neave started up. It was dark in his dressing-room; the window shone pale. How long had he been asleep? He listened, and through the big, airy, darkened house there floated far-away voices, far-away sounds. Perhaps, he thought vaguely, he had been asleep for a long time. He'd been forgotten. What had all this to do with him – this house and Charlotte, the girls and Harold – what did he know about them? They were strangers to him. Life had passed him by. Charlotte was not his wife. His wife!

. . . A dark porch, half hidden by a passion-vine, that drooped sorrowful, mournful, as though it understood. Small, warm arms were round his neck. A face, little and pale, lifted to his, and a voice breathed, 'Good-bye, my treasure.'

My treasure! 'Good-bye, my treasure!' Which of them had spoken? Why had they said good-bye? There had been some terrible mistake. *She* was his wife, that little pale girl, and all the rest of his life had been a dream.

Then the door opened, and young Charles, standing in the light, put his hands by his side and shouted like a young soldier, 'Dinner is on the table, sir!'

'I'm coming, I'm coming,' said old Mr. Neave.

Drawn by W. Smithson Broadhead

"Mr. Neave lowered himself into the cane lounge by the window, stretched out his legs, and
made his little evening joke"

The Sphere 20 August 1921 p197

HER FIRST BALL

Exactly when the ball began Leila would have found it hard to say. Perhaps her first real partner was the cab. It did not matter that she shared the cab with the Sheridan girls and their brother. She sat back in her own little corner of it, and the bolster on which her hand rested felt like the sleeve of an unknown young man's dress suit; and away they bowled, past waltzing lamp-posts and houses and fences and trees.

'Have you really never been to a ball before, Leila? But, my child, how too weird –' cried the Sheridan girls.

'Our nearest neighbour was fifteen miles,' said Leila softly, gently opening and shutting her fan.

Oh, dear, how hard it was to be indifferent like the others! She tried not to smile too much; she tried not to care. But every single thing was so new and exciting . . . Meg's tuberoses, Jose's long loop of amber, Laura's little dark head, pushing above her white fur like a flower through snow. She would remember for ever. It even gave her a pang to see her cousin Laurie throw away the wisps of tissue paper he pulled from the fastenings of his new gloves. She would like to have kept those wisps as a keepsake, as a remembrance. Laurie leaned forward and put his hand on Laura's knee.

'Look here, darling,' he said. 'The third and the ninth as usual. Twig?'

Oh, how marvellous to have a brother! In her excitement Leila felt that if there had been time, if it hadn't been impossible, she couldn't have helped crying because she was an only child, and no brother had ever said 'Twig?' to her; no sister would ever say, as Meg said to Jose that moment, 'I've never known your hair go up more successfully than it has to-night!'

But, of course, there was no time. They were at the drill hall already; there were cabs in front of them and cabs behind. The road was bright on either side with moving fan-like lights, and on the pavement gay couples seemed to float through the air; little satin shoes chased each other like birds.

'Hold on to me, Leila; you'll get lost,' said Laura.

'Come on, girls, let's make a dash for it,' said Laurie.

Leila put two fingers on Laura's pink velvet cloak, and they were somehow lifted past the big golden lantern, carried along the passage, and pushed into the little room marked 'Ladies'. Here the crowd was so great there was hardly space to take off their things; the noise was deafening. Two benches on either side were stacked high with wraps. Two old women in white aprons ran up and down tossing fresh armfuls. And everybody was pressing forward trying to get at the little dressing-table and mirror at the far end.

A great quivering jet of gas lighted the ladies' room. It couldn't wait; it was dancing already. When the door opened again and there came a burst of tuning from the drill hall, it leaped almost to the ceiling.

Dark girls, fair girls were patting their hair, tying ribbons again, tucking handkerchiefs down the fronts of their bodices, smoothing marble-white gloves. And because they were all laughing it seemed to Leila that they were all lovely.

'Aren't there any invisible hair-pins?' cried a voice. 'How most extraordinary! I can't see a single invisible hair-pin.'

'Powder my back, there's a darling,' cried some one else.

'But I must have a needle and cotton. I've torn simply miles and miles of the frill,' wailed a third.

Then, 'Pass them along, pass them along!' The straw basket of programmes was tossed from arm to arm. Darling little pink-and-silver programmes, with pink pencils and fluffy tassels. Leila's fingers shook as she took one out of the basket. She wanted to ask some one, 'Am I meant to have one too?' but she had just time to read: 'Waltz 3. *Two, Two in a Canoe*. Polka 4. *Making the Feathers Fly*,' when Meg cried, 'Ready, Leila?' and they pressed their way through the crush in the passage towards the big double doors of the drill hall.

Dancing had not begun yet, but the band had stopped tuning, and the noise was so great it seemed that when it did begin to play it would never be heard. Leila, pressing close to Meg, looking over Meg's shoulder, felt that even the little quivering coloured flags strung across the ceiling were talking. She quite forgot to be shy; she forgot how in the middle of dressing she had sat down on the bed with one shoe off and one shoe on and begged her mother to ring up her cousins and say she couldn't go after all. And the rush of longing she had had to be sitting on the verandah of their forsaken up-country home, listening to the baby owls crying

'More pork' in the moonlight, was changed to a rush of joy so sweet that it was hard to bear alone. She clutched her fan, and, gazing at the gleaming, golden floor, the azaleas, the lanterns, the stage at one end with its red carpet and gilt chairs and the band in a corner, she thought breathlessly, 'How heavenly; how simply heavenly!'

All the girls stood grouped together at one side of the doors, the men at the other, and the chaperones in dark dresses, smiling rather foolishly, walked with little careful steps over the polished floor towards the stage.

'This is my little country cousin Leila. Be nice to her. Find her partners; she's under my wing,' said Meg, going up to one girl after another.

Strange faces smiled at Leila – sweetly, vaguely. Strange voices answered, 'Of course, my dear.' But Leila felt the girls didn't really see her. They were looking towards the men. Why didn't the men begin? What were they waiting for? There they stood, smoothing their gloves, patting their glossy hair and smiling among themselves. Then, quite suddenly, as if they had only just made up their minds that that was what they had to do, the men came gliding over the parquet. There was a joyful flutter among the girls. A tall, fair man flew up to Meg, seized her programme, scribbled something; Meg passed him on to Leila. 'May I have the pleasure?' He ducked and smiled. There came a dark man wearing an eyeglass, then cousin Laurie with a friend, and Laura with a little freckled fellow whose tie was crooked. Then quite an old man – fat, with a big bald patch on his head – took her programme and murmured, 'Let me see, let me see!' And he was a long time comparing his programme, which looked black with names, with hers. It seemed to give him so much trouble that Leila was ashamed. 'Oh, please don't bother,' she said eagerly. But instead of replying the fat man wrote something, glanced at her again. 'Do I remember this bright little face?' he said softly. 'Is it known to me of yore?' At that moment the band began playing; the fat man disappeared. He was tossed away on a great wave of music that came flying over the gleaming floor, breaking the groups up into couples, scattering them, sending them spinning. . . .

Leila had learned to dance at boarding school. Every Saturday afternoon the boarders were hurried off to a little corrugated iron mission hall where Miss Eccles (of London) held her 'select' classes. But the difference between that dusty-smelling hall – with calico texts on the walls, the poor terrified little woman in a brown velvet toque with rabbit's ears thumping the cold piano, Miss Eccles poking the girls' feet with her long white wand – and this was so tremendous that Leila was sure if her partner didn't come and she had to listen to that marvellous music and to watch the others sliding, gliding over the golden floor, she would die at least, or faint, or lift her arms and fly out of one of those dark windows that showed the stars.

'Ours, I think –' Some one bowed, smiled, and offered her his arm; she hadn't to die after all. Some one's hand pressed her waist, and she floated away like a flower that is tossed into a pool.

'Quite a good floor, isn't it?' drawled a faint voice close to her ear.

'I think it's most beautifully slippery,' said Leila.

'Pardon!' The faint voice sounded surprised. Leila said it again. And there was a tiny pause before the voice echoed, 'Oh, quite!' and she was swung round again.

He steered so beautifully. That was the great difference between dancing with girls and men, Leila decided. Girls banged into each other, and stamped on each other's feet; the girl who was gentleman always clutched you so.

The azaleas were separate flowers no longer; they were pink and white flags streaming by.

'Were you at the Bells' last week?' the voice came again. It sounded tired. Leila wondered whether she ought to ask him if he would like to stop.

'No, this is my first dance,' said she.

Her partner gave a little gasping laugh. 'Oh, I say,' he protested.

'Yes, it is really the first dance I've ever been to.' Leila was most fervent. It was such a relief to be able to tell somebody. 'You see, I've lived in the country all my life up till now. . . .'

At that moment the music stopped, and they went to sit on two chairs against the wall. Leila tucked her pink satin feet under and fanned herself, while she blissfully watched the other couples passing and disappearing through the swing doors.

'Enjoying yourself, Leila?' asked Jose, nodding her golden head.

Laura passed and gave her the faintest little wink; it made Leila wonder for a moment whether she was quite grown up after all. Certainly her partner did not say very much.

He coughed, tucked his handkerchief away, pulled down his waistcoat, took a minute thread off his sleeve. But it didn't matter. Almost immediately the band started, and her second partner seemed to spring from the ceiling.

'Floor's not bad,' said the new voice. Did one always begin with the floor? And then, 'Were you at the Neaves' on Tuesday?' And again Leila explained. Perhaps it was a little strange that her partners were not more interested. For it was thrilling. Her first ball! She was only at the beginning of everything. It seemed to her that she had never known what the night was like before. Up till now it had been dark, silent, beautiful very often – oh yes – but mournful somehow. Solemn. And now it would never be like that again – it had opened dazzling bright.

'Care for an ice?' said her partner. And they went through the swing doors, down the passage, to the supper room. Her cheeks burned, she was fearfully thirsty. How sweet the ices looked on little glass plates, and how cold the frosted spoon was, iced too! And when they came back to the hall there was the fat man waiting for her by the door. It gave her quite a shock again to see how old he was; he ought to have been on the stage with the fathers and mothers. And when Leila compared him with her other partners he looked shabby. His waistcoat was creased, there was a button off his glove, his coat looked as if it was dusty with French chalk.

'Come along, little lady,' said the fat man. He scarcely troubled to clasp her, and they moved away so gently, it was more like walking than dancing. But he said not a word about the floor. 'Your first dance, isn't it?' he murmured.

'How *did* you know?'

'Ah,' said the fat man, 'that's what it is to be old!' He wheezed faintly as he steered her past an awkward couple. 'You see, I've been doing this kind of thing for the last thirty years.'

'Thirty years?' cried Leila. Twelve years before she was born!

'It hardly bears thinking about, does it?' said the fat man gloomily. Leila looked at his bald head, and she felt quite sorry for him.

'I think it's marvellous to be still going on,' she said kindly.

'Kind little lady,' said the fat man, and he pressed her a little closer, and hummed a bar of the waltz. 'Of course,' he said, 'you can't hope to last anything like as long as that. No-o,' said the fat man, 'long before that you'll be sitting up there on the stage, looking on, in your nice black velvet. And these pretty arms will have turned into little short fat ones, and you'll beat time with such a different kind of fan – a black bony one.' The fat man seemed to shudder. 'And you'll smile away like the poor old dears up there, and point to your daughter, and tell the elderly lady next to you how some dreadful man tried to kiss her at the club ball. And your heart will ache, ache' – the fat man squeezed her closer still, as if he really was sorry for that poor heart – 'because no one wants to kiss you now. And you'll say how unpleasant these polished floors are to walk on, how dangerous they are. Eh, Mademoiselle Twinkletoes?' said the fat man softly.

Leila gave a light little laugh, but she did not feel like laughing. Was it – could it all be true? It sounded terribly true. Was this first ball only the beginning of her last ball after all?

At that the music seemed to change; it sounded sad, sad; it rose upon a great sigh. Oh, how quickly things changed! Why didn't happiness last for ever? For ever wasn't a bit too long.

'I want to stop,' she said in a breathless voice. The fat man led her to the door.

'No,' she said, 'I won't go outside. I won't sit down. I'll just stand here, thank you.' She leaned against the wall, tapping with her foot, pulling up her gloves and trying to smile. But deep inside her a little girl threw her pinafore over her head and sobbed. Why had he spoiled it all?

'I say, you know,' said the fat man, 'you mustn't take me seriously, little lady.'

'As if I should!' said Leila, tossing her small dark head and sucking her underlip. . . .

Again the couples paraded. The swing doors opened and shut. Now new music was given out by the bandmaster. But Leila didn't want to dance any more. She wanted to be home, or sitting on the verandah listening to those baby owls. When she looked through the dark windows at the stars, they had long beams like wings. . . .

But presently a soft, melting, ravishing tune began, and a young man with curly hair bowed before her. She would have to dance, out of politeness, until she could find Meg. Very stiffly she walked into the middle; very haughtily she put her hand on his sleeve. But in one minute, in one turn, her feet glided, glided. The lights, the azaleas, the dresses, the pink faces, the velvet chairs, all became one beautiful flying wheel. And when her next partner bumped her into the fat man and he said, 'Par*don*', she smiled at him more radiantly than ever. She didn't even recognise him again.

AT THE BAY

Very early morning. The sun was not yet risen, and the whole of Crescent Bay was hidden under a white sea-mist. The big bush-covered hills at the back were smothered. You could not see where they ended and the paddocks and bungalows began. The sandy road was gone and the paddocks and bungalows the other side of it; there were no white dunes covered with reddish grass beyond them; there was nothing to mark which was beach and where was the sea. A heavy dew had fallen. The grass was blue. Big drops hung on the bushes and just did not fall; the silvery, fluffy toi-toi was limp on its long stalks, and all the marigolds and the pinks in the bungalow gardens were bowed to the earth with wetness. Drenched were the cold fuchsias, round pearls of dew lay on the flat nasturtium leaves. It looked as though the sea had beaten up softly in the darkness, as though one immense wave had come rippling, rippling – how far? Perhaps if you had waked up in the middle of the night you might have seen a big fish flicking in at the window and gone again. . . .

Ah-Aah! sounded the sleepy sea. And from the bush there

came the sound of little streams flowing, quickly, lightly, slipping between the smooth stones, gushing into ferny basins and out again; and there was the splashing of big drops on large leaves, and something else – what was it? – a faint stirring and shaking, the snapping of a twig and then such silence that it seemed some one was listening.

Round the corner of Crescent Bay, between the piled-up masses of broken rock, a flock of sheep came pattering. They were huddled together, a small, tossing, woolly mass, and their thin, stick-like legs trotted along quickly as if the cold and the quiet had frightened them. Behind them an old sheep-dog, his soaking paws covered with sand, ran along with his nose to the ground, but carelessly, as if thinking of something else. And then in the rocky gateway the shepherd himself appeared. He was a lean, upright old man, in a frieze coat that was covered with a web of tiny drops, velvet trousers tied under the knee, and a wide-awake with a folded blue handkerchief round the brim. One hand was crammed into his belt, the other grasped a beautifully smooth yellow stick. And as he walked, taking his time, he kept up a very soft light whistling, an airy, far-away fluting that sounded mournful and tender. The old dog cut an ancient caper or two and then drew up sharp, ashamed of his levity, and walked a few dignified paces by his master's side. The sheep ran forward in little pattering rushes; they began to bleat, and ghostly flocks and herds answered them from under the sea. 'Baa! Baaa!' For a time they seemed to be always on the same piece of ground. There ahead was stretched the sandy road with shallow puddles; the same soaking bushes showed on either side and the same shadowy palings. Then something immense came into view; an enormous shock-haired giant with his arms stretched out. It was the big gum-tree outside Mrs. Stubbs's shop, and as they passed by there was a strong whiff of eucalyptus. And now big spots of light gleamed in the mist. The shepherd stopped whistling; he rubbed his red nose and wet beard on his wet sleeve and, screwing up his eyes, glanced in the direction of the sea. The sun was rising. It was marvellous how quickly the mist thinned, sped away, dissolved from the shallow plain, rolled up from the bush and was gone as if in a hurry to escape; big twists and curls jostled and shouldered each other as the silvery beams broadened. The far-away sky – a bright, pure blue – was reflected in the puddles, and the drops, swimming along the telegraph poles, flashed into points of light. Now the leaping, glittering sea was so bright it made one's eyes ache to look at it. The shepherd drew a pipe, the bowl as small as an acorn, out of his breast pocket, fumbled for a chunk of speckled tobacco, pared off a few shavings and stuffed the bowl. He was a grave, fine-looking old man. As he lit up and the blue smoke wreathed his head, the dog, watching, looked proud of him.

'Baa! Baaa!' The sheep spread out into a fan. They were just clear of the summer colony before the first sleeper turned over and lifted a drowsy head; their cry sounded in the dreams of little children . . . who lifted their arms to drag down, to cuddle the darling little woolly lambs of sleep. Then the first inhabitant appeared; it was the Burnells' cat Florrie, sitting on the gatepost, far too early as usual, looking for their milk-girl. When she saw the old sheep-dog she sprang up quickly, arched her back, drew in her tabby head, and seemed to give a little fastidious shiver. 'Ugh! What a coarse, revolting creature!' said Florrie. But the old sheep-dog, not looking up, waggled past, flinging out his legs from side to side. Only one of his ears twitched to prove that he saw, and thought her a silly young female.

The breeze of morning lifted in the bush and the smell of leaves and wet black earth mingled with the sharp smell of the sea. Myriads of birds were singing. A goldfinch flew over the shepherd's head and, perching on the tiptop of a spray, it turned to the sun, ruffling its small breast feathers. And now they had passed the fisherman's hut, passed the charred-looking little *whare* where Leila the milk-girl lived with her old Gran. The sheep strayed over a yellow swamp and Wag, the sheep-dog, padded after, rounded them up and headed them for the steeper, narrower rocky pass that led out of Crescent Bay and towards Daylight Cove. 'Baa! Baaa!' Faint the cry came as they rocked along the fast-drying road. The shepherd put away his pipe, dropping it into his breast-pocket so that the little bowl hung over. And straightway the soft airy whistling began again. Wag ran out along a ledge of rock after something that smelled, and ran back again disgusted. Then pushing, nudging, hurrying, the sheep rounded the bend and the shepherd followed after out of sight.

II

A few moments later the back door of one of the bungalows opened, and a figure in a broad-striped bathing suit flung down the paddock, cleared the stile, rushed through the tussock grass into the hollow, staggered up the sandy hillock, and raced for dear life over the big porous stones, over the cold, wet pebbles, on to the hard sand that gleamed like oil. Splish-Splosh! Splish-Splosh! The water bubbled round his legs as Stanley Burnell waded out exulting. First man in as usual! He'd beaten them all again. And he swooped down to souse his head and neck.

'Hail, brother! All hail, Thou Mighty One!' A velvety bass voice came booming over the water.

Great Scott! Damnation take it! Stanley lifted up to see a dark head bobbing far out and an arm lifted. It was Jonathan Trout – there before him! 'Glorious morning!' sang the voice.

'Yes, very fine!' said Stanley briefly. Why the dickens didn't the fellow stick to his part of the sea? Why should he come barging over to this exact spot? Stanley gave a kick, a lunge and struck out, swimming overarm. But Jonathan was a match for him. Up he came, his black hair sleek on his forehead, his short beard sleek.

'I had an extraordinary dream last night!' he shouted.

What was the matter with the man? This mania for conversation irritated Stanley beyond words. And it was always the same – always some piffle about a dream he'd had, or some cranky idea he'd got hold of, or some rot he'd been reading. Stanley turned over on his back and kicked with his legs till he was a living waterspout. But even then . . . 'I dreamed I was hanging over a terrifically high cliff, shouting to some one below.' You would be! thought Stanley. He could stick no more of it. He stopped splashing. 'Look here, Trout,' he said, 'I'm in rather a hurry this morning.'

'You're WHAT?' Jonathan was so surprised – or pretended to be – that he sank under the water, then reappeared again blowing.

'All I mean is,' said Stanley, 'I've no time to – to – to fool about. I want to get this over. I'm in a hurry. I've work to do this morning – see?'

Jonathan was gone before Stanley had finished. 'Pass, friend!' said the bass voice gently, and he slid away through the water with scarcely a ripple . . . . But curse the fellow! He'd ruined Stanley's bathe. What an unpractical idiot the man was! Stanley struck out to sea again, and then as quickly swam in again, and away he rushed up the beach. He felt cheated.

Jonathan stayed a little longer in the water. He floated, gently moving his hands like fins, and letting the sea rock his long, skinny body. It was curious, but in spite of everything he was fond of Stanley Burnell. True, he had a fiendish desire to tease him sometimes, to poke fun at him, but at bottom he was sorry for the fellow. There was something pathetic in his determination to make a job of everything. You couldn't help feeling he'd be caught out one day, and then what an almighty cropper he'd come! At that moment an immense wave lifted Jonathan, rode past him, and broke along the beach with a joyful sound. What a beauty! And now there came another. That was the way to live – carelessly, recklessly, spending oneself. He got on to his feet and began to wade towards the shore, pressing his toes into the firm, wrinkled sand. To take things easy, not to fight against the ebb and flow of life, but to give way to it – that was what was needed. It was this tension that was all wrong. To live – to live! And the perfect morning, so fresh and fair, basking in the light, as though laughing at its own beauty, seemed to whisper, 'Why not?'

But now he was out of the water Jonathan turned blue with cold. He ached all over; it was as though some one was wringing the blood out of him. And stalking up the beach, shivering, all his muscles tight, he too felt his bathe was spoilt. He'd stayed in too long.

III

Beryl was alone in the living-room when Stanley appeared, wearing a blue serge suit, a stiff collar and a spotted tie. He looked almost uncannily clean and brushed; he was going to town for the day. Dropping into his chair, he pulled out his watch and put it beside his plate.

'I've just got twenty-five minutes,' he said. 'You might go and see if the porridge is ready, Beryl?'

'Mother's just gone for it,' said Beryl. She sat down at the table and poured out his tea.

'Thanks!' Stanley took a sip. 'Hallo!' he said in an astonished voice, 'you've forgotten the sugar.'

'Oh, sorry!' But even then Beryl didn't help him; she pushed the basin across. What did this mean? As Stanley helped himself his blue eyes widened; they seemed to quiver. He shot a quick glance at his sister-in-law and leaned back.

'Nothing wrong, is there?' he asked carelessly, fingering his collar.

Beryl's head was bent; she turned her plate in her fingers.

'Nothing,' said her light voice. Then she too looked up, and smiled at Stanley. 'Why should there be?'

'O-oh! No reason at all as far as I know. I thought you seemed rather –'

At that moment the door opened and the three little girls appeared, each carrying a porridge plate. They were dressed alike in blue jerseys and knickers; their brown legs were bare, and each had her hair plaited and pinned up in what was called a horse's tail. Behind them came Mrs. Fairfield with the tray.

'Carefully, children,' she warned. But they were taking the very greatest care. They loved being allowed to carry things. 'Have you said good morning to your father?'

'Yes, grandma.' They settled themselves on the bench opposite Stanley and Beryl.

'Good morning, Stanley!' Old Mrs. Fairfield gave him his plate.

'Morning, mother! How's the boy?'

'Splendid! He only woke up once last night. What a perfect morning!' The old woman paused, her hand on the loaf of bread, to gaze out of the open door into the garden. The sea sounded. Through the wide-open window streamed the sun on to the yellow varnished walls and bare floor. Everything on the table flashed and glittered. In the middle there was an old salad bowl filled with yellow and red nasturtiums. She smiled, and a look of deep content shone in her eyes.

'You might *cut* me a slice of that bread, mother,' said Stanley. 'I've only twelve and a half minutes before the coach passes. Has anyone given my shoes to the servant girl?'

'Yes, they're ready for you.' Mrs. Fairfield was quite unruffled.

'Oh, Kezia! Why are you such a messy child!' cried Beryl despairingly.

'Me, Aunt Beryl?' Kezia stared at her. What had she done now? She had only dug a river down the middle of her porridge, filled it, and was eating the banks away. But she did that every single morning, and no one had said a word up till now.

'Why can't you eat your food properly like Isabel and Lottie?' How unfair grown-ups are!

'But Lottie always makes a floating island, don't you, Lottie?'

'I don't,' said Isabel smartly. 'I just sprinkle mine with sugar and put on the milk and finish it. Only babies play with their food.'

Stanley pushed back his chair and got up.

'Would you get me those shoes, mother? And, Beryl, if you've finished, I wish you'd cut down to the gate and stop the coach. Run in to your mother, Isabel, and ask her where my bowler hat's been put. Wait a minute – have you children been playing with my stick?'

'No, father!'

'But I put it here,' Stanley began to bluster. 'I remember distinctly putting it in this corner. Now, who's had it? There's no time to lose. Look sharp! The stick's got to be found.'

Even Alice, the servant-girl, was drawn into the chase. 'You haven't been using it to poke the kitchen fire with by any chance?'

Stanley dashed into the bedroom where Linda was lying. 'Most extraordinary thing. I can't keep a single possession to myself. They've made away with my stick, now!'

'Stick, dear? What stick?' Linda's vagueness on these occasions could not be real, Stanley decided. Would nobody sympathise with him?

'Coach! Coach, Stanley!' Beryl's voice cried from the gate.

Stanley waved his arm to Linda. 'No time to say good-bye!' he cried. And he meant that as a punishment to her.

He snatched his bowler hat, dashed out of the house, and swung down the garden path. Yes, the coach was there waiting, and Beryl, leaning over the open gate, was laughing up at somebody or other just as if nothing had happened. The heartlessness of women! The way they took it for granted it was your job to slave away for them while they didn't even take the trouble to see that your walking-stick wasn't lost. Kelly trailed his whip across the horses.

'Good-bye, Stanley,' called Beryl, sweetly and gaily. It was easy enough to say good-bye! And there she stood, idle, shading her eyes with her hand. The worst of it was Stanley had to shout good-bye too, for the sake of appearances. Then he saw her turn, give a little skip and run back to the house. She was glad to be rid of him!

Yes, she was thankful. Into the living-room she ran and called 'He's gone!' Linda cried from her room: 'Beryl! Has Stanley gone?' Old Mrs. Fairfield appeared, carrying the boy in his little flannel coatee.

'Gone?'

'Gone!'

Oh, the relief, the difference it made to have the man out of the house. Their very voices were changed as they called to one another; they sounded warm and loving and as if they shared a secret. Beryl went over to the table. 'Have another cup of tea, mother. It's still hot.' She wanted, somehow, to celebrate the fact that they could do what they liked now. There was no man to disturb them; the whole perfect day was theirs.

'No, thank you, child,' said old Mrs. Fairfield, but the way at that moment she tossed the boy up and said 'a-goos-a-goos-a-ga!' to him meant that she felt the same. The little girls ran into the paddock like chickens let out of a coop.

Even Alice, the servant-girl, washing up the dishes in the kitchen, caught the infection and used the precious tank water in a perfectly reckless fashion.

'Oh, these men!' said she, and she plunged the teapot into the bowl and held it under the water even after it had stopped bubbling, as if it too was a man and drowning was too good for them.

IV

'Wait for me, Isa-bel! Kezia, wait for me!'

There was poor little Lottie, left behind again, because she found it so fearfully hard to get over the stile by herself. When she stood on the first step her knees began to wobble; she grasped the post. Then you had to put one leg over. But which leg? She never could decide. And when she did finally put one leg over with a sort of stamp of despair – then the feeling was awful. She was half in the paddock still and half in the tussock grass. She clutched the post desperately and lifted up her voice. 'Wait for me!'

'No, don't you wait for her, Kezia!' said Isabel. 'She's such a little silly. She's always making a fuss. Come on!' And she tugged Kezia's jersey. 'You can use my bucket if you come with me,' she said kindly. 'It's bigger than yours.' But Kezia couldn't leave Lottie all by herself. She ran back to her. By this time Lottie was very red in the face and breathing heavily.

'Here, put your other foot over,' said Kezia.

'Where?'

Lottie looked down at Kezia as if from a mountain height.

'Here where my hand is.' Kezia patted the place.

'Oh, *there* do you mean?' Lottie gave a deep sigh and put the second foot over.

'Now – sort of turn round and sit down and slide,' said Kezia.

'But there's nothing to sit down *on*, Kezia,' said Lottie.

She managed it at last, and once it was over she shook herself and began to beam.

'I'm getting better at climbing over stiles, aren't I, Kezia?'

Lottie's was a very hopeful nature.

The pink and the blue sunbonnet followed Isabel's bright red sunbonnet up that sliding, slipping hill. At the top they paused to decide where to go and to have a good stare at who was there already. Seen from behind, standing against the skyline, gesticulating largely with their spades, they looked like minute puzzled explorers.

The whole family of Samuel Josephs was there already with their lady-help, who sat on a camp-stool and kept order with a whistle that she wore tied round her neck, and a small cane with which she directed operations. The Samuel Josephs never played by themselves or managed their own game. If they did, it ended in the boys pouring water down the girls' necks or the girls trying to put little black crabs into the boys' pockets. So Mrs. S. J. and the poor lady-help drew up what she called a 'brogramme' every morning to keep them 'abused and out of bischief'. It was all competitions or races or round games. Everything began with a piercing blast of the lady-help's whistle and ended with another. There were even prizes – large, rather dirty paper parcels which the lady-help with a sour little smile drew out of a bulging string kit. The Samuel Josephs fought fearfully for the prizes and cheated and pinched one another's arms – they were all expert pinchers. The only time the Burnell children ever played with them Kezia had got a prize, and when she undid three bits of paper she found a very small rusty button-hook. She couldn't understand why they made such a fuss. . . .

But they never played with the Samuel Josephs now or even went to their parties. The Samuel Josephs were always giving children's parties at the Bay and there was always the same food. A big washhand basin of very brown fruit-salad, buns cut into four and a washhand jug full of something the lady-help called 'Limmonadear'. And you went away in the evening with half the frill torn off your frock or something spilled all down the front of your open-work pinafore, leaving the Samuel Josephs leaping like savages on their lawn. No! They were too awful.

On the other side of the beach, close down to the water, two little boys, their knickers rolled up, twinkled like spiders. One was digging, the other pattered in and out of the water, filling a small bucket. They were the Trout boys, Pip and Rags. But Pip was so busy digging and Rags was so busy helping that they didn't see their little cousins until they were quite close.

'Look!' said Pip. 'Look what I've discovered.' And he showed them an old wet, squashed-looking boot. The three little girls stared.

'Whatever are you going to do with it?' asked Kezia.

'Keep it, of course!' Pip was very scornful. 'It's a find – see?'

Yes, Kezia saw that. All the same . . .

'There's lots of things buried in the sand,' explained Pip. 'They get chucked up from wrecks. Treasure. Why – you might find –'

'But why does Rags have to keep on pouring water in?' asked Lottie.

'Oh, that's to moisten it,' said Pip, 'to make the work a bit easier. Keep it up, Rags.'

And good little Rags ran up and down, pouring in the water that turned brown like cocoa.

'Here, shall I show you what I found yesterday?' said Pip mysteriously, and he stuck his spade into the sand. 'Promise not to tell.'

They promised.

'Say, cross my heart straight dinkum.'

The little girls said it.

Pip took something out of his pocket, rubbed it a long time on the front of his jersey, then breathed on it and rubbed it again.

'Now turn round!' he ordered.

They turned round.

'All look the same way! Keep still! Now!'

And his hand opened; he held up to the light something that flashed, that winked, that was a most lovely green.

'It's a nemeral,' said Pip solemnly.

'Is it really, Pip?' Even Isabel was impressed.

The lovely green thing seemed to dance in Pip's fingers. Aunt Beryl had a nemeral in a ring, but it was a very small one. This one was as big as a star and far more beautiful.

V

As the morning lengthened whole parties appeared over the sand-hills and came down on the beach to bathe. It was understood that at eleven o'clock the women and children of the summer colony had the sea to themselves. First the women undressed, pulled on their bathing dresses and covered their heads in hideous caps like sponge bags; then the children were unbuttoned. The beach was strewn with little heaps of clothes and shoes; the big summer hats, with stones on them to keep them from blowing away, looked like immense shells. It was strange that even the sea seemed to sound differently when all those leaping, laughing figures ran into the waves. Old Mrs. Fairfield, in a lilac cotton dress and a black hat tied under the chin, gathered her little brood and got them ready. The little Trout boys whipped their shirts over their heads, and away the five sped, while their grandma sat with one hand in her knitting-bag ready to draw out the ball of wool when she was satisfied they were safely in.

The firm compact little girls were not half so brave as the tender, delicate-looking boys. Pip and Rags, shivering, crouching down, slapping the water, never hesitated. But Isabel, who could swim twelve strokes, and Kezia, who could nearly swim eight, only followed on the strict understanding they were not to be splashed. As for Lottie, she didn't follow at all. She liked to be left to go in her own way, please. And that way was to sit down at the edge of the water, her legs straight, her knees pressed together, and to make vague motions with her arms as if she expected to be wafted out to sea. But when a bigger wave than usual, an old whiskery one, came lolloping along in her direction, she scrambled to her feet with a face of horror and flew up the beach again.

'Here, mother, keep those for me, will you?'

Two rings and a thin gold chain were dropped into Mrs. Fairfield's lap.

'Yes, dear. But aren't you going to bathe here?'

'No-o,' Beryl drawled. She sounded vague. 'I'm undressing farther along. I'm going to bathe with Mrs. Harry Kember.'

'Very well.' But Mrs. Fairfield's lips set. She disapproved of Mrs. Harry Kember. Beryl knew it.

Poor old mother, she smiled, as she skimmed over the stones. Poor old mother! Old! Oh, what joy, what bliss it was to be young. . . .

'You look very pleased,' said Mrs. Harry Kember. She sat hunched up on the stones, her arms round her knees, smoking.

'It's such a lovely day,' said Beryl, smiling down at her.

'Oh my *dear*!' Mrs. Harry Kember's voice sounded as though she knew better than that. But then her voice always sounded as though she knew something more about you than you did yourself. She was a long, strange-looking woman with narrow hands and feet. Her face, too, was long and narrow and exhausted-looking; even her fair curled fringe looked burnt out and withered. She was the only woman at the Bay who smoked, and she smoked incessantly, keeping the cigarette between her lips while she talked, and only taking it out when the ash was so long you could not understand why it did not fall. When she was not playing bridge – she played bridge every day of her life – she spent her time lying in the full glare of the sun. She could stand any amount of it; she never had enough. All the same, it did not seem to warm her. Parched, withered, cold, she lay stretched on the stones like a piece of tossed-up driftwood. The women at the Bay thought she was very, very fast. Her lack of vanity, her slang, the way she treated men as though she was one of them, and the fact that she didn't care twopence about her house and called the servant Gladys 'Glad-eyes', was disgraceful. Standing on the verandah steps Mrs. Kember would call in her indifferent, tired voice, 'I say, Glad-eyes, you might heave me a handker-chief if I've got one, will you?' And Glad-eyes, a red bow in her hair instead of a cap, and white shoes, came running with an impudent smile. It was an absolute scandal! True, she had no children, and her husband. . . Here the voices were always raised; they became fervent. How can he have married her? How can he, how can he? It must have been money, of course, but even then!

Mrs. Kember's husband was at least ten years younger than she was, and so incredibly handsome that he looked like a mask or a most perfect illustration in an American novel rather than a man. Black hair, dark blue eyes, red lips, a slow sleepy smile, a fine tennis player, a perfect dancer, and with it all a mystery. Harry Kember was like a man walking in his sleep. Men couldn't stand him, they couldn't get a word out of the chap; he ignored his wife just as she ignored him. How did he live? Of course there were stories, but such stories! They simply couldn't be told. The women he'd been seen with, the places he'd been seen in . . . but nothing was ever certain, nothing definite. Some of the women at the Bay privately thought he'd commit a murder one day. Yes, even while they talked to Mrs. Kember and took in the awful concoction she was wearing, they saw her, stretched as she lay on the beach; but cold, bloody, and still with a cigarette stuck in the corner of her mouth.

Mrs. Kember rose, yawned, unsnapped her belt buckle, and tugged at the tape of her blouse. And Beryl stepped out of her skirt and shed her jersey, and stood up in her short white petticoat, and her camisole with ribbon bows on the shoulders.

'Mercy on us,' said Mrs. Harry Kember, 'what a little beauty you are!'

'Don't!' said Beryl softly; but, drawing off one stocking and then the other, she felt a little beauty.

'My dear – why not?' said Mrs. Harry Kember, stamping on her own petticoat. Really – her underclothes! A pair of blue cotton knickers and a linen bodice that reminded one somehow of a pillow-case. . . . 'And you don't wear stays, do you?' She touched Beryl's waist, and Beryl sprang away with a small affected cry. Then 'Never!' she said firmly.

'Lucky little creature,' sighed Mrs. Kember, unfastening her own.

Beryl turned her back and began the complicated movements of some one who is trying to take off her clothes and to pull on her bathing-dress all at one and the same time.

'Oh, my dear – don't mind me,' said Mrs. Harry Kember. 'Why be shy? I shan't eat you. I shan't be shocked like those other ninnies.' And she gave her strange neighing laugh and grimaced at the other women.

But Beryl was shy. She never undressed in front of anybody. Was that silly? Mrs. Harry Kember made her feel it was silly, even something to be ashamed of. Why be shy indeed! She glanced quickly at her friend standing so boldly in her torn chemise and lighting a fresh cigarette; and a quick, bold, evil feeling started up in her breast. Laughing recklessly, she drew on the limp, sandy-feeling bathing-dress that was not quite dry and fastened the twisted buttons.

'That's better,' said Mrs. Harry Kember. They began to go down the beach together. 'Really, it's a sin for you to wear clothes, my dear. Somebody's got to tell you some day.'

The water was quite warm. It was that marvellous transparent blue, flecked with silver, but the sand at the bottom looked gold; when you kicked with your toes there rose a little puff of gold-dust. Now the waves just reached her breast. Beryl stood, her arms outstretched, gazing out, and as each wave came she gave the slightest little jump, so that it seemed it was the wave which lifted her so gently.

'I believe in pretty girls having a good time,' said Mrs. Harry Kember. 'Why not? Don't you make a mistake, my dear. Enjoy yourself.' And suddenly she turned turtle, disappeared, and swam away quickly, quickly, like a rat. Then she flicked round and began swimming back. She was going to say something else. Beryl felt that she was being poisoned by this cold woman, but she longed to hear. But oh, how strange, how horrible! As Mrs. Harry Kember came up close she looked, in her black waterproof bathing-cap, with her sleepy face lifted above the water, just her chin touching, like a horrible caricature of her husband.

VI

In a steamer chair, under a manuka tree that grew in the middle of the front grass patch, Linda Burnell dreamed the morning away. She did nothing. She looked up at the dark, close, dry leaves of the manuka, at the chinks of blue between, and now and again a tiny yellowish flower dropped on her. Pretty – yes, if you held one of those flowers on the palm of your hand and looked at it closely, it was an exquisite small thing. Each pale yellow petal shone as if each was the careful work of a loving hand. The tiny tongue in the centre gave it the shape of a bell. And when you turned it over the outside was a deep bronze colour. But as soon as they flowered, they fell and were scattered. You brushed them off your frock as you talked; the horrid little things got caught in one's hair. Why, then, flower at all? Who takes the trouble – or the joy – to make all these things that are wasted, wasted. . . . It was uncanny.

On the grass beside her, lying between two pillows, was the boy. Sound asleep he lay, his head turned away from his mother. His fine dark hair looked more like a shadow than like real hair, but his ear was a bright, deep coral. Linda clasped her hands above her head and crossed her feet. It was very pleasant to know that all these bungalows were empty, that everybody was down on the beach, out of sight, out of hearing. She had the garden to herself; she was alone.

Dazzling white the picotees shone; the golden-eyed marigolds glittered; the nasturtiums wreathed the verandah poles in green and gold flame. If only one had time to look at these flowers long enough, time to get over the sense of novelty and strangeness, time to know them! But as soon as one paused to part the petals, to discover the under-side of the leaf, along came Life and one was swept away. And, lying in her cane chair, Linda felt so light; she felt like a leaf. Along came Life like a wind and she was seized and shaken; she had to go. Oh dear, would it always be so? Was there no escape?

. . . Now she sat on the verandah of their Tasmanian home, leaning against her father's knee. And he promised, 'As soon as you and I are old enough, Linny, we'll cut off somewhere, we'll escape. Two boys together. I have a fancy I'd like to sail up a river in China.' Linda saw that river, very wide, covered with little rafts and boats. She saw the yellow hats of the boatmen and she heard their high, thin voices as they called . . .

'Yes, papa.'

But just then a very broad young man with bright ginger hair walked slowly past their house, and slowly, solemnly even, uncovered. Linda's father pulled her ear teasingly, in the way he had.

'Linny's beau,' he whispered.

'Oh, papa, fancy being married to Stanley Burnell!'

Well, she was married to him. And what was more she loved him. Not the Stanley whom every one saw, not the everyday one; but a timid, sensitive, innocent Stanley who knelt down every night to say his prayers, and who longed to be good. Stanley was simple. If he believed in people – as he believed in her, for instance – it was with his whole heart. He could not be disloyal; he could not tell a lie. And how terribly he suffered if he thought anyone – she – was not being dead straight, dead sincere with him! 'This is too subtle for me!' He flung out the words, but his open, quivering, distraught look was like the look of a trapped beast.

But the trouble was – here Linda felt almost inclined to laugh, though Heaven knows it was no laughing matter – she saw *her* Stanley so seldom. There were glimpses, moments, breathing spaces of calm, but all the rest of the time it was like living in a house that couldn't be cured of the habit of catching on fire, on a ship that got wrecked every day. And it was always Stanley who was in the thick of the danger. Her whole time was spent in rescuing him, and restoring him, and calming him down, and listening to his story. And what was left of her time was spent in the dread of having children.

Linda frowned; she sat up quickly in her steamer chair and clasped her ankles. Yes, that was her real grudge against life; that was what she could not understand. That was the question she asked and asked, and listened in vain for the answer. It was all very well to say it was the common lot of women to bear children. It wasn't true. She, for one, could prove that wrong. She was broken, made weak, her courage was gone, through child-bearing. And what made it doubly hard to bear was, she did not love her children. It was useless pretending. Even if she had had the strength she never would have nursed and played with the little girls. No, it was as though a cold breath had chilled her through and through on each of those awful journeys; she had no warmth left to give them. As to the boy – well, thank Heaven, mother had taken him; he was mother's, or Beryl's, or anybody's who wanted him. She had hardly held him in her arms. She was so indifferent about him that as he lay there . . . Linda glanced down.

The boy had turned over. He lay facing her, and he was no longer asleep. His dark-blue, baby eyes were open; he looked as though he was peeping at his mother. And suddenly his face dimpled; it broke into a wide, toothless smile, a perfect beam, no less.

'I'm here!' that happy smile seemed to say. 'Why don't you like me?'

There was something so quaint, so unexpected about that smile that Linda smiled herself. But she checked herself and said to the boy coldly, 'I don't like babies.'

'Don't like babies?' The boy couldn't believe her. 'Don't like *me*?' He waved his arms foolishly at his mother.

Linda dropped off her chair on to the grass.

'Why do you keep on smiling?' she said severely. 'If you knew what I was thinking about, you wouldn't.'

But he only squeezed up his eyes, slyly, and rolled his head on the pillow. He didn't believe a word she said.

'We know all about that!' smiled the boy.

Linda was so astonished at the confidence of this little creature. . . . Ah no, be sincere. That was not what she felt; it was something far different, it was something so new, so . . . The tears danced in her eyes; she breathed in a small whisper to the boy, 'Hallo, my funny!'

But by now the boy had forgotten his mother. He was serious again. Something pink, something soft waved in front of him. He made a grab at it and it immediately disappeared. But when he lay back, another, like the first, appeared. This time he determined to catch it. He made a tremendous effort and rolled right over.

VII

The tide was out; the beach was deserted; lazily flopped the warm sea. The sun beat down, beat down hot and fiery on the fine sand, baking the grey and blue and black and white-veined pebbles. It sucked up the little drop of water that lay in the hollow of the curved shells; it bleached the pink convolvulus that threaded through and through the sand-hills. Nothing seemed to move but the small sand-hoppers. Pit-pit-pit! They were never still.

Over there on the weed-hung rocks that looked at low tide like shaggy beasts come down to the water to drink, the sunlight seemed to spin like a silver coin dropped into each of the small rock pools. They danced, they quivered, and minute ripples laved the porous shores. Looking down, bending over, each pool was like a lake with pink and blue houses clustered on the shores; and oh! the vast mountainous country behind those houses – the ravines, the passes, the dangerous creeks and fearful tracks that led to the water's edge. Underneath waved the sea-forest – pink thread-like trees, velvet anemones, and orange berry-spotted weeds. Now a stone on the bottom moved, rocked, and there was a glimpse of a black feeler; now a thread-like creature wavered by and was lost. Something was happening to the pink, waving trees; they were changing to a cold moonlight blue. And now there sounded the faintest 'plop'. Who made that sound? What was going on down there? And how strong, how damp the seaweed smelt in the hot sun. . . .

The green blinds were drawn in the bungalows of the summer colony. Over the verandahs, prone on the paddock, flung over the fences, there were exhausted-looking bathing-dresses and rough striped towels. Each back window seemed to have a pair of sand-shoes on the sill and some lumps of rock or a bucket or a collection of pawa shells. The bush quivered in a haze of heat; the sandy road was empty except for the Trouts' dog Snooker, who lay stretched in the very middle of it. His blue eye was turned up, his legs stuck out stiffly, and he gave an occasional desperate-sounding puff, as much as to say he had decided to make an end of it and was only waiting for some kind cart to come along.

'What are you looking at, my grandma? Why do you keep stopping and sort of staring at the wall?'

Kezia and her grandmother were taking their siesta together. The little girl, wearing only her short drawers and her under-bodice, her arms and legs bare, lay on one of the puffed-up pillows of her grandma's bed, and the old woman, in a white ruffled dressing-gown, sat in a rocker at the window, with a long piece of pink knitting in her lap. This room that they shared, like the other rooms of the bungalow, was of light varnished wood and the floor was bare. The furniture was of the shabbiest, the simplest. The dressing-table, for instance, was a packing-case in a sprigged muslin petticoat, and the mirror above was very strange; it was as though a little piece of forked lightning was imprisoned in it. On the table there stood a jar of sea-pinks, pressed so tightly together they looked more like a velvet pincushion, and a special shell which Kezia had given her grandma for a pin-tray, and another even more special which she had thought would make a very nice place for a watch to curl up in.

'Tell me, grandma,' said Kezia.

The old woman sighed, whipped the wool twice round her thumb, and drew the bone needle through. She was casting on.

'I was thinking of your Uncle William, darling,' she said quietly.

'My Australian Uncle William?' said Kezia. She had another.

'Yes, of course.'

'The one I never saw?'

'That was the one.'

'Well, what happened to him?' Kezia knew perfectly well, but she wanted to be told again.

'He went to the mines, and he got a sunstroke there and died,' said old Mrs. Fairfield.

Kezia blinked and considered the picture again . . . a little man fallen over like a tin soldier by the side of the big black hole.

'Does it make you sad to think about him, grandma?' She hated her grandma to be sad.

It was the old woman's turn to consider. Did it make her sad? To look back, back. To stare down the years, as Kezia had seen her doing. To look after *them* as a woman does, long after *they* were out of sight. Did it make her sad? No, life was like that.

'No, Kezia.'

'But why?' asked Kezia. She lifted one bare arm and began to draw things in the air. 'Why did Uncle William have to die? He wasn't old.'

Mrs. Fairfield began counting the stitches in threes. 'It just happened,' she said in an absorbed voice.

'Does everybody have to die?' asked Kezia.

'Everybody!'

'*Me?*' Kezia sounded fearfully incredulous.

'Some day, my darling.'

'But, grandma.' Kezia waved her left leg and waggled the toes. They felt sandy. 'What if I just won't?'

The old woman sighed again and drew a long thread from the ball.

'We're not asked, Kezia,' she said sadly. 'It happens to all of us sooner or later.'

Kezia lay still thinking this over. She didn't want to die. It meant she would have to leave here, leave everywhere, for ever, leave – leave her grandma. She rolled over quickly.

'Grandma,' she said in a startled voice.

'What, my pet!'

'*You're* not to die.' Kezia was very decided.

'Ah, Kezia' – her grandma looked up and smiled and shook her head – 'don't let's talk about it.'

'But you're not to. You couldn't leave me. You couldn't not be there.' This was awful. 'Promise me you won't ever do it, grandma,' pleaded Kezia.

The old woman went on knitting.

'Promise me! Say never!'

But still her grandma was silent.

Kezia rolled off the bed; she couldn't bear it any longer, and lightly she leapt on to her grandma's knees, clasped her hands round the old woman's throat and began kissing her, under the chin, behind the ear, and blowing down her neck.

'Say never . . . say never . . . say never –' She gasped between the kisses. And then she began, very softly and lightly, to tickle her grandma.

'Kezia!' The old woman dropped her knitting. She swung back in the rocker. She began to tickle Kezia. 'Say never, say never, say never,' gurgled Kezia, while they lay there laughing in each other's arms. 'Come, that's enough, my squirrel! That's enough, my wild pony!' said old Mrs. Fairfield, setting her cap straight. 'Pick up my knitting.'

Both of them had forgotten what the 'never' was about.

VIII

The sun was still full on the garden when the back door of the Burnells' shut with a bang, and a very gay figure walked down the path to the gate. It was Alice, the servant-girl, dressed for her afternoon out. She wore a white cotton dress with such large red spots on it and so many that they made you shudder, white shoes and a leghorn turned up under the brim with poppies. Of course she wore gloves, white ones, stained at the fastenings with iron-mould, and in one hand she carried a very dashed-looking sunshade which she referred to as her *perishall*.

Beryl, sitting in the window, fanning her freshly-washed hair, thought she had never seen such a guy. If Alice had only blacked her face with a piece of cork before she started out, the picture would have been complete. And where did a girl like that go to in a place like this? The heart-shaped Fijian fan beat scornfully at that lovely bright mane. She supposed Alice had picked up some horrible common larrikin and they'd go off into the bush together. Pity to make herself so conspicuous; they'd have hard work to hide with Alice in that rig-out.

But no, Beryl was unfair. Alice was going to tea with Mrs. Stubbs, who'd sent her an 'invite' by the little boy who called for orders. She had taken ever such a liking to Mrs. Stubbs ever since the first time she went to the shop to get something for her mosquitoes.

'Dear heart!' Mrs. Stubbs had clapped her hand to her side. 'I never seen anyone so eaten. You might have been attacked by canningbals.'

Alice did wish there'd been a bit of life on the road though.

79

Made her feel so queer, having nobody behind her. Made her feel all weak in the spine. She couldn't believe that some one wasn't watching her. And yet it was silly to turn round; it gave you away. She pulled up her gloves, hummed to herself and said to the distant gum-tree, 'Shan't be long now.' But that was hardly company.

Mrs. Stubbs's shop was perched on a little hillock just off the road. It had two big windows for eyes, a broad verandah for a hat, and the sign on the roof, scrawled MRS. STUBBS'S, was like a little card stuck rakishly in the hat crown.

On the verandah there hung a long string of bathing-dresses, clinging together as though they'd just been rescued from the sea rather than waiting to go in, and beside them there hung a cluster of sand-shoes so extraordinarily mixed that to get at one pair you had to tear apart and forcibly separate at least fifty. Even then it was the rarest thing to find the left that belonged to the right. So many people had lost patience and gone off with one shoe that fitted and one that was a little too big. . . . Mrs. Stubbs prided herself on keeping something of everything. The two windows, arranged in the form of precarious pyramids, were crammed so tight, piled so high, that it seemed only a conjurer could prevent them from toppling over. In the left-hand corner of one window, glued to the pane by four gelatine lozenges, there was – and there had been from time immemorial – a notice.

LOST! HANSOME GOLE BROOCH

SOLID GOLD

ON OR NEAR BEACH

REWARD OFFERED

Alice pressed open the door. The bell jangled, the red serge curtains parted, and Mrs. Stubbs appeared. With her broad smile and the long bacon knife in her hand, she looked like a friendly brigand. Alice was welcomed so warmly that she found it quite difficult to keep up her 'manners'. They consisted of persistent little coughs and hems, pulls at her gloves, tweaks at her skirt, and a curious difficulty in seeing what was set before her or understanding what was said.

Tea was laid on the parlour table – ham, sardines, a whole pound of butter, and such a large johnny cake that it looked like an advertisement for somebody's baking-powder. But the Primus stove roared so loudly that it was useless to try to talk above it. Alice sat down on the edge of a basket-chair while Mrs. Stubbs pumped the stove still higher. Suddenly Mrs. Stubbs whipped the cushion off a chair and disclosed a large brown-paper parcel.

'I've just had some new photers taken, my dear,' she shouted cheerfully to Alice. 'Tell me what you think of them.'

In a very dainty, refined way Alice wet her finger and put the tissue back from the first one. Life! How many there were! There were three dozzing at least. And she held hers up to the light.

Mrs. Stubbs sat in an arm-chair, leaning very much to one side. There was a look of mild astonishment on her large face, and well there might be. For though the arm-chair stood on a carpet, to the left of it, miraculously skirting the carpet-border, there was a dashing water-fall. On her right stood a Grecian pillar with a giant fern-tree on either side of it, and in the background towered a gaunt mountain, pale with snow.

'It is a nice style, isn't it?' shouted Mrs. Stubbs; and Alice had just screamed 'Sweetly' when the roaring of the Primus stove died down, fizzled out, ceased, and she said 'Pretty' in a silence that was frightening.

'Draw up your chair, my dear,' said Mrs. Stubbs, beginning to pour out. 'Yes,' she said thoughtfully, as she handed the tea, 'but I don't care about the size. I'm having an enlargemint. All very well for Christmas cards, but I never was the one for small photers myself. You get no comfort out of them. To say the truth, I find them dis'eartening.'

Alice quite saw what she meant.

'Size,' said Mrs. Stubbs. 'Give me size. That was what my poor dear husband was always saying. He couldn't stand anything small. Gave him the creeps. And, strange as it may seem, my dear' – here Mrs. Stubbs creaked and seemed to expand herself at the memory – 'it was dropsy that carried him off at the larst. Many's the time they drawn one and a half pints from 'im at the 'ospital . . . . It seemed like a judgmint.'

Alice burned to know exactly what it was that was drawn from him. She ventured, 'I suppose it was water.'

But Mrs. Stubbs fixed Alice with her eyes and replied meaningly, 'It was *liquid*, my dear.'

Liquid! Alice jumped away from the word like a cat and came back to it, nosing and wary.

'That's 'im!' said Mrs. Stubbs, and she pointed dramatically to the life-size head and shoulders of a burly man with a dead white rose in the button-hole of his coat that made you think of a curl of cold mutting fat. Just below, in silver letters on a red cardboard ground, were the words, 'Be not afraid, it is I.'

'It's ever such a fine face,' said Alice faintly.

The pale-blue bow on the top of Mrs. Stubbs's fair frizzy hair quivered. She arched her plump neck. What a neck she had! It was bright pink where it began and then it changed to warm apricot, and that faded to the colour of a brown egg and then to a deep creamy.

'All the same, my dear,' she said surprisingly, 'freedom's best!' Her soft, fat chuckle sounded like a purr. 'Freedom's best,' said Mrs. Stubbs again.

Freedom! Alice gave a loud, silly little titter. She felt awkward. Her mind flew back to her own kitching. Ever so queer! She wanted to be back in it again.

IX

A strange company assembled in the Burnells' washhouse after tea. Round the table there sat a bull, a rooster, a donkey that kept forgetting it was a donkey, a sheep and a bee. The washhouse was the perfect place for such a meeting because they could make as much noise as they liked, and nobody ever interrupted. It was a small tin shed standing apart from the bungalow. Against the wall there was a deep trough and in the corner a copper with a basket of clothes-pegs on top of it. The little window, spun over with cobwebs, had a piece of candle and a mouse-trap on the dusty sill. There were clothes-lines criss-crossed overhead and, hanging from a peg on the wall, a very big, a huge, rusty horseshoe. The table was in the middle with a form at either side.

'You can't be a bee, Kezia. A bee's not an animal. It's a ninseck.'

'Oh, but I do want to be a bee frightfully,' wailed Kezia. . . . A tiny bee, all yellow-furry, with striped legs. She drew her legs up under her and leaned over the table. She felt she was a bee.

'A ninseck must be an animal,' she said stoutly. 'It makes a noise. It's not like a fish.'

'I'm a bull, I'm a bull!' cried Pip. And he gave such a tremendous bellow – how did he make that noise? – that Lottie looked quite alarmed.

'I'll be a sheep,' said little Rags. 'A whole lot of sheep went past this morning.'

'How do you know?'

'Dad heard them. Baa!' He sounded like the little lamb that trots behind and seems to wait to be carried.

'Cock-a-doodle-do!' shrilled Isabel. With her red cheeks and bright eyes she looked like a rooster.

'What'll I be?' Lottie asked everybody, and she sat there smiling, waiting for them to decide for her. It had to be an easy one.

'Be a donkey, Lottie.' It was Kezia's suggestion. 'Hee-haw! You can't forget that.'

'Hee-haw!' said Lottie solemnly. 'When do I have to say it?'

'I'll explain, I'll explain,' said the bull. It was he who had the cards. He waved them round his head. 'All be quiet! All listen!' And he waited for them. 'Look here, Lottie.' He turned up a card. 'It's got two spots on it – see? Now, if you put that card in the middle and somebody else has one with two spots as well, you say "Hee-haw," and the card's yours.'

'Mine?' Lottie was round-eyed. 'To keep?'

'No, silly. Just for the game, see? Just while we're playing.' The bull was very cross with her.

'Oh, Lottie, you *are* a little silly,' said the proud rooster.

Lottie looked at both of them. Then she hung her head; her lip quivered. 'I don't want to play,' she whispered. The others glanced at one another like conspirators. All of them knew what that meant. She would go away and be discovered somewhere standing with her pinny thrown over her head, in a corner, or against a wall, or even behind a chair.

'Yes, you *do*, Lottie. It's quite easy,' said Kezia.

And Isabel, repentant, said exactly like a grown-up, 'Watch *me*, Lottie, and you'll soon learn.'

'Cheer up, Lot,' said Pip. 'There, I know what I'll do. I'll give you the first one. It's mine, really, but I'll give it to you. Here you are.' And he slammed the card down in front of Lottie.

Lottie revived at that. But now she was in another difficulty. 'I haven't got a hanky,' she said; 'I want one badly, too.'

'Here, Lottie, you can use mine.' Rags dipped into his sailor blouse and brought up a very wet-looking one, knotted together. 'Be very careful,' he warned her. 'Only use that corner. Don't undo it. I've got a little starfish inside I'm going to try and tame.'

'Oh, come on, you girls,' said the bull. 'And mind – you're not to look at your cards. You've got to keep your hands under the table till I say "Go."'

Smack went the cards round the table. They tried with all their might to see, but Pip was too quick for them. It was very exciting, sitting there in the washhouse; it was all they could do not to burst into a little chorus of animals before Pip had finished dealing.

'Now, Lottie, you begin.'

Timidly Lottie stretched out a hand, took the top card off her pack, had a good look at it – it was plain she was counting the spots – and put it down.

'No, Lottie, you can't do that. You mustn't look first. You must turn it the other way over.'

'But then everybody will see it the same time as me,' said Lottie.

The game proceeded. Mooe-ooo-er! The bull was terrible. He charged over the table and seemed to eat the cards up.

Bss-ss! said the bee.

Cock-a-doodle-do! Isabel stood up in her excitement and moved her elbows like wings.

Baa! Little Rags put down the King of Diamonds and Lottie put down the one they called the King of Spain. She had hardly any cards left.

'Why don't you call out, Lottie?'

'I've forgotten what I am,' said the donkey woefully.

'Well, change! Be a dog instead! Bow-wow!'

'Oh yes. That's *much* easier.' Lottie smiled again. But when she and Kezia both had a one Kezia waited on purpose. The others made signs to Lottie and pointed. Lottie turned very red; she looked bewildered, and at last she said, 'Hee-haw! Ke-zia.'

'Ss! Wait a minute!' They were in the very thick of it when the bull stopped them, holding up his hand. 'What's that? What's that noise?'

'What noise? What do you mean?' asked the rooster.

'Ss! Shut up! Listen!' They were mouse-still. 'I thought I heard a – a sort of knocking,' said the bull.

'What was it like?' asked the sheep faintly.

No answer.

The bee gave a shudder. 'Whatever did we shut the door for?' she said softly. Oh, why, why had they shut the door?

While they were playing, the day had faded; the gorgeous sunset had blazed and died. And now the quick dark came racing over the sea, over the sand-hills, up the paddock. You were frightened to look in the corners of the washhouse, and yet you had to look with all your might. And somewhere, far away, grandma was lighting a lamp. The blinds were being pulled down; the kitchen fire leapt in the tins on the mantelpiece.

'It would be awful now,' said the bull, 'if a spider was to fall from the ceiling on to the table, wouldn't it?'

'Spiders don't fall from ceilings.'

'Yes, they do. Our Min told us she'd seen a spider as big as a saucer, with long hairs on it like a gooseberry.'

Quickly all the little heads were jerked up; all the little bodies drew together, pressed together.

'Why doesn't somebody come and call us?' cried the rooster.

Oh, those grown-ups, laughing and snug, sitting in the lamp-light, drinking out of cups! They'd forgotten about them. No, not really forgotten. That was what their smile meant. They had decided to leave them there all by themselves.

Suddenly Lottie gave such a piercing scream that all of them jumped off the forms, all of them screamed too. 'A face – a face looking!' shrieked Lottie.

It was true, it was real. Pressed against the window was a pale face, black eyes, a black beard.

'Grandma! Mother! Somebody!'

But they had not got to the door, tumbling over one another, before it opened for Uncle Jonathan. He had come to take the little boys home.

X

He had meant to be there before, but in the front garden he had come upon Linda walking up and down the grass, stopping to pick off a dead pink or give a top-heavy carnation something to lean against, or to take a deep breath of something, and then walking on again, with her little air of remoteness. Over her white frock she wore a yellow, pink-fringed shawl from the Chinaman's shop.

'Hallo, Jonathan!' called Linda. And Jonathan whipped off his shabby panama, pressed it against his breast, dropped on one knee, and kissed Linda's hand.

'Greeting, my Fair One! Greeting, my Celestial Peach Blossom!' boomed the bass voice gently. 'Where are the other noble dames?'

'Beryl's out playing bridge and mother's giving the boy his bath. . . . Have you come to borrow something?'

The Trouts were for ever running out of things and sending across to the Burnells' at the last moment.

But Jonathan only answered, 'A little love, a little kindness'; and he walked by his sister-in-law's side.

Linda dropped into Beryl's hammock under the manuka tree, and Jonathan stretched himself on the grass beside her, pulled a long stalk and began chewing it. They knew each other well. The voices of children cried from the other gardens. A fisherman's light cart shook along the sandy road, and from far away they heard a dog barking; it was muffled as though the dog had its head in a sack. If you listened you could just hear the soft swish of the sea at full tide sweeping the pebbles. The sun was sinking.

'And so you go back to the office on Monday, do you, Jonathan?' asked Linda.

'On Monday the cage door opens and clangs to upon the victim for another eleven months and a week,' answered Jonathan.

Linda swung a little. 'It must be awful,' she said slowly.

'Would ye have me laugh, my fair sister? Would ye have me weep?'

Linda was so accustomed to Jonathan's way of talking that she paid no attention to it.

'I suppose,' she said vaguely, 'one gets used to it. One gets used to anything.'

'Does one? Hum!' The 'Hum' was so deep it seemed to boom from underneath the ground. 'I wonder how it's done,' brooded Jonathan; 'I've never managed it.'

Looking at him as he lay there, Linda thought again how attractive he was. It was strange to think that he was only an ordinary clerk, that Stanley earned twice as much money as he. What was the matter with Jonathan? He had no ambition; she supposed that was it. And yet one felt he was gifted, exceptional. He was passionately fond of music; every spare penny he had went on books. He was always full of new ideas, schemes, plans. But nothing came of it all. The new fire blazed in Jonathan; you almost heard it roaring softly as he explained, described and dilated on the new thing; but a moment later it had fallen in and there was nothing but ashes, and Jonathan went about with a look like hunger in his black eyes. At these times he exaggerated his absurd manner of speaking, and he sang in church – he was the leader of the choir – with such fearful dramatic intensity that the meanest hymn put on an unholy splendour.

'It seems to me just as imbecile, just as infernal, to have to go to the office on Monday,' said Jonathan, 'as it always has done and always will do. To spend all the best years of one's life sitting on a stool from nine to five, scratching in somebody's ledger! It's a queer use to make of one's . . . one and only life, isn't it? Or do I fondly dream?' He rolled over on the grass and looked up at Linda. 'Tell me, what is the difference between my life and that of an ordinary prisoner? The only difference I can see is that I put myself in jail and nobody's ever going to let me out. That's a more intolerable situation than the other. For if I'd been – pushed in, against my will – kicking, even – once the door was locked, or at any rate in five years or so, I might have accepted the fact and begun to take an interest in the flight of flies or counting the warder's steps along the passage with particular attention to variations of tread and so on. But as it is, I'm like an insect that's flown into a room of its own accord. I dash against the walls, dash against the windows, flop against the ceiling, do everything on God's earth, in fact, except fly out again. And all the while I'm thinking, like that moth, or that butterfly, or whatever it is, 'The shortness of life! The shortness of life!' I've only one night or one day, and there's this vast dangerous garden, waiting out there, undiscovered, unexplored.'

'But, if you feel like that, why –' began Linda quickly.

'*Ah!*' cried Jonathan. And that 'Ah!' was somehow almost exultant. 'There you have me. Why? Why indeed? There's the maddening, mysterious question. Why don't I fly out again? There's the window or the door or whatever it was I came in by. It's not hopelessly shut – is it? Why don't I find it and be off? Answer me that, little sister.' But he gave her no time to answer.

'I'm exactly like that insect again. For some reason' – Jonathan paused between the words – 'it's not allowed, it's forbidden, it's against the insect law, to stop banging and flopping and crawling up the pane even for an instant. Why don't I leave the office? Why don't I seriously consider, this moment, for instance, what it is that prevents me leaving? It's not as though I'm tremendously tied. I've two boys to provide for, but, after all, they're boys. I could cut off to sea, or get a job up-country, or –' Suddenly he smiled at Linda and said in a changed voice, as if he were confiding a secret, 'Weak . . . weak. No stamina. No anchor. No guiding principle, let us call it.' But then the dark velvety voice rolled out:

> *Would ye hear the story*
> *How it unfolds itself . . .*

and they were silent.

The sun had set. In the western sky there were great masses of crushed-up rose-coloured clouds. Broad beams of light shone through the clouds and beyond them as if they would cover the whole sky. Overhead the blue faded; it turned a pale gold, and the bush outlined against it gleamed dark and brilliant like metal. Sometimes when those beams of light show in the sky they are very awful. They remind you that up there sits Jehovah, the jealous God, the Almighty, Whose eye is upon you, ever watchful, never weary. You remember that at His coming the whole earth will shake into one ruined graveyard; the cold, bright angels will drive you this way and that, and there will be no time to explain what could be explained so simply. . . . But to-night it seemed to Linda there was something infinitely joyful and loving in those silver beams. And now no sound came from the sea. It breathed softly as if it would draw that tender, joyful beauty into its own bosom.

'It's all wrong, it's all wrong,' came the shadowy voice of Jonathan. 'It's not the scene, it's not the setting for . . . three stools, three desks, three inkpots and a wire blind.'

Linda knew that he would never change, but she said, 'Is it too late, even now?'

'I'm old – I'm old,' intoned Jonathan. He bent towards her, he passed his hand over his head. 'Look!' His black hair was speckled all over with silver, like the breast plumage of a black fowl.

Linda was surprised. She had no idea that he was grey. And yet, as he stood up beside her and sighed and stretched, she saw him, for the first time, not resolute, not gallant, not careless, but touched already with age. He looked very tall on the darkening grass, and the thought crossed her mind, 'He is like a weed.'

Jonathan stooped again and kissed her fingers.

'Heaven reward thy sweet patience, lady mine,' he murmured. 'I must go seek those heirs to my fame and fortune . . . .' He was gone.

XI

Light shone in the windows of the bungalow. Two square patches of gold fell upon the pinks and the peaked marigolds. Florrie, the cat, came out on to the veranda, and sat on the top step, her white paws close together, her tail curled round. She looked content, as though she had been waiting for this moment all day.

'Thank goodness, it's getting late,' said Florrie. 'Thank goodness, the long day is over.' Her greengage eyes opened.

Presently there sounded the rumble of the coach, the crack of Kelly's whip. It came near enough for one to hear the voices of the men from town, talking loudly together. It stopped at the Burnells' gate.

Stanley was half-way up the path before he saw Linda. 'Is that you, darling?'

'Yes, Stanley.'

He leapt across the flower-bed and seized her in his arms. She was enfolded in that familiar, eager, strong embrace.

'Forgive me, darling, forgive me,' stammered Stanley, and he put his hand under her chin and lifted her face to him.

'Forgive you?' smiled Linda. 'But whatever for?'

'Good God! You can't have forgotten,' cried Stanley Burnell. 'I've thought of nothing else all day. I've had the hell of a day. I made up my mind to dash out and telegraph, and then I thought the wire mightn't reach you before I did. I've been in tortures, Linda.'

'But, Stanley,' said Linda, 'what must I forgive you for?'

'Linda!' – Stanley was very hurt – 'didn't you realise – you must have realised – I went away without saying good-bye to you this morning? I can't imagine how I can have done such a thing. My confounded temper, of course. But – well' – and he sighed and took her in his arms again – 'I've suffered for it enough to-day.'

'What's that you've got in your hand?' asked Linda. 'New gloves? Let me see.'

'Oh, just a cheap pair of wash-leather ones,' said Stanley humbly. 'I noticed Bell was wearing some in the coach this morning, so, as I was passing the shop, I dashed in and got myself a pair. What are you smiling at? You don't think it was wrong of me, do you?'

'On the *con*-trary, darling,' said Linda, 'I think it was most sensible.'

She pulled one of the large, pale gloves on her own fingers and looked at her hand, turning it this way and that. She was still smiling.

Stanley wanted to say, 'I was thinking of you the whole time I bought them.' It was true, but for some reason he couldn't say it. 'Let's go in,' said he.

XII

Why does one feel so different at night? Why is it so exciting to be awake when everybody else is asleep? Late – it is very late! And yet every moment you feel more and more wakeful, as though you were slowly, almost with every breath, waking up into a new, wonderful, far more thrilling and exciting world than the daylight one. And what is this queer sensation that you're a conspirator? Lightly, stealthily you move about your room. You take something off the dressing-table and put it down again without a sound. And everything, even the bed-post, knows you, responds, shares your secret. . . .

You're not very fond of your room by day. You never think about it. You're in and out, the door opens and slams, the cupboard creaks. You sit down on the side of your bed, change your shoes and dash out again. A dive down to the glass, two pins in your hair, powder your nose and off again. But now – it's suddenly dear to you. It's a darling little funny room. It's yours. Oh, what a joy it is to own things! Mine – my own!

'My very own for ever?'

'Yes.' Their lips met.

No, of course, that had nothing to do with it. That was all nonsense and rubbish. But, in spite of herself, Beryl saw so plainly two people standing in the middle of her room. Her arms were round his neck; he held her. And now he whispered, 'My beauty, my little beauty!' She jumped off her bed, ran over to the window and kneeled on the window-seat, with her elbows on the sill. But the beautiful night, the garden, every bush, every leaf, even the white palings, even the stars, were conspirators too. So bright was the moon that the flowers were bright as by day; the shadow of the nasturtiums, exquisite lily-like leaves and wide-open flowers, lay across the silvery verandah. The manuka tree, bent by the southerly winds, was like a bird on one leg stretching out a wing.

But when Beryl looked at the bush, it seemed to her the bush was sad.

'We are dumb trees, reaching up in the night, imploring we know not what,' said the sorrowful bush.

It is true when you are by yourself and you think about life, it is always sad. All that excitement and so on has a way of suddenly leaving you, and it's as though, in the silence, somebody called your name, and you heard your name for the first time. 'Beryl!'

'Yes, I'm here. I'm Beryl. Who wants me?'

'Beryl!'

'Let me come.'

It is lonely living by oneself. Of course, there are relations, friends, heaps of them; but that's not what she means. She wants some one who will find the Beryl they none of them know, who will expect her to be that Beryl always. She wants a lover.

'Take me away from all these other people, my love. Let us go far away. Let us live our life, all new, all ours, from the very beginning. Let us make our fire. Let us sit down to eat together. Let us have long talks at night.'

And the thought was almost, 'Save me, my love. Save me!'

. . . 'Oh, go on! Don't be a prude, my dear. You enjoy yourself while you're young. That's my advice.' And a high rush of silly laughter joined Mrs. Harry Kember's loud, indifferent neigh.

You see, it's so frightfully difficult when you've nobody. You're so at the mercy of things. You can't just be rude. And you've always this horror of seeming inexperienced and stuffy like the other ninnies at the Bay. And – and it's fascinating to know you've power over people. Yes, that is fascinating. . . .

Oh why, oh why doesn't 'he' come soon?

If I go on living here, thought Beryl, anything may happen to me.

'But how do you know he is coming at all?' mocked a small voice within her.

But Beryl dismissed it. She couldn't be left. Other people, perhaps, but not she. It wasn't possible to think that Beryl Fairfield never married, that lovely fascinating girl.

'Do you remember Beryl Fairfield?'

'Remember her! As if I could forget her! It was one summer at the Bay that I saw her. She was standing on the beach in a blue' – no, pink – 'muslin frock, holding on a big cream' – no, black – 'straw hat. But it's years ago now.'

'She's as lovely as ever, more so if anything.'

Beryl smiled, bit her lip, and gazed over the garden. As she gazed, she saw somebody, a man, leave the road, step along the paddock beside their palings as if he was coming straight towards her. Her heart beat. Who was it? Who could it be? It couldn't be a burglar, certainly not a burglar, for he was smoking and he strolled lightly. Beryl's heart leapt; it seemed to turn right over, and then to stop. She recognised him.

'Good evening, Miss Beryl,' said the voice softly.

'Good evening.'

'Won't you come for a little walk?' it drawled.

Come for a walk – at that time of night! 'I couldn't. Everybody's in bed. Everybody's asleep.'

'Oh,' said the voice lightly, and a whiff of sweet smoke reached her. 'What does everybody matter? Do come! It's such a fine night. There's not a soul about.'

Beryl shook her head. But already something stirred in her, something reared its head.

The voice said, 'Frightened?' It mocked, 'Poor little girl!'

'Not in the least,' said she. As she spoke that weak thing within her seemed to uncoil, to grow suddenly tremendously strong; she longed to go!

And just as if this was quite understood by the other, the voice said, gently and softly, but finally, 'Come along!'

Beryl stepped over her low window, crossed the verandah, ran down the grass to the gate. He was there before her.

'That's right,' breathed the voice, and it teased, 'You're not frightened, are you? You're not frightened?'

She was; now she was here she was terrified, and it seemed to her everything was different. The moonlight stared and glittered; the shadows were like bars of iron. Her hand was taken.

'Not in the least,' she said lightly. 'Why should I be?'

Her hand was pulled gently, tugged. She held back.

'No, I'm not coming any farther,' said Beryl.

'Oh, rot!' Harry Kember didn't believe her. 'Come along! We'll just go as far as that fuchsia bush. Come along!'

The fuchsia bush was tall. It fell over the fence in a shower. There was a little pit of darkness beneath.

'No, really, I don't want to,' said Beryl.

For a moment Harry Kember didn't answer. Then he came close to her, turned to her, smiled and said quickly, 'Don't be silly! Don't be silly!'

His smile was something she'd never seen before. Was he drunk? That bright, blind, terrifying smile froze her with horror. What was she doing? How had she got here? The stern garden asked her as the gate pushed open, and quick as a cat Harry Kember came through and snatched her to him.

'Cold little devil! Cold little devil!' said the hateful voice.

But Beryl was strong. She slipped, ducked, wrenched free.

'You are vile, vile,' said she.

'Then why in God's name did you come?' stammered Harry Kember.

Nobody answered him.

A cloud, small, serene, floated across the moon. In that moment of darkness the sea sounded deep, troubled. Then the cloud sailed away, and the sound of the sea was a vague murmur, as though it waked out of a dark dream. All was still.

MARRIAGE À LA MODE

On his way to the station William remembered with a fresh pang of disappointment that he was taking nothing down to the kiddies. Poor little chaps! It was hard lines on them. Their first words always were as they ran to greet him, 'What have you got for me, daddy?' and he had nothing. He would have to buy them some sweets at the station. But that was what he had done for the past four Saturdays; their faces had fallen last time when they saw the same old boxes produced again.

And Paddy had said, 'I had red ribbing on mine *bee*-fore!'

And Johnny had said, 'It's always pink on mine. I hate pink.'

But what was William to do? The affair wasn't so easily settled. In the old days, of course, he would have taken a taxi off to a decent toyshop and chosen them something in five minutes. But nowadays they had Russian toys, French toys, Serbian toys – toys from God knows where. It was over a year since Isabel had scrapped the old donkeys and engines and so on because they were so 'dreadfully sentimental' and 'so appallingly bad for the babies' sense of form.'

'It's so important,' the new Isabel had explained, 'that they should like the right things from the very beginning. It saves so much time later on. Really, if the poor pets have to spend their infant years staring at these horrors, one can imagine them growing up and asking to be taken to the Royal Academy.'

And she spoke as though a visit to the Royal Academy was certain immediate death to anyone. . . .

'Well, I don't know,' said William slowly. 'When I was their age I used to go to bed hugging an old towel with a knot in it.'

The new Isabel looked at him, her eyes narrowed, her lips apart.

'*Dear* William! I'm sure you did!' She laughed in the new way.

Sweets it would have to be, however, thought William gloomily, fishing in his pocket for change for the taxi-man. And he saw the kiddies handing the boxes round – they were awfully generous little chaps – while Isabel's precious friends didn't hesitate to help themselves. . . .

What about fruit? William hovered before a stall just inside the station. What about a melon each? Would they have to share that, too? Or a pineapple for Pad, and a melon for Johnny? Isabel's friends could hardly go sneaking up to the nursery at the children's meal-times. All the same, as he bought the melon William had a horrible vision of one of Isabel's young poets lapping up a slice, for some reason, behind the nursery door.

With his two very awkward parcels he strode off to his train. The platform was crowded, the train was in. Doors banged open and shut. There came such a loud hissing from the engine that people looked dazed as they scurried to and fro. William made straight for a first-class smoker, stowed away his suit-case and parcels, and taking a huge wad of papers out of his inner pocket, he flung down in the corner and began to read.

'Our client moreover is positive. . . . We are inclined to reconsider . . . in the event of –' Ah, that was better. William pressed back his flattened hair and stretched his legs across the carriage floor. The familiar dull gnawing in his breast quietened down. 'With regard to our decision –' He took out a blue pencil and scored a paragraph slowly.

Two men came in, stepped across him, and made for the farther corner. A young fellow swung his golf clubs into the rack and sat down opposite. The train gave a gentle lurch, they were off. William glanced up and saw the hot, bright station slipping away. A red-faced girl raced along by the carriages, there was something strained and almost desperate in the way she waved and called. 'Hysterical!' thought William dully. Then a greasy, black-faced workman at the end of the platform grinned at the passing train. And William thought, 'A filthy life!' and went back to his papers.

When he looked up again there were fields, and beasts standing for shelter under the dark trees. A wide river, with naked children splashing in the shallows, glided into sight and was gone again. The sky shone pale, and one bird drifted high like a dark fleck in a jewel.

'We have examined our client's correspondence files. . . .' The last sentence he had read echoed in his mind. 'We have examined . . .' William hung on to that sentence, but it was no good; it snapped in the middle, and the fields, the sky, the sailing bird, the water, all said, 'Isabel'. The same thing happened every Saturday afternoon. When he was on his way to meet Isabel there began those countless imaginary meetings. She was at the station, standing just a little apart from everybody else; she was sitting in the open taxi outside; she was at the garden gate; walking across the parched grass; at the door, or just inside the hall.

And her clear, light voice said, 'It's William,' or 'Hillo, William!' or 'So William has come!' He touched her cool hand, her cool cheek.

The exquisite freshness of Isabel! When he had been a little boy, it was his delight to run into the garden after a shower of rain and shake the rose-bush over him. Isabel was that rose-bush, petal-soft, sparkling and cool. And he was still that little boy. But there was no running into the garden now, no laughing and shaking. The dull, persistent gnawing in his breast started again. He drew up his legs, tossed the papers aside, and shut his eyes.

'What is it, Isabel? What is it?' he said tenderly. They were in their bedroom in the new house. Isabel sat on a painted stool before the dressing-table that was strewn with little black and green boxes.

'What is what, William?' And she bent forward, and her fine light hair fell over her cheeks.

'Ah, you know!' He stood in the middle of the strange room and he felt a stranger. At that Isabel wheeled round quickly and faced him.

'Oh, William!' she cried imploringly, and she held up the hairbrush: 'Please! Please don't be so dreadfully stuffy

" 'Oh, William!' she cried, imploringly,
and she held up the hairbrush. "Please!
Please don't be so dreadfully stuffy and—
tragic' "

Drawn by W. Smithson Broadhead

The Sphere 31 December 1921 p364

and – tragic. You're always saying or looking or hinting that I've changed. Just because I've got to know really congenial people, and go about more, and am frightfully keen on – on everything, you behave as though I'd – ' Isabel tossed back her hair and laughed – 'killed our love or something. It's so awfully absurd' – she bit her lip – 'and it's so maddening, William. Even this new house and the servants you grudge me.'

'Isabel!'

'Yes, yes, it's true in a way,' said Isabel quickly. 'You think they are another bad sign. Oh, I know you do. I feel it,' she said softly, 'every time you come up the stairs. But we couldn't have gone on living in that other poky little hole, William. Be practical, at least! Why, there wasn't enough room for the babies even.'

No, it was true. Every morning when he came back from chambers it was to find the babies with Isabel in the back drawing-room. They were having rides on the leopard skin thrown over the sofa back, or they were playing shops with Isabel's desk for a counter, or Pad was sitting on the hearthrug rowing away for dear life with a little brass fire shovel, while Johnny shot at pirates with the tongs. Every evening they each had a pick-a-back up the narrow stairs to their fat old Nanny.

Yes, he supposed it was a poky little house. A little white house with blue curtains and a window-box of petunias. William met their friends at the door with 'Seen our petunias? Pretty terrific for London, don't you think?'

But the imbecile thing, the absolutely extraordinary thing was that he hadn't the slightest idea that Isabel wasn't as happy as he. God, what blindness! He hadn't the remotest notion in those days that she really hated that inconvenient little house, that she thought the fat Nanny was ruining the babies, that she was desperately lonely, pining for new people and new music and pictures and so on. If they hadn't gone to that studio party at Moira Morrison's – if Moira Morrison hadn't said as they were leaving, 'I'm going to rescue your wife, selfish man. She's like an exquisite little Titania' – if Isabel hadn't gone with Moira to Paris – if – if . . .

The train stopped at another station. Bettingford. Good heavens! They'd be there in ten minutes. William stuffed the papers back into his pockets; the young man opposite had long since disappeared. Now the other two got out. The late afternoon sun shone on women in cotton frocks and little sunburnt, barefoot children. It blazed on a silky yellow flower with coarse leaves which sprawled over a bank of rock. The air ruffling through the window smelled of the sea. Had Isabel the same crowd with her this week-end, wondered William?

And he remembered the holidays they used to have, the four of them, with a little farm girl, Rose, to look after the babies. Isabel wore a jersey and her hair in a plait; she looked about fourteen. Lord! how his nose used to peel! And the amount they ate, and the amount they slept in that immense feather bed with their feet locked together. . . . William couldn't help a grim smile as he thought of Isabel's horror if she knew the full extent of his sentimentality.

* * *

'Hillo, William!' She was at the station after all, standing just as he had imagined, apart from the others, and – William's heart leapt – she was alone.

'Hallo, Isabel!' William stared. He thought she looked so beautiful that he had to say something. 'You look very cool.'

'Do I?' said Isabel. 'I don't feel very cool. Come along, your horrid old train is late. The taxi's outside.' She put her hand lightly on his arm as they passed the ticket collector. 'We've all come to meet you,' she said. 'But we've left Bobby Kane at the sweet shop, to be called for.'

'Oh!' said William. It was all he could say for the moment.

There in the glare waited the taxi, with Bill Hunt and Dennis Green sprawling on one side, their hats tilted over their faces, while on the other, Moira Morrison, in a bonnet like a huge strawberry, jumped up and down.

'No ice! No ice! No ice!' she shouted gaily.

And Dennis chimed in from under his hat. '*Only* to be had from the fishmonger's.'

And Bill Hunt, emerging, added, 'With *whole* fish in it.'

'Oh, what a bore!' wailed Isabel. And she explained to William how they had been chasing round the town for ice while she waited for him. 'Simply everything is running down the steep cliffs into the sea, beginning with the butter.'

'We shall have to anoint ourselves with butter,' said Dennis. 'May thy head, William, lack not ointment.'

'Look here,' said William, 'how are we going to sit? I'd better get up by the driver.'

'No, Bobby Kane's by the driver,' said Isabel. 'You're to sit between Moira and me.' The taxi started. 'What have you got in those mysterious parcels?'

'De-cap-it-ated heads!' said Bill Hunt, shuddering beneath his hat.

'Oh, fruit!' Isabel sounded very pleased. 'Wise William! A melon and a pineapple. How too nice!'

'No, wait a bit,' said William, smiling. But he really was anxious. 'I brought them down for the kiddies.'

'Oh, my dear!' Isabel laughed, and slipped her hand through his arm. 'They'd be rolling in agonies if they were to eat them. No' – she patted his hand – 'you must bring them something next time. I refuse to part with my pineapple.'

'Cruel Isabel! Do let me smell it!' said Moira. She flung her arms across William appealingly. 'Oh!' The strawberry bonnet fell forward: she sounded quite faint.

'A Lady in Love with a Pine-apple,' said Dennis, as the taxi drew up before a little shop with a striped blind. Out came Bobby Kane, his arms full of little packets.

'I do hope they'll be good. I've chosen them because of the colours. There are some round things which really look too divine. And just look at this nougat,' he cried ecstatically, 'just look at it! It's a perfect little ballet!'

But at that moment the shopman appeared. 'Oh, I forgot. They're none of them paid for,' said Bobby, looking frightened. Isabel gave the shopman a note, and Bobby was radiant again. 'Hallo, William! I'm sitting by the driver.' And bare-headed, all in white, with his sleeves rolled up to the shoulders, he leapt into his place. 'Avanti!' he cried. . . .

After tea the others went off to bathe, while William stayed and made his peace with the kiddies. But Johnny and Paddy were asleep, the rose-red glow had paled, bats were flying, and still the bathers had not returned. As William wandered downstairs, the maid crossed the hall carrying a lamp. He followed her into the sitting-room. It was a long room, coloured yellow. On the wall opposite William some one had painted a young man, over life-size, with very wobbly legs, offering a wide-eyed daisy to a young woman who had one very short arm and one very long, thin one. Over the chairs and sofa there hung strips of black material, covered with big splashes like broken eggs, and everywhere one looked there seemed to be an ash-tray full of cigarette ends. William sat down in one of the arm-chairs. Nowadays, when one felt with one hand down the sides, it wasn't to come upon a sheep with three legs or a cow that had lost one horn, or a very fat dove out of the Noah's Ark. One fished up yet another little paper-covered book of smudged-looking poems. . . . He thought of the wad of papers in his pocket, but he was too hungry and tired to read. The door was open; sounds came from the kitchen. The servants were talking as if they were alone in the house. Suddenly there came a loud screech of laughter and an equally loud 'Sh!' They had remembered him. William got up and went through the french windows into the garden, and as he stood there in the shadow he heard the bathers coming up the sandy road; their voices rang through the quiet.

'I think it's up to Moira to use her little arts and wiles.'

A tragic moan from Moira.

'We ought to have a gramophone for the week-ends that played "The Maid of the Mountains."'

'Oh no! Oh no!' cried Isabel's voice. 'That's not fair to William. Be nice to him, my children! He's only staying until to-morrow evening.'

'Leave him to me,' cried Bobby Kane. 'I'm awfully good at looking after people.'

The gate swung open and shut. William moved on the terrace; they had seen him. 'Hallo, William!' And Bobby Kane, flapping his towel, began to leap and pirouette on the parched lawn. 'Pity you didn't come, William. The water was divine. And we all went to a little pub afterwards and had sloe gin.'

The others had reached the house. 'I say, Isabel,' called Bobby, 'would you like me to wear my Nijinsky dress to-night?'

'No,' said Isabel, 'nobody's going to dress. We're all starving. William's starving, too. Come along, *mes amis*, let's begin with sardines.'

'I've found the sardines,' said Moira, and she ran into the hall, holding a box high in the air.

'A Lady with a Box of Sardines,' said Dennis gravely.

'Well, William, and how's London?' asked Bill Hunt, drawing the cork out of a bottle of whisky.

'Oh, London's not much changed,' answered William.

'Good old London,' said Bobby, very hearty, spearing a sardine.

But a moment later William was forgotten. Moira Morrison began wondering what colour one's legs really were under water.

'Mine are the palest, palest mushroom colour.'

Bill and Dennis ate enormously. And Isabel filled glasses, and changed plates, and found matches, smiling blissfully. At one moment she said, 'I do wish, Bill, you'd paint it.'

'Paint what?' said Bill loudly, stuffing his mouth with bread.

'Us,' said Isabel, 'round the table. It would be so fascinating in twenty years' time.'

Bill screwed up his eyes and chewed. 'Light's wrong,' he said rudely, 'far too much yellow'; and went on eating. And that seemed to charm Isabel, too.

But after supper they were all so tired they could do nothing but yawn until it was late enough to go to bed. . . .

It was not until William was waiting for his taxi the next afternoon that he found himself alone with Isabel. When he brought his suit-case down into the hall, Isabel left the others and went over to him. She stooped down and picked up the suit-case. 'What a weight!' she said, and she gave a little awkward laugh. 'Let me carry it! To the gate.'

'No, why should you?' said William. 'Of course not. Give it to me.'

'Oh, please do let me,' said Isabel. 'I want to, really.' They walked together silently. William felt there was nothing to say now.

'There,' said Isabel triumphantly, setting the suit-case down, and she looked anxiously along the sandy road. 'I hardly seem to have seen you this time,' she said breathlessly. 'It's so short, isn't it? I feel you've only just come. Next time –' The taxi came into sight. 'I hope they look after you properly in London. I'm so sorry the babies have been out all day, but Miss Neil had arranged it. They'll hate missing you. Poor William, going back to London.' The taxi turned. 'Good-bye!' She gave him a little hurried kiss; she was gone.

Fields, trees, hedges streamed by. They shook through the empty, blind-looking little town, ground up the steep pull to the station. The train was in. William made straight for a first-class smoker, flung back into the corner, but this time he let the papers alone. He folded his arms against the dull, persistent gnawing, and began in his mind to write a letter to Isabel.

* * *

The post was late as usual. They sat outside the house in long chairs under coloured parasols. Only Bobby Kane lay on the turf at Isabel's feet. It was dull, stifling; the day drooped like a flag.

'Do you think there will be Mondays in Heaven?' asked Bobby childishly.

And Dennis murmured, 'Heaven will be one long Monday.'

But Isabel couldn't help wondering what had happened to the salmon they had for supper last night. She had meant to have fish mayonnaise for lunch and now . . .

Moira was asleep. Sleeping was her latest discovery. 'It's *so* wonderful. One simply shuts one's eyes, that's all. It's *so* delicious.'

When the old ruddy postman came beating along the sandy road on his tricycle one felt the handle-bars ought to have been oars.

Bill Hunt put down his book. 'Letters,' he said complacently, and they all waited. But, heartless postman – O malignant world! There was only one, a fat one for Isabel. Not even a paper.

'And mine's only from William,' said Isabel mournfully.

'From William – already?'

'He's sending you back your marriage lines as a gentle reminder.'

'Does everybody have marriage lines? I thought they were only for servants.'

'Pages and pages! Look at her! A Lady reading a Letter,' said Dennis.

My darling, precious Isabel. Pages and pages there were. As Isabel read on her feeling of astonishment changed to a stifled feeling. What on earth had induced William . . . ? How extraordinary it was. . . . What could have made him . . . ? She felt confused, more and more excited, even frightened. It was just like William. Was it? It was absurd, of course, it must be absurd, ridiculous. 'Ha, ha, ha! Oh dear!' What was she to do? Isabel flung back in her chair and laughed till she couldn't stop laughing.

'Do, do tell us,' said the others. 'You must tell us.'

'I'm longing to,' gurgled Isabel. She sat up, gathered the letter, and waved it at them. 'Gather round,' she said. 'Listen, it's too marvellous. A love-letter!'

'A love-letter! But how divine!' *Darling, precious Isabel.* But she had hardly begun before their laughter interrupted her.

'Go on, Isabel, it's perfect.'

'It's the most marvellous find.'

'Oh, do go on, Isabel!'

God forbid, my darling, that I should be a drag on your happiness.

'Oh! oh! oh!'

'Sh! sh! sh!'

114

And Isabel went on. When she reached the end they were hysterical: Bobby rolled on the turf and almost sobbed.

'You must let me have it just as it is, entire, for my new book,' said Dennis firmly. 'I shall give it a whole chapter.'

'Oh, Isabel,' moaned Moira, 'that wonderful bit about holding you in his arms!'

'I always thought those letters in divorce cases were made up. But they pale before this.'

'Let me hold it. Let me read it, mine own self,' said Bobby Kane.

But, to their surprise, Isabel crushed the letter in her hand. She was laughing no longer. She glanced quickly at them all; she looked exhausted. 'No, not just now. Not just now,' she stammered.

And before they could recover she had run into the house, through the hall, up the stairs into her bedroom. Down she sat on the side of the bed. 'How vile, odious, abominable, vulgar,' muttered Isabel. She pressed her eyes with her knuckles and rocked to and fro. And again she saw them, but not four, more like forty, laughing, sneering, jeering, stretching out their hands while she read them William's letter. Oh, what a loathsome thing to have done. How could she have done it! *God forbid, my darling, that I should be a drag on your happiness.* William! Isabel pressed her face into the pillow. But she felt that even the grave bedroom knew her for what she was, shallow, tinkling, vain. . . .

Presently from the garden below there came voices.

'Isabel, we're all going for a bathe. Do come!'

'Come, thou wife of William!'

'Call her once before you go, call once yet!'

Isabel sat up. Now was the moment, now she must decide. Would she go with them, or stay here and write to William. Which, which should it be? 'I must make up my mind.' Oh, but how could there be any question? Of course she would stay here and write.

'Titania!' piped Moira.

'Isa-bel?'

No, it was too difficult. 'I'll – I'll go with them, and write to William later. Some other time. Later. Not now. But I shall *certainly* write,' thought Isabel hurriedly.

And, laughing in the new way, she ran down the stairs.

Drawn by W. Smithson Broadhead
"Isabel sat up. Now was the moment, now she must decide"

The Sphere 31 December 1921 p365

THE VOYAGE

The Picton boat was due to leave at half-past eleven. It was a beautiful night, mild, starry, only when they got out of the cab and started to walk down the Old Wharf that jutted out into the harbour, a faint wind blowing off the water ruffled under Fenella's hat, and she put up her hand to keep it on. It was dark on the Old Wharf, very dark; the wool sheds, the cattle trucks, the cranes standing up so high, the little squat railway engine, all seemed carved out of solid darkness. Here and there on a rounded wood-pile, that was like the stalk of a huge black mushroom, there hung a lantern, but it seemed afraid to unfurl its timid, quivering light in all that blackness; it burned softly, as if for itself.

Fenella's father pushed on with quick, nervous strides. Beside him her grandma bustled along in her crackling black ulster; they went so fast that she had now and again to give an undignified little skip to keep up with them. As well as her luggage strapped into a neat sausage, Fenella carried clasped to her her grandma's umbrella, and the handle, which was a swan's head, kept giving her shoulder a sharp little peck as if it too wanted her to hurry. . . . Men, their caps pulled down, their collars turned up, swung by; a few women all muffled scurried along; and one tiny boy, only his little black arms and legs showing out of a white woolly shawl, was jerked along angrily between his father and mother; he looked like a baby fly that had fallen into the cream.

Then suddenly, so suddenly that Fenella and her grandma both leapt, there sounded from behind the largest wool shed, that had a trail of smoke hanging over it, *Mia-oo-oo-O-O!*

'First whistle,' said her father briefly, and at that moment they came in sight of the Picton boat. Lying beside the dark wharf, all strung, all beaded with round golden lights, the Picton boat looked as if she was more ready to sail among stars than out into the cold sea. People pressed along the gangway. First went her grandma, then her father, then Fenella. There was a high step down on to the deck, and an old sailor in a jersey standing by gave her his dry, hard hand. They were there; they stepped out of the way of the hurrying people, and standing under a little iron stairway that led to the upper deck they began to say good-bye.

'There, mother, there's your luggage!' said Fenella's father, giving grandma another strapped-up sausage.

'Thank you, Frank.'

'And you've got your cabin tickets safe?'

'Yes, dear.'

'And your other tickets?'

Grandma felt for them inside her glove and showed him the tips.

'That's right.'

He sounded stern, but Fenella, eagerly watching him, saw that he looked tired and sad. *Mia-oo-oo-O-O!* The second whistle blared just above their heads, and a voice like a cry shouted, 'Any more for the gangway?'

'You'll give my love to father,' Fenella saw her father's lips say. And her grandma, very agitated, answered, 'Of course I will, dear. Go now. You'll be left. Go now, Frank. Go now.'

'It's all right, mother. I've got another three minutes.' To her surprise Fenella saw her father take off his hat. He clasped grandma in his arms and pressed her to him. 'God bless you, mother!' she heard him say.

And grandma put her hand, with the black thread glove that was worn through on her ring finger, against his cheek, and she sobbed, 'God bless you, my own brave son!'

This was so awful that Fenella quickly turned her back on them, swallowed once, twice, and frowned terribly at a little green star on a mast head. But she had to turn round again; her father was going.

'Good-bye, Fenella. Be a good girl.' His cold, wet moustache brushed her cheek. But Fenella caught hold of the lapels of his coat.

'How long am I going to stay?' she whispered anxiously. He wouldn't look at her. He shook her off gently, and gently said, 'We'll see about that. Here! Where's your hand?' He pressed something into her palm. 'Here's a shilling in case you should need it.'

A shilling! She must be going away for ever! 'Father!' cried Fenella. But he was gone. He was the last off the ship. The sailors put their shoulders to the gangway. A huge coil of dark rope went flying through the air and fell 'thump' on the wharf. A bell rang; a whistle shrilled. Silently the dark wharf began to slip, to slide, to edge away from them. Now there was a rush of water between. Fenella strained to see with all her might. 'Was that father turning round?' – or waving? – or standing alone? – or walking off by himself? The strip of water grew broader, darker. Now the Picton boat began to swing round steady, pointing out to sea. It was no good looking any longer. There was nothing to be seen but a few lights, the face of the town clock hanging in the air, and more lights, little patches of them, on the dark hills.

The freshening wind tugged at Fenella's skirts; she went back to her grandma. To her relief grandma seemed no longer sad. She had put the two sausages of luggage one on top of the other, and she was sitting on them, her hands folded, her head a little on one side. There was an intent, bright look on her face. Then Fenella saw that her lips were moving and guessed that she was praying. But the old woman gave her a bright nod as if to say the prayer was nearly over. She unclasped her hands, sighed, clasped them again, bent forward, and at last gave herself a soft shake.

'And now, child,' she said, fingering the bow of her bonnet-strings, 'I think we ought to see about our cabins. Keep close to me, and mind you don't slip.'

'Yes, grandma!'

'And be careful the umbrella isn't caught in the stair rail. I saw a beautiful umbrella broken in half like that on my way over!

'Yes, grandma.'

Dark figures of men lounged against the rails. In the glow of their pipes a nose shone out, or the peak of a cap, or a pair

Drawn by W. Smithson Broadhead

" She had put the two sausages of luggage one on top of the other, and she was
sitting on them, her hands folded, her head a little on one side "

The Sphere 24 December 1921 p341

of surprised-looking eyebrows. Fenella glanced up. High in the air, a little figure, his hands thrust in his short jacket pockets, stood staring out to sea. The ship rocked ever so little, and she thought the stars rocked too. And now a pale steward in a linen coat, holding a tray high in the palm of his hand, stepped out of a lighted doorway and skimmed past them. They went through that doorway. Carefully over the high brass-bound step on to the rubber mat and then down such a terribly steep flight of stairs that grandma had to put both feet on each step, and Fenella clutched the clammy brass rail and forgot all about the swan-necked umbrella.

At the bottom grandma stopped; Fenella was rather afraid she was going to pray again. But no, it was only to get out the cabin tickets. They were in the saloon. It was glaring bright and stifling; the air smelled of paint and burnt chop-bones and indiarubber. Fenella wished her grandma would go on, but the old woman was not to be hurried. An immense basket of ham sandwiches caught her eye. She went up to them and touched the top one delicately with her finger.

'How much are the sandwiches?' she asked.

'Tuppence!' bawled a rude steward, slamming down a knife and fork.

Grandma could hardly believe it.

'Twopence *each*?' she asked.

'That's right,' said the steward, and he winked at his companion.

Grandma made a small, astonished face. Then she whispered primly to Fenella, 'What wickedness!' And they sailed out at the further door and along a passage that had cabins on either side. Such a very nice stewardess came to meet them. She was dressed all in blue and her collar and cuffs were fastened with large brass buttons. She seemed to know grandma well.

'Well, Mrs. Crane,' said she, unlocking their washstand. 'We've got you back again. It's not often you give yourself a cabin.'

'No,' said grandma. 'But this time my dear son's thoughtfulness –'

'I hope –' began the stewardess. Then she turned round and took a long, mournful look at grandma's blackness and at Fenella's black coat and skirt, black blouse, and hat with a crape rose.

Grandma nodded. 'It was God's will,' said she.

The stewardess shut her lips and, taking a deep breath, she seemed to expand.

'What I always say is,' she said, as though it was her own discovery, 'sooner or later each of us has to go, and that's a certingty.' She paused. 'Now, can I bring you anything, Mrs. Crane? A cup of tea? I know it's no good offering you a little something to keep the cold out.'

Grandma shook her head. 'Nothing, thank you. We've got a few wine biscuits and Fenella has a very nice banana.'

'Then I'll give you a look later on,' said the stewardess, and she went out, shutting the door.

What a very small cabin it was! It was like being shut up in a box with grandma. The dark round eye above the washstand gleamed at them dully. Fenella felt shy. She stood against the door, still clasping her luggage and the umbrella.

Were they going to get undressed in here? Already her grandma had taken off her bonnet, and, rolling up the strings, she fixed each with a pin to the lining before she hung the bonnet up. Her white hair shone like silk; the little bun at the back was covered with a black net. Fenella hardly ever saw her grandma with her head uncovered; she looked strange.

'I shall put on the woollen fascinator your dear mother crocheted for me,' said grandma, and, unstrapping the sausage, she took it out and wound it round her head; the fringe of grey bobbles danced at her eyebrows as she smiled tenderly and mournfully at Fenella. Then she undid her bodice, and something under that, and something else underneath that. Then there seemed a short, sharp tussle, and grandma flushed faintly. Snip! Snap! She had undone her stays. She breathed a sigh of relief, and sitting on the plush couch, she slowly and carefully pulled off her elastic-sided boots and stood them side by side.

By the time Fenella had taken off her coat and skirt and put on her flannel dressing-gown grandma was quite ready.

'Must I take off my boots, grandma? They're lace.'

Grandma gave them a moment's deep consideration. 'You'd feel a great deal more comfortable if you did, child,' said she. She kissed Fenella. 'Don't forget to say your prayers. Our dear Lord is with us when we are at sea even more than when we are on dry land. And because I am an experienced traveller,' said grandma briskly, 'I shall take the upper berth.'

'But, grandma, however will you get up there?'

Three little spider-like steps were all Fenella saw. The old woman gave a small silent laugh before she mounted them nimbly, and she peered over the high bunk at the astonished Fenella.

'You didn't think your grandma could do that, did you?' said she. And as she sank back Fenella heard her light laugh again.

The hard square of brown soap would not lather, and the water in the bottle was like a kind of blue jelly. How hard it was, too, to turn down those stiff sheets; you simply had to tear your way in. If everything had been different, Fenella might have got the giggles. . . . At last she was inside, and while she lay there panting, there sounded from above a long, soft whispering, as though some one was gently, gently rustling among tissue paper to find something. It was grandma saying her prayers. . . .

A long time passed. Then the stewardess came in; she trod softly and leaned her hand on grandma's bunk.

'We're just entering the Straits,' she said.

'Oh!'

'It's a fine night, but we're rather empty. We may pitch a little.'

And indeed at that moment the Picton boat rose and rose and hung in the air just long enough to give a shiver before she swung down again, and there was the sound of heavy water slapping against her sides. Fenella remembered she had left that swan-necked umbrella standing up on the little couch. If it fell over, would it break? But grandma remembered too, at the same time.

'I wonder if you'd mind, stewardess, laying down my umbrella,' she whispered.

'Not at all, Mrs. Crane.' And the stewardess, coming back to grandma, breathed, 'Your little granddaughter's in such a beautiful sleep.'

'God be praised for that!' said grandma.

'Poor little motherless mite!' said the stewardess. And grandma was still telling the stewardess all about what happened when Fenella fell asleep.

But she hadn't been asleep long enough to dream before she woke up again to see something waving in the air above her head. What was it? What could it be? It was a small grey foot. Now another joined it. They seemed to be feeling about for something; there came a sigh.

'I'm awake, grandma,' said Fenella.

'Oh, dear, am I near the ladder?' asked grandma. 'I thought it was this end.'

'No, grandma, it's the other. I'll put your foot on it. Are we there?' asked Fenella.

'In the harbour,' said grandma. 'We must get up, child. You'd better have a biscuit to steady yourself before you move.'

But Fenella had hopped out of her bunk. The lamp was still burning, but night was over, and it was cold. Peering through that round eye, she could see far off some rocks. Now they were scattered over with foam; now a gull flipped by; and now there came a long piece of real land.

'It's land, grandma,' said Fenella, wonderingly, as though they had been at sea for weeks together. She hugged herself; she stood on one leg and rubbed it with the toes of the other foot; she was trembling. Oh, it had all been so sad lately.

Was it going to change? But all her grandma said was, 'Make haste, child. I should leave your nice banana for the stewardess as you haven't eaten it.' And Fenella put on her black clothes again, and a button sprang off one of her gloves and rolled to where she couldn't reach it. They went up on deck.

But if it had been cold in the cabin, on deck it was like ice. The sun was not up yet, but the stars were dim, and the cold pale sky was the same colour as the cold pale sea. On the land a white mist rose and fell. Now they could see quite plainly dark bush. Even the shapes of the umbrella ferns showed, and those strange silvery withered trees that are like skeletons . . . . Now they could see the landing-stage and some little houses, pale too, clustered together, like shells on the lid of a box. The other passengers tramped up and down, but more slowly than they had the night before, and they looked gloomy.

And now the landing-stage came out to meet them. Slowly it swam towards the Picton boat, and a man holding a coil of rope, and a cart with a small drooping horse and another man sitting on the step, came too.

'It's Mr. Penreddy, Fenella, come for us,' said grandma. She sounded pleased. Her white waxen cheeks were blue with cold, her chin trembled, and she had to keep wiping her eyes and her little pink nose.

'You've got my –'

'Yes, grandma.' Fenella showed it to her.

The rope came flying through the air, and 'smack' it fell on to the deck. The gangway was lowered. Again Fenella followed her grandma on to the wharf over to the little cart, and a moment later they were bowling away. The hooves of the little horse drummed over the wooden piles, then sank softly into the sandy road. Not a soul was to be seen; there was not even a feather of smoke. The mist rose and fell and the sea still sounded asleep as slowly it turned on the beach.

'I seen Mr. Crane yestiddy,' said Mr. Penreddy. 'He looked himself then. Missus knocked him up a batch of scones last week.'

And now the little horse pulled up before one of the shell-like houses. They got down. Fenella put her hand on the gate, and the big, trembling dew-drops soaked through her glove-tips. Up a little path of round white pebbles they went, with drenched sleeping flowers on either side. Grandma's delicate white picotees were so heavy with dew that they were fallen, but their sweet smell was part of the cold morning. The blinds were down in the little house; they mounted the steps on to the verandah. A pair of old bluchers was on one side of the door, and a large red watering-can on the other.

'Tut! tut! Your grandpa,' said grandma. She turned the handle. Not a sound. She called, 'Walter!' And immediately a deep voice that sounded half stifled called back, 'Is that you, Mary?'

'Wait, dear,' said grandma. 'Go in there.' She pushed Fenella gently into a small dusky sitting-room.

On the table a white cat, that had been folded up like a camel, rose, stretched itself, yawned, and then sprang on to the tips of its toes. Fenella buried one cold little hand in the white, warm fur, and smiled timidly while she stroked and listened to grandma's gentle voice and the rolling tones of grandpa.

130

Drawn by W. Smithson Broadhead

" There, lying to one side of an immense bed, lay grandpa. Just his head with a white tuft, and his rosy face and long silver beard . . ."

The Sphere 24 December 1921 p340

A door creaked. 'Come in, dear.' The old woman beckoned, Fenella followed. There, lying to one side of an immense bed, lay grandpa. Just his head with a white tuft, and his rosy face and long silver beard showed over the quilt. He was like a very old wide-awake bird.

'Well, my girl!' said grandpa. 'Give us a kiss!' Fenella kissed him. 'Ugh!' said grandpa. 'Her little nose is as cold as a button. What's that she's holding? Her grandma's umbrella?'

Fenella smiled again, and crooked the swan neck over the bed-rail. Above the bed there was a big text in a deep-black frame:-

> *Lost! One Golden Hour*
> *Set with Sixty Diamond Minutes.*
> No *Reward Is Offered*
> *For It Is* GONE FOR EVER!

'Yer grandma painted that,' said grandpa. And he ruffled his white tuft and looked at Fenella so merrily she almost thought he winked at her.

A MARRIED MAN'S STORY

It is evening. Supper is over. We have left the small, cold dining-room, we have come back to the sitting-room where there is a fire. All is as usual. I am sitting at my writing-table which is placed across a corner so that I am behind it, as it were, and facing the room. The lamp with the green shade is alight; I have before me two large books of reference, both open, a pile of papers. . . . All the paraphernalia, in fact, of an extremely occupied man. My wife, with her little boy on her lap, is in a low chair before the fire. She is about to put him to bed before she clears away the dishes and piles them up in the kitchen for the servant girl to-morrow morning. But the warmth, the quiet, and the sleepy baby, have made her dreamy. One of his red woollen boots is off, one is on. She sits, bent forward, clasping the little bare foot, staring into the glow, and as the fire quickens, falls, flares again, her shadow – an immense *Mother and Child* – is here and gone again upon the wall. . . .

Outside it is raining. I like to think of that cold drenched window behind the blind, and beyond, the dark bushes in the garden, their broad leaves bright with rain, and beyond the fence, the gleaming road with the two hoarse little gutters singing against each other, and the wavering reflections of the lamps, like fishes' tails. While I am here, I am there, lifting my face to the dim sky, and it seems to me it must be raining all over the world – that the whole earth is drenched, is sounding with a soft, quick patter or hard, steady drumming, or gurgling and something that is like sobbing and laughing mingled together, and that light playful splashing that is of water falling into still lakes and flowing rivers. And all at one and the same moment I am arriving in a strange city, slipping under the hood of the cab while the driver whips the cover off the breathing horse, running from shelter to shelter, dodging some one, swerving by some one else. I am conscious of tall houses, their doors and shutters sealed against the night, of dripping balconies and sodden flower-pots. I am brushing through deserted gardens and falling into moist smelling summer-houses (you know how soft and almost crumbling the wood of a summer-house is in the rain), I am standing on the dark quayside, giving my ticket into the wet red hand of the old sailor in an oilskin. How strong the sea smells! How loudly the tied-up boats knock against one another! I am crossing the wet stackyard, hooded in an old sack, carrying a lantern, while the house-dog, like a soaking doormat, springs, shakes himself over me. And now I am walking along a deserted road – it is impossible to miss the puddles, and the trees are stirring – stirring.

But one could go on with such a catalogue for ever – on and on – until one lifted the single arum lily leaf and discovered the tiny snails clinging, until one counted . . . and what then? Aren't those just the signs, the traces of my feeling?

The bright green streaks made by someone who walks over the dewy grass? Not the feeling itself. And as I think that, a mournful, glorious voice begins to sing in my bosom. Yes, perhaps that is nearer what I mean. What a voice! What power! What velvety softness! Marvellous!

Suddenly my wife turns round quickly. She knows – how long has she known? – that I am not 'working'. It is strange that with her full, open gaze she should smile so timidly – and that she should say in such a hesitating voice, 'What are you thinking?'

I smile and draw two fingers across my forehead in the way I have. 'Nothing,' I answer softly.

At that she stirs and, still trying not to make it sound important, she says, 'Oh, but you must have been thinking of something!'

Then I really meet her gaze, meet it fully, and I fancy her face quivers. Will she never grow accustomed to these simple – one might say – everyday little lies? Will she never learn not to expose herself – or to build up defences?

'Truly, I was thinking of nothing.'

There! I seem to see it dart at her. She turns away, pulls the other red sock off the baby, sits him up, and begins to unbutton him behind. I wonder if that little soft rolling bundle sees anything, feels anything? Now she turns him over on her knee, and in this light, his soft arms and legs waving, he is extraordinarily like a young crab. A queer thing is I can't connect him with my wife and myself; I've never accepted him as ours. Each time when I come into the hall and see the perambulator, I catch myself thinking: 'H'm, some one has brought a baby!' Or, when his crying wakes me at night, I feel inclined to blame my wife for having brought the baby in from outside. The truth is, that though one might suspect her of strong maternal feelings, my wife doesn't seem to me the type of woman who bears children in her own body. There's an immense difference! Where is that . . . animal ease and playfulness, that quick kissing and cuddling one has been taught to expect of young mothers? She hasn't a sign of it. I believe that when she ties its bonnet she feels like an aunt and not a mother. But of course I may be wrong; she may be passionately devoted. . . . I don't think so. At any rate, isn't it a trifle indecent to feel like this about one's own wife? Indecent or not, one has these feelings. And one other thing. How can I reasonably expect my wife, *a broken-hearted woman*, to spend her time tossing the baby? But that is beside the mark. She never even began to toss when her heart was whole.

And now she has carried the baby to bed. I hear her soft, deliberate steps moving between the dining-room and the kitchen, there and back again, to the tune of the clattering dishes. And now all is quiet. What is happening now? Oh, I know just as surely as if I'd gone to see – she is standing in the middle of the kitchen facing the rainy window. Her head is bent, with one finger she is tracing something – nothing – on the table. It is cold in the kitchen; the gas jumps; the tap drips; it's a forlorn picture. And nobody is going to come behind her, to take her in his arms, to kiss her soft hair, to lead her to the fire and to rub her hands warm again. Nobody is going to call her or to wonder what she is doing out there.

And she knows it. And yet, being a woman, deep down, deep down, she really does expect the miracle to happen; she really could embrace that dark, dark deceit, rather than live – like this.

To live like this. . . . I write those words very carefully, very beautifully. For some reason I feel inclined to sign them, or to write underneath – Trying a New Pen. But seriously, isn't it staggering to think what may be contained in one innocent-looking little phrase? It tempts me – it tempts me terribly. Scene: The supper-table. My wife has just handed me my tea. I stir it, lift the spoon, idly chase and then carefully capture a speck of tea-leaf, and having brought it ashore, I murmur, quite gently, 'How long shall we continue to live – like – this?' And immediately there is that famous 'blinding flash and deafening roar. Huge pieces of débris (I must say I like débris) are flung into the air . . . and when the dark clouds of smoke have drifted away . . .' But this will never happen; I shall never know it. It will be found upon me 'intact' as they say. 'Open my heart and you will see . . .'

Why? Ah, there you have me! There is the most difficult question of all to answer. Why do people stay together? Putting aside 'for the sake of the children,' and 'the habit of years' and 'economic reasons' as lawyers' nonsense – it's not much more – if one really does try to find out why it is that people don't leave each other, one discovers a mystery. It is because they can't; they are bound. And nobody on earth knows what are the bonds that bind them except those two. Am I being obscure? Well, the thing itself isn't so frightfully

crystal clear, is it? Let me put it like this. Supposing you are
taken, absolutely, first into his confidence and then into hers.
Supposing you know all there is to know about the situation.
And having given it not only your deepest sympathy but
your most honest impartial criticism, you declare, very calmly
(but not without the slightest suggestion of relish – for there is
– I swear there is – in the very best of us – something that leaps
up and cries 'A-ahh !' for joy at the thought of destroying),
'Well, my opinion is that you two people ought to part. You'll
do no earthly good together. Indeed, it seems to me, it's the
duty of either to set the other free.' What happens then? He
– and she – agree. It is their conviction too. You are only
saying what they have been thinking all last night. And away
they go to act on your advice, immediately. . . . And the next
time you hear of them they are still together. You see – you've
reckoned without the unknown quantity – which is their secret
relation to each other – and that they can't disclose even
if they want to. Thus far you may tell and no further. Oh, don't
misunderstand me! It need not necessarily have anything
to do with their sleeping together. . . . But this brings me to a
thought I've often half entertained. Which is that human
beings, as we know them, don't choose each other at all. It
is the owner, the second self inhabiting them, who makes
the choice for his own particular purposes, and – this may
sound absurdly far-fetched – it's the second self in the other
which responds. Dimly – dimly – or so it has seemed to me –
we realise this, at any rate to the extent that we realise the
hopelessness of trying to escape. So that, what it all amounts to
is – if the impermanent selves of my wife and me are happy

– *tant mieux pour nous* – if miserable – *tant pis.* . . . But I don't know, I don't know. And it may be that it's something entirely individual in me – this sensation (yes, it is even a sensation) of how extraordinarily *shell-like* we are as we are – little creatures, peering out of the sentry-box at the gate, ogling through our glass case at the entry, wan little servants, who never can say for certain, even, if the master is out or in. . . .

The door opens . . . My wife. She says, 'I am going to bed.'

And I look up vaguely, and vaguely say, 'You are going to bed.'

'Yes.' A tiny pause. 'Don't forget – will you? – to turn out the gas in the hall.'

And again I repeat, 'The gas in the hall.'

There was a time – the time before – when this habit of mine – it really has become a habit now – it wasn't one then – was one of our sweetest jokes together. It began, of course, when on several occasions I really was deeply engaged and I didn't hear. I emerged only to see her shaking her head and laughing at me, 'You haven't heard a word!'

'No. What did you say?'

Why should she think that so funny and charming? She did – it delighted her. 'Oh, my darling, it's so like you! It's so – so –' And I knew she loved me for it. I knew she positively looked forward to coming in and disturbing me, and so – as one does – I played up. I was guaranteed to be wrapped away every evening at 10.30 p.m. But now? For some reason I feel it would be crude to stop my performance. It's simplest to play on. But what is she waiting for to-night? Why doesn't she go? Why prolong this? She is going. No, her hand on the door-knob, she turns round again, and she says in the most curious, small, breathless voice, 'You're not cold?'

Oh, it's not fair to be as pathetic as that! That was simply damnable. I shuddered all over before I managed to bring out a slow 'No-o!' while my left hand ruffles the reference pages.

She is gone; she will not come back again to-night. It is not only I who recognise that – the room changes too. It relaxes, like an old actor. Slowly the mask is rubbed off; the look of strained attention changes to an air of heavy, sullen brooding. Every line, every fold breathes fatigue. The mirror is quenched; the ash whitens; only my sly lamp burns on . . . . But what a cynical indifference to me it all shows! Or should I perhaps be flattered? No, we understand each other. You know those stories of little children who are suckled by wolves and accepted by the tribe, and how for ever after they move freely among their fleet, grey brothers? Something like that has happened to me. But wait! That about the wolves won't do. Curious! Before I wrote it down, while it was still in my head, I was delighted with it. It seemed to express, and more, to suggest, just what I wanted to say. But written, I can smell the falseness immediately and the . . . source of the smell is in that word fleet. Don't you agree? Fleet, grey brothers! 'Fleet'. A word I never use. When I wrote 'wolves' it skimmed across my mind like a shadow and I couldn't resist it. Tell me! Tell me! Why is it so difficult to write simply – and not only simply but *sotto voce*, if you know what I mean? That is how I long to write. No fine effects – no bravura. But just the plain truth, as only a liar can tell it.

I light a cigarette, lean back, inhale deeply – and find myself wondering if my wife is asleep. Or is she lying in her cold bed, staring into the dark, with those trustful, bewildered eyes? Her eyes are like the eyes of a cow that is being driven along a road. 'Why am I being driven – what harm have I done?' But I really am not responsible for that look; it's her natural expression. One day, when she was turning out a cupboard, she found a little old photograph of herself, taken when she was a girl at school. In her confirmation dress, she explained. And there were the eyes, even then. I remember saying to her, 'Did you always look so sad?' Leaning over my shoulder, she laughed lightly, 'Do I look sad? I think it's just . . . me.' And she waited for me to say something about it. But I was marvelling at her courage at having shown it to me at all. It was a hideous photograph! And I wondered again if she realised how plain she was, and comforted herself with the idea that people who loved each other didn't criticise but accepted everything, or if she really rather liked her appearance and expected me to say something complimentary.

Oh, that was base of me! How could I have forgotten all the numberless times when I have known her turn away to avoid the light, press her face into my shoulders. And, above all, how could I have forgotten the afternoon of our wedding-day when we sat on the green bench in the Botanical Gardens and listened to the band, how, in an interval between two pieces, she suddenly turned to me and said in the voice in which one says, 'Do you think the grass is damp?' or 'Do you think it's time for tea?' . . . 'Tell me, do you think physical beauty is so very important?' I don't like to think how often she had rehearsed that question. And do you know what I answered? At that moment, as if at my command, there came a great gush of hard, bright sound from the band, and I managed to shout above it cheerfully, 'I didn't hear what you said.' Devilish! Wasn't it? Perhaps not wholly. She looked like the poor patient who hears the surgeon say, 'It will certainly be necessary to perform the operation – but not now!'

But all this conveys the impression that my wife and I were never really happy together. Not true! Not true! We were marvellously, radiantly happy. We were a model couple. If you had seen us together, any time, any place, if you had followed us, tracked us down, spied, taken us off our guard, you still would have been forced to confess, 'I have never seen a more ideally suited pair.' Until last autumn.

But really to explain what happened then I should have to go back and back – I should have to dwindle until my two hands clutched the bannisters, the stair-rail was higher than my head, and I peered through to watch my father padding softly up and down. There were coloured windows on the landings. As he came up, first his bald head was scarlet, then it was yellow. How frightened I was! And when they put me to bed, it was to dream that we were living inside one of my father's big coloured bottles. For he was a chemist. I was born nine years after my parents were married. I was an only child, and the effort to produce even me – small, withered bud I must have been – sapped all my mother's strength. She never left her room again. Bed, sofa, window, she moved between the three. Well I can see her, on the window days, sitting, her cheek in her hand, staring out. Her room looked over the street. Opposite there was a wall plastered with advertisements for travelling shows and circuses and so on. I stand beside her, and we gaze at the slim lady in a red dress hitting a dark gentleman over the head with her parasol, or at the tiger peering through the jungle while the clown, close by, balances a bottle on his nose, or at a little golden-haired girl sitting on the knee of an old black man in a broad cotton hat. . . . She says nothing. On sofa days there is a flannel dressing-gown that I loathe, and a cushion that keeps on slipping off the hard sofa. I pick it up. It has flowers and writing sewn on. I ask what the writing says, and she whispers, 'Sweet Repose!' In bed her fingers plait, in tight little plaits, the fringe of the quilt and her lips are thin. And that is all there is of my mother, except the last queer 'episode' that comes later.

My father . . . Curled up in the corner on the lid of a round box that held sponges, I stared at my father so long, it's as though his image, cut off at the waist by the counter, has remained solid in my memory. Perfectly bald, polished head, shaped like a thin egg, creased, creamy cheeks, little bags under the eyes, large pale ears like handles. His manner was discreet, sly, faintly amused and tinged with impudence. Long before I could appreciate it I knew the mixture . . . I even used to copy him in my corner, bending forward, with a small reproduction of his faint sneer. In the evening his customers were, chiefly, young women; some of them came in every day for his famous fivepenny pick-me-up. Their gaudy looks, their voices, their free ways, fascinated me. I longed to be my

143

father, handing them across the counter the little glass of bluish stuff they tossed off so greedily. God knows what it was made of. Years after I drank some, just to see what it tasted like, and I felt as though some one had given me a terrific blow on the head; I felt stunned.

One of those evenings I remember vividly. It was cold; it must have been autumn, for the flaring gas was lighted after my tea. I sat in my corner and my father was mixing something; the shop was empty. Suddenly the bell jangled and a young woman rushed in, crying so loud, sobbing so hard, that it didn't sound real. She wore a green cape trimmed with fur and a hat with cherries dangling. My father came from behind the screen. But she couldn't stop herself at first. She stood in the middle of the shop and wrung her hands and moaned; I've never heard such crying since. Presently she managed to gasp out, 'Give me a pick-me-up!' Then she drew a long breath, trembled away from him and quavered, 'I've had *bad news!*' And in the flaring gaslight I saw the whole side of her face was puffed up and purple; her lip was cut, and her eyelid looked as though it was gummed fast over the wet eye. My father pushed the glass across the counter, and she took the purse out of her stocking and paid him. But she couldn't drink; clutching the glass, she stared in front of her as if she could not believe what she saw. Each time she put her head back the tears spurted out again. Finally she put the glass down. It was no use. Holding the cape with one hand, she ran in the same way out of the shop again. My father gave no sign. But long after she had gone I crouched in my corner, and when I think back it's as though I felt my whole body vibrating

– 'So that's what it is outside,' I thought. 'That's what it's like out there.'

Do you remember your childhood? I am always coming across these marvellous accounts by writers who declare that they remember 'everything'. I certainly don't. The dark stretches, the blanks, are much bigger than the bright glimpses. I seem to have spent most of my time like a plant in a cupboard. Now and again, when the sun shone, a careless hand thrust me out on to the window-sill, and a careless hand whipped me in again – and that was all. But what happened in the darkness – I wonder? Did one grow? Pale stem . . . timid leaves . . . white reluctant bud. No wonder I was hated at school. Even the masters shrank from me. I somehow knew that my soft hesitating voice disgusted them. I knew, too, how they turned away from my shocked, staring eyes. I was small and thin, and I smelled of the shop; my nickname was Gregory Powder. School was a tin building, stuck on the raw hillside. There were dark red streaks like blood in the oozing clay banks of the playground. I hide in the dark passage, where the coats hang, and am discovered there by one of the masters. 'What are you doing there in the dark?' His terrible voice kills me; I die before his eyes. I am standing in a ring of thrust-out heads; some are grinning, some look greedy, some are spitting. And it is always cold. Big crushed-up clouds press across the sky; the rusty water in the school tank is frozen; the bell sounds numb. One day they put a dead bird in my overcoat pocket. I found it just when I reached home. Oh, what a strange flutter there was at my heart when I drew out that terribly soft, cold little body, with the legs thin as pins and the claws wrung. I sat on the back door step in the yard and put the bird in my cap. The feathers round the neck looked wet and there was a tiny tuft just above the closed eyes that stood up too. How tightly the beak was shut! I could not see the mark where it was divided. I stretched out one wing and touched the soft, secret down underneath; I tried to make the claws curl round my little finger. But I didn't feel sorry for it – no! I wondered. The smoke from our kitchen chimney poured downwards, and flakes of soot floated – soft, light in the air. Through a big crack in the cement yard a poor-looking plant with dull, reddish flowers had pushed its way. I looked at the dead bird again. . . . And that is the first time that I remember singing – rather . . . listening to a silent voice inside a little cage that was me.

But what has all this to do with my married happiness? How can all this affect my wife and me? Why – to tell what happened last autumn – do I run all this way back into the Past? The Past – what is the Past? I might say the star-shaped flake of soot on a leaf of the poor-looking plant, and the bird lying on the quilted lining of my cap, and my father's pestle and my mother's cushion belong to it. But that is not to say they are any less mine than they were when I looked upon them with my very eyes, and touched them with these fingers. No, they are more – they are a living part of me. Who am I, in fact, as I sit here at this table, but my own past? If I deny that, I am nothing. And if I were to try to divide my life into childhood, youth, early manhood and so on, it would be a kind of affectation; I should know I was doing it just because of the pleasantly important sensation it gives one to rule lines, and to use green ink for childhood, red for the next stage, and purple for the period of adolescence. For, one thing I have learnt, one thing I do believe is, Nothing Happens Suddenly. Yes, that is my religion, I suppose.

My mother's death, for instance. Is it more distant from me to-day than it was then? It is just as close, as strange, as puzzling, and in spite of all the countless times I have recalled the circumstances, I know no more now than I did then, whether I dreamed them, or whether they really occurred. It happened when I was thirteen and I slept in a little strip of a room on what was called the half-landing. One night I woke up with a start to see my mother, in her nightgown, without even the hated flannel dressing-gown, sitting on my bed. But the strange thing which frightened me was, she wasn't looking at me. Her head was bent; the short, thin trail of hair lay between her shoulders; her hands were pressed between her knees, and my bed shook; she was shivering. It was the first time I had ever seen her out of her own room. I said, or I think I said, 'Is that you, Mother?' And as she turned round, I saw in the moonlight how queer she looked. Her face looked small – quite different. She looked like one of the boys at the school baths, who sits on a step, shivering just like that, and wants to go in and yet is frightened.

'Are you awake?' she said. Her eyes opened; I think she smiled. She leaned towards me. 'I've been poisoned,' she whispered. 'Your father's poisoned me.' And she nodded. Then, before I could say a word, she was gone; I thought I heard the door shut. I sat quite still, I couldn't move, I think I expected something else to happen. For a long time I listened for something; there wasn't a sound. The candle was by my bed, but I was too frightened to stretch out my hand for the matches. But even while I wondered what I ought to do, even while my heart thumped – everything became confused. I lay down and pulled the blankets round me. I fell asleep, and the next morning my mother was found dead of failure of the heart.

Did that visit happen? Was it a dream? Why did she come to tell me? Or why, if she came, did she go away so quickly? And her expression – so joyous under the frightened look – was that real? I believed it fully the afternoon of the funeral, when I saw my father dressed up for his part, hat and all. That tall hat so gleaming black and round was like a cork covered with black sealing-wax, and the rest of my father was awfully like a bottle, with his face for the label – *Deadly Poison*. It flashed into my mind as I stood opposite him in the hall. And Deadly Poison, or old D. P., was my private name for him from that day.

Late, it grows late. I love the night. I love to feel the tide of darkness rising slowly and slowly washing, turning over and over, lifting, floating, all that lies strewn upon the dark beach, all that lies hid in rocky hollows. I love, I love this strange feeling of drifting – whither? After my mother's death I hated to go to bed. I used to sit on the window-sill, folded up, and watch the sky. It seemed to me the moon moved much faster than the sun. And one big, bright green star I chose for my own. My star! But I never thought of it beckoning to me or twinkling merrily for my sake. Cruel, indifferent, splendid – it burned in the airy night. No matter – it was mine! But, growing close up against the window, there was a creeper with small, bunched-up pink and purple flowers. These did know me. These, when I touched them at night, welcomed my fingers; the little tendrils, so weak, so delicate, knew I would not hurt them. When the wind moved the leaves I felt I understood their shaking. When I came to the window, it seemed to me the flowers said among themselves, 'The boy is here.'

As the months passed there was often a light in my father's room below. And I heard voices and laughter. 'He's got some woman with him,' I thought. But it meant nothing to me. Then the gay voice, the sound of the laughter, gave me the idea it was one of the girls who used to come to the shop in the evenings – and gradually I began to imagine which girl it was. It was the dark one in the red coat and skirt, who once had given me a penny. A merry face stooped over me – warm breath tickled my neck – there were little beads of black on her long lashes, and when she opened her arms to kiss me there came a marvellous wave of scent ! Yes, that was the one.

Time passed, and I forgot the moon and my green star and my shy creeper – I came to the window to wait for the light in my father's window, to listen for the laughing voice, until one night I dozed and I dreamed she came again – again she drew me to her, something soft, scented, warm and merry hung over me like a cloud. But when I tried to see, her eyes only mocked me, her red lips opened and she hissed, 'Little sneak! Little sneak!' But not as if she were angry, – as if she understood, and her smile somehow was like a rat – hateful!

The night after, I lighted the candle and sat down at the table instead. By and by, as the flame steadied, there was a small lake of liquid wax, surrounded by a white, smooth wall. I took a pin and made little holes in this wall and then sealed them up faster than the wax could escape. After a time I fancied the candle flame joined in the game; it leapt up, quivered, wagged; it even seemed to laugh. But while I played with the candle and smiled and broke off the tiny white peaks of wax that rose above the wall and floated them on my lake, a feeling of awful dreariness fastened on me – yes, that's the word. It crept up from my knees to my thighs, into my arms; I ached all over with misery. And I felt so strangely that I couldn't move. Something bound me there by the table – I couldn't even let the pin drop that I held between my finger and thumb. For a moment I came to a stop, as it were.

Then the shrivelled case of the bud split and fell, the plant in the cupboard came into flower. 'Who am I?' I thought. 'What is all this?' And I looked at my room, at the broken bust of the man called Hahnemann on top of the cupboard, at my little bed with the pillow like an envelope. I saw it all, but not as I had seen before. . . . Everything lived, everything. But that was not all. I was equally alive and – it's the only way I can express it – the barriers were down between us – I had come into my own world!

The barriers were down. I had been all my life a little outcast; but until that moment no one had 'accepted' me; I had lain in the cupboard – or the cave forlorn. But now I was taken, I was accepted, claimed. I did not consciously turn away from the world of human beings; I had never known it; but I from that night did beyond words consciously turn towards my silent brothers. . . .

unfinished

THE GARDEN-PARTY

And after all the weather was ideal. They could not have had a more perfect day for a garden-party if they had ordered it. Windless, warm, the sky without a cloud. Only the blue was veiled with a haze of light gold, as it is sometimes in early summer. The gardener had been up since dawn, mowing the lawns and sweeping them, until the grass and the dark flat rosettes where the daisy plants had been seemed to shine. As for the roses, you could not help feeling they understood that roses are the only flowers that impress people at garden-parties; the only flowers that everybody is certain of knowing. Hundreds, yes, literally hundreds, had come out in a single night; the green bushes bowed down as though they had been visited by archangels.

Breakfast was not yet over before the men came to put up the marquee.

'Where do you want the marquee put, mother?'

'My dear child, it's no use asking me. I'm determined to leave everything to you children this year. Forget I am your mother. Treat me as an honoured guest.'

But Meg could not possibly go and supervise the men. She had washed her hair before breakfast, and she sat drinking her coffee in a green turban, with a dark wet curl stamped on each cheek. Jose, the butterfly, always came down in a silk petticoat and a kimono jacket.

'You'll have to go, Laura; you're the artistic one.'

Away Laura flew, still holding her piece of bread-and-butter. It's so delicious to have an excuse for eating out of doors, and besides, she loved having to arrange things; she always felt she could do it so much better than anybody else.

Four men in their shirt-sleeves stood grouped together on the garden path. They carried staves covered with rolls of canvas, and they had big tool-bags slung on their backs. They looked impressive. Laura wished now that she was not holding that piece of bread-and-butter, but there was nowhere to put it, and she couldn't possibly throw it away. She blushed and tried to look severe and even a little bit short-sighted as she came up to them.

'Good morning,' she said, copying her mother's voice. But that sounded so fearfully affected that she was ashamed, and stammered like a little girl, 'Oh – er – have you come – is it about the marquee?'

'That's right, miss,' said the tallest of the men, a lanky, freckled fellow, and he shifted his tool-bag, knocked back his straw hat and smiled down at her. 'That's about it.'

His smile was so easy, so friendly, that Laura recovered. What nice eyes he had, small, but such a dark blue! And now she looked at the others, they were smiling too. 'Cheer up, we won't bite,' their smile seemed to say. How very nice workmen were! And what a beautiful morning! She mustn't mention the morning; she must be business-like. The marquee.

154

'Well, what about the lily-lawn? Would that do?'

And she pointed to the lily-lawn with the hand that didn't hold the bread-and-butter. They turned, they stared in the direction. A little fat chap thrust out his under-lip, and the tall fellow frowned.

'I don't fancy it,' said he. 'Not conspicuous enough. You see, with a thing like a marquee,' and he turned to Laura in his easy way, 'you want to put it somewhere where it'll give you a bang slap in the eye, if you follow me.'

Laura's upbringing made her wonder for a moment whether it was quite respectful of a workman to talk to her of bangs slap in the eye. But she did quite follow him.

'A corner of the tennis-court,' she suggested. 'But the band's going to be in one corner.'

'H'm, going to have a band, are you?' said another of the workmen. He was pale. He had a haggard look as his dark eyes scanned the tennis-court. What was he thinking?

'Only a very small band,' said Laura gently. Perhaps he wouldn't mind so much if the band was quite small. But the tall fellow interrupted.

'Look here, miss, that's the place. Against those trees. Over there. That'll do fine.'

Against the karakas. Then the karaka-trees would be hidden. And they were so lovely, with their broad, gleaming leaves, and their clusters of yellow fruit. They were like trees you imagined growing on a desert island, proud, solitary, lifting their leaves and fruits to the sun in a kind of silent splendour. Must they be hidden by a marquee?

They must. Already the men had shouldered their staves

155

and were making for the place. Only the tall fellow was left. He bent down, pinched a sprig of lavender, put his thumb and forefinger to his nose and snuffed up the smell. When Laura saw that gesture she forgot all about the karakas in her wonder at him caring for things like that – caring for the smell of lavender. How many men that she knew would have done such a thing. Oh, how extraordinarily nice workmen were, she thought. Why couldn't she have workmen for friends rather than the silly boys she danced with and who came to Sunday night supper? She would get on much better with men like these.

It's all the fault, she decided, as the tall fellow drew something on the back of an envelope, something that was to be looped up or left to hang, of these absurd class distinctions. Well, for her part, she didn't feel them. Not a bit, not an atom. . . . And now there came the chock-chock of wooden hammers. Some one whistled, some one sang out, 'Are you right there, matey?' 'Matey!' The friendliness of it, the – the – Just to prove how happy she was, just to show the tall fellow how at home she felt, and how she despised stupid conventions, Laura took a big bite of her bread-and-butter as she stared at the little drawing. She felt just like a work-girl.

'Laura, Laura, where are you? Telephone, Laura!' a voice cried from the house.

'Coming!' Away she skimmed, over the lawn, up the path, up the steps, across the verandah, and into the porch. In the hall her father and Laurie were brushing their hats ready to go to the office.

'I say, Laura,' said Laurie very fast, 'you might just give a squiz at my coat before this afternoon. See if it wants pressing.'

'I will,' said she. Suddenly she couldn't stop herself. She ran at Laurie and gave him a small, quick squeeze. 'Oh, I do love parties, don't you?' gasped Laura.

'Ra-ther,' said Laurie's warm, boyish voice, and he squeezed his sister too, and gave her a gentle push. 'Dash off to the telephone, old girl.'

The telephone. 'Yes, yes; oh yes. Kitty? Good morning, dear. Come to lunch? Do, dear. Delighted of course. It will only be a very scratch meal – just the sandwich crusts and broken meringue-shells and what's left over. Yes, isn't it a perfect morning? Your white? Oh, I certainly should. One moment – hold the line. Mother's calling.' And Laura sat back. 'What, mother? Can't hear.'

Mrs. Sheridan's voice floated down the stairs. 'Tell her to wear that sweet hat she had on last Sunday.'

'Mother says you're to wear that *sweet* hat you had on last Sunday. Good. One o'clock. Bye-bye.'

Laura put back the receiver, flung her arms over her head, took a deep breath, stretched and let them fall. 'Huh,' she sighed, and the moment after the sigh she sat up quickly. She was still, listening. All the doors in the house seemed to be open. The house was alive with soft, quick steps and running voices. The green baize door that led to the kitchen regions swung open and shut with a muffled thud. And now there came a long, chuckling absurd sound. It was the heavy piano being moved on its stiff castors. But the air! If you stopped to notice, was the air always like this? Little faint winds were playing chase in at the tops of the windows, out at the doors. And there were two tiny spots of sun, one on the inkpot, one on a silver photograph frame, playing too. Darling little spots. Especially the one on the inkpot lid. It was quite warm. A warm little silver star. She could have kissed it.

The front door bell pealed, and there sounded the rustle of Sadie's print skirt on the stairs. A man's voice murmured; Sadie answered, careless, 'I'm sure I don't know. Wait. I'll ask Mrs. Sheridan.'

'What is it, Sadie?' Laura came into the hall.

'It's the florist, Miss Laura.'

It was, indeed. There, just inside the door, stood a wide, shallow tray full of pots of pink lilies. No other kind. Nothing but lilies – canna lilies, big pink flowers, wide open, radiant, almost frighteningly alive on bright crimson stems.

'O-oh, Sadie!' said Laura, and the sound was like a little moan. She crouched down as if to warm herself at that blaze of lilies; she felt they were in her fingers, on her lips, growing in her breast.

'It's some mistake,' she said faintly. 'Nobody ever ordered so many. Sadie, go and find mother.'

But at that moment Mrs. Sheridan joined them.

'It's quite right,' she said calmly. 'Yes, I ordered them. Aren't they lovely?' She pressed Laura's arm. 'I was passing the shop yesterday, and I saw them in the window. And I suddenly thought for once in my life I shall have enough canna lilies. The garden-party will be a good excuse.'

'But I thought you said you didn't mean to interfere,' said Laura. Sadie had gone. The florist's man was still outside at his van. She put her arm round her mother's neck and gently, very gently, she bit her mother's ear.

'My darling child, you wouldn't like a logical mother, would you? Don't do that. Here's the man.'

He carried more lilies still, another whole tray.

'Bank them up, just inside the door, on both sides of the porch, please,' said Mrs. Sheridan. 'Don't you agree, Laura?'

'Oh, I *do*, mother.'

In the drawing-room Meg, Jose and good little Hans had at last succeeded in moving the piano.

'Now, if we put this chesterfield against the wall and move everything out of the room except the chairs, don't you think?'

'Quite.'

'Hans, move these tables into the smoking-room, and bring a sweeper to take these marks off the carpet and – one moment, Hans –' Jose loved giving orders to the servants, and they loved obeying her. She always made them feel they were taking part in some drama. 'Tell mother and Miss Laura to come here at once.'

'Very good, Miss Jose.'

She turned to Meg. 'I want to hear what the piano sounds like, just in case I'm asked to sing this afternoon. Let's try over "This life is Weary."'

Pom! Ta-ta-ta *Tee*-ta! The piano burst out so passionately that Jose's face changed. She clasped her hands. She looked mournfully and enigmatically at her mother and Laura as they came in.

> This Life is *Wee*-ary,
> A Tear – a Sigh.
> A Love that *Chan*-ges,
>> This Life is *Wee*-ary,
> A Tear – a Sigh.
> A Love that *Chan*-ges,
> And then . . . Good-bye!

But at the word 'Good-bye,' and although the piano sounded more desperate than ever, her face broke into a brilliant, dreadfully unsympathetic smile.

'Aren't I in good voice, mummy?' she beamed.

> This Life is *Wee*-ary,
> Hope comes to Die.
> A Dream – a *Wa*-kening.

But now Sadie interrupted them. 'What is it, Sadie?'

'If you please, m'm, cook says have you got the flags for the sandwiches?'

'The flags for the sandwiches, Sadie?' echoed Mrs. Sheridan dreamily. And the children knew by her face that she hadn't got them. 'Let me see.' And she said to Sadie firmly, 'Tell cook I'll let her have them in ten minutes.'

Sadie went.

'Now, Laura,' said her mother quickly, 'come with me into the smoking-room. I've got the names somewhere on the back of an envelope. You'll have to write them out for me. Meg, go upstairs this minute and take that wet thing off your head. Jose, run and finish dressing this instant. Do you hear me, children, or shall I have to tell your father when he comes home to-night? And – and, Jose, pacify cook if you do go into the kitchen, will you? I'm terrified of her this morning.'

The envelope was found at last behind the dining-room clock, though how it had got there Mrs. Sheridan could not imagine.

'One of you children must have stolen it out of my bag, because I remember vividly – cream-cheese and lemon-curd. Have you done that?'

'Yes.'

'Egg and –' Mrs. Sheridan held the envelope away from her. 'It looks like mice. It can't be mice, can it?'

'Olive, pet,' said Laura, looking over her shoulder.

'Yes, of course, olive. What a horrible combination it sounds. Egg and olive.'

They were finished at last, and Laura took them off to the kitchen. She found Jose there pacifying the cook, who did not look at all terrifying.

'I have never seen such exquisite sandwiches,' said Jose's rapturous voice. 'How many kinds did you say there were, cook? Fifteen?'

'Fifteen, Miss Jose.'

'Well, cook, I congratulate you.'

Cook swept up crusts with the long sandwich knife, and smiled broadly.

'Godber's has come,' announced Sadie, issuing out of the pantry. She had seen the man pass the window.

That meant the cream puffs had come. Godber's were

famous for their cream puffs. Nobody ever thought of making them at home.

'Bring them in and put them on the table, my girl,' ordered cook.

Sadie brought them in and went back to the door. Of course Laura and Jose were far too grown-up to really care about such things. All the same, they couldn't help agreeing that the puffs looked very attractive. Very. Cook began arranging them, shaking off the extra icing sugar.

'Don't they carry one back to all one's parties?' said Laura.

'I suppose they do,' said practical Jose, who never liked to be carried back. 'They look beautifully light and feathery, I must say.'

'Have one each, my dears,' said cook in her comfortable voice. 'Yer ma won't know.'

Oh, impossible. Fancy cream puffs so soon after breakfast. The very idea made one shudder. All the same, two minutes later Jose and Laura were licking their fingers with that absorbed inward look that only comes from whipped cream.

'Let's go into the garden, out by the back way,' suggested Laura. 'I want to see how the men are getting on with the marquee. They're such awfully nice men.'

But the back door was blocked by cook, Sadie, Godber's man and Hans.

Something had happened.

'Tuk-tuk-tuk,' clucked cook like an agitated hen. Sadie had her hand clapped to her cheek as though she had toothache. Hans's face was screwed up in the effort to understand. Only Godber's man seemed to be enjoying himself; it was his story.

'What's the matter? What's happened?'

'There's been a horrible accident,' said cook. 'A man killed.'

'A man killed! Where? How? When?'

But Godber's man wasn't going to have his story snatched from under his very nose.

'Know those little cottages just below here, miss?' Know them? Of course, she knew them. 'Well, there's a young chap living there, name of Scott, a carter. His horse shied at a traction-engine, corner of Hawke Street this morning, and he was thrown out on the back of his head. Killed.'

'Dead!' Laura stared at Godber's man.

'Dead when they picked him up,' said Godber's man with relish. 'They were taking the body home as I come up here.' And he said to the cook, 'He's left a wife and five little ones.'

'Jose, come here.' Laura caught hold of her sister's sleeve and dragged her through the kitchen to the other side of the green baize door. There she paused and leaned against it. 'Jose!' she said, horrified, 'however are we going to stop everything?'

'Stop everything, Laura!' cried Jose in astonishment. 'What do you mean?'

'Stop the garden-party, of course.' Why did Jose pretend?

But Jose was still more amazed. 'Stop the garden-party? My dear Laura, don't be so absurd. Of course we can't do anything of the kind. Nobody expects us to. Don't be so extravagant.'

'But we can't possibly have a garden-party with a man dead just outside the front gate.'

163

That really was extravagant, for the little cottages were in a lane to themselves at the very bottom of a steep rise that led up to the house. A broad road ran between. True, they were far too near. They were the greatest possible eyesore, and they had no right to be in that neighbourhood at all. They were little mean dwellings painted a chocolate brown. In the garden patches there was nothing but cabbage stalks, sick hens and tomato cans. The very smoke coming out of their chimneys was poverty-stricken. Little rags and shreds of smoke, so unlike the great silvery plumes that uncurled from the Sheridans' chimneys. Washerwomen lived in the lane and sweeps and a cobbler, and a man whose house-front was studded all over with minute bird-cages. Children swarmed. When the Sheridans were little they were forbidden to set foot there because of the revolting language and of what they might catch. But since they were grown up, Laura and Laurie on their prowls sometimes walked through. It was disgusting and sordid. They came out with a shudder. But still one must go everywhere; one must see everything. So through they went.

'And just think of what the band would sound like to that poor woman,' said Laura.

'Oh, Laura!' Jose began to be seriously annoyed. 'If you're going to stop a band playing every time some one has an accident, you'll lead a very strenuous life. I'm every bit as sorry about it as you. I feel just as sympathetic.' Her eyes hardened. She looked at her sister just as she used to when they were little and fighting together. 'You won't bring a drunken workman back to life by being sentimental,' she said softly.

'Drunk! Who said he was drunk?' Laura turned furiously on Jose. She said just as they had used to say on those occasions, 'I'm going straight up to tell mother.'

'Do, dear,' cooed Jose.

'Mother, can I come into your room?' Laura turned the big glass door-knob.

'Of course, child. Why, what's the matter? What's given you such a colour?' And Mrs. Sheridan turned round from her dressing-table. She was trying on a new hat.

'Mother, a man's been killed,' began Laura.

'*Not* in the garden?' interrupted her mother.

'No, no!'

'Oh, what a fright you gave me!' Mrs. Sheridan sighed with relief, and took off the big hat and held it on her knees.

'But listen, mother,' said Laura. Breathless, half-choking, she told the dreadful story. 'Of course, we can't have our party, can we?' she pleaded. 'The band and everybody arriving. They'd hear us, mother; they're nearly neighbours!'

To Laura's astonishment her mother behaved just like Jose; it was harder to bear because she seemed amused. She refused to take Laura seriously.

'But, my dear child, use your common sense. It's only by accident we've heard of it. If some one had died there normally – and I can't understand how they keep alive in those poky little holes – we should still be having our party, shouldn't we?'

Laura had to say 'yes' to that, but she felt it was all wrong. She sat down on her mother's sofa and pinched the cushion frill.

'Mother, isn't it terribly heartless of us?' she asked.

'Darling!' Mrs. Sheridan got up and came over to her, carrying the hat. Before Laura could stop her she had popped it on. 'My child!' said her mother, 'the hat is yours. It's made for you. It's much too young for me. I have never seen you look such a picture. Look at yourself!' And she held up her hand-mirror.

'But, mother,' Laura began again. She couldn't look at herself; she turned aside.

This time Mrs. Sheridan lost patience just as Jose had done.

'You are being very absurd, Laura,' she said coldly. 'People like that don't expect sacrifices from us. And it's not very sympathetic to spoil everybody's enjoyment as you're doing now.'

'I don't understand,' said Laura, and she walked quickly out of the room into her own bedroom. There, quite by chance, the first thing she saw was this charming girl in the mirror, in her black hat trimmed with gold daisies, and a long black velvet ribbon. Never had she imagined she could look like that. Is mother right? she thought. And now she hoped her mother was right. Am I being extravagant? Perhaps it was extravagant. Just for a moment she had another glimpse of that poor woman and those little children, and the body being carried into the house. But it all seemed blurred, unreal, like a picture in the newspaper. I'll remember it again after the party's over, she decided. And somehow that seemed quite the best plan. . . .

Lunch was over by half-past one. By half-past two they

were all ready for the fray. The green-coated band had arrived and was established in a corner of the tennis-court.

'My dear!' trilled Kitty Maitland, 'aren't they too like frogs for words? You ought to have arranged them round the pond with the conductor in the middle on a leaf.'

Laurie arrived and hailed them on his way to dress. At the sight of him Laura remembered the accident again. She wanted to tell him. If Laurie agreed with the others, then it was bound to be all right. And she followed him into the hall.

'Laurie!'

'Hallo!' He was half-way upstairs, but when he turned round and saw Laura he suddenly puffed out his cheeks and goggled his eyes at her. 'My word, Laura! You do look stunning,' said Laurie. 'What an absolutely topping hat!'

Laura said faintly 'Is it?' and smiled up at Laurie, and didn't tell him after all.

Soon after that people began coming in streams. The band struck up; the hired waiters ran from the house to the marquee. Wherever you looked there were couples strolling, bending to the flowers, greeting, moving on over the lawn. They were like bright birds that had alighted in the Sheridans' garden for this one afternoon, on their way to – where? Ah, what happiness it is to be with people who all are happy, to press hands, press cheeks, smile into eyes.

'Darling Laura, how well you look!'

'What a becoming hat, child!'

'Laura, you look quite Spanish. I've never seen you look so striking.'

And Laura, glowing, answered softly, 'Have you had tea?

Won't you have an ice? The passion-fruit ices really are rather special.' She ran to her father and begged him. 'Daddy darling, can't the band have something to drink?'

And the perfect afternoon slowly ripened, slowly faded, slowly its petals closed.

'Never a more delightful garden-party . . .' 'The greatest success . . .' 'Quite the most . . .'

Laura helped her mother with the good-byes. They stood side by side in the porch till it was all over.

'All over, all over, thank heaven,' said Mrs. Sheridan. 'Round up the others, Laura. Let's go and have some fresh coffee. I'm exhausted. Yes, it's been very successful. But oh, these parties, these parties! Why will you children insist on giving parties!' And they all of them sat down in the deserted marquee.

'Have a sandwich, daddy dear. I wrote the flag.'

'Thanks.' Mr. Sheridan took a bite and the sandwich was gone. He took another. 'I suppose you didn't hear of a beastly accident that happened to-day?' he said.

'My dear,' said Mrs. Sheridan, holding up her hand, 'we did. It nearly ruined the party. Laura insisted we should put it off.'

'Oh, mother!' Laura didn't want to be teased about it.

'It was a horrible affair all the same,' said Mr. Sheridan. 'The chap was married too. Lived just below in the lane, and leaves a wife and half a dozen kiddies, so they say.'

An awkward little silence fell. Mrs. Sheridan fidgeted with her cup. Really, it was very tactless of father. . . .

Suddenly she looked up. There on the table were all those

sandwiches, cakes, puffs, all uneaten, all going to be wasted. She had one of her brilliant ideas.

'I know,' she said. 'Let's make up a basket. Let's send that poor creature some of this perfectly good food. At any rate, it will be the greatest treat for the children. Don't you agree? And she's sure to have neighbours calling in and so on. What a point to have it all ready prepared. Laura!' She jumped up. 'Get me the big basket out of the stairs cupboard.'

'But, mother, do you really think it's a good idea?' said Laura.

Again, how curious, she seemed to be different from them all. To take scraps from their party. Would the poor woman really like that?

'Of course! What's the matter with you to-day? An hour or two ago you were insisting on us being sympathetic, and now –'

Oh well! Laura ran for the basket. It was filled, it was heaped by her mother.

'Take it yourself, darling,' said she. 'Run down just as you are. No, wait, take the arum lilies too. People of that class are so impressed by arum lilies.'

'The stems will ruin her lace frock,' said practical Jose.

So they would. Just in time. 'Only the basket, then. And, Laura!' – her mother followed her out of the marquee – 'don't on any account –'

'What mother?'

No, better not put such ideas into the child's head! 'Nothing! Run along.'

It was just growing dusky as Laura shut their garden gates.

A big dog ran by like a shadow. The road gleamed white, and down below in the hollow the little cottages were in deep shade. How quiet it seemed after the afternoon. Here she was going down the hill to somewhere where a man lay dead, and she couldn't realise it. Why couldn't she? She stopped a minute. And it seemed to her that kisses, voices, tinkling spoons, laughter, the smell of crushed grass were somehow inside her. She had no room for anything else. How strange! She looked up at the pale sky, and all she thought was, 'Yes, it was the most successful party.'

Now the broad road was crossed. The lane began, smoky and dark. Women in shawls and men's tweed caps hurried by. Men hung over the palings; the children played in the doorways. A low hum came from the mean little cottages. In some of them there was a flicker of light, and a shadow, crab-like, moved across the window. Laura bent her head and hurried on. She wished now she had put on a coat. How her frock shone! And the big hat with the velvet streamer – if only it was another hat! Were the people looking at her? They must be. It was a mistake to have come; she knew all along it was a mistake. Should she go back even now?

No, too late. This was the house. It must be. A dark knot of people stood outside. Beside the gate an old, old woman with a crutch sat in a chair, watching. She had her feet on a newspaper. The voices stopped as Laura drew near. The group parted. It was as though she was expected, as though they had known she was coming here.

Laura was terribly nervous. Tossing the velvet ribbon over her shoulder, she said to a woman standing by, 'Is this Mrs.

Scott's house?' and the woman, smiling queerly, said, 'It is, my lass.'

Oh, to be away from this! She actually said, 'Help me, God,' as she walked up the tiny path and knocked. To be away from those staring eyes, or to be covered up in anything, one of those women's shawls even. I'll just leave the basket and go, she decided. I shan't even wait for it to be emptied.

Then the door opened. A little woman in black showed in the gloom.

Laura said, 'Are you Mrs. Scott?' But to her horror the woman answered, 'Walk in, please, miss,' and she was shut in the passage.

'No,' said Laura, 'I don't want to come in. I only want to leave this basket. Mother sent –'

The little woman in the gloomy passage seemed not to have heard her. 'Step this way, please, miss,' she said in an oily voice, and Laura followed her.

She found herself in a wretched little low kitchen, lighted by a smoky lamp. There was a woman sitting before the fire.

'Em,' said the little creature who had let her in. 'Em! It's a young lady.' She turned to Laura. She said meaningly, 'I'm 'er sister, miss. You'll excuse 'er, won't you?'

'Oh, but of course!' said Laura. 'Please, please don't disturb her. I – I only want to leave –'

But at that moment the woman at the fire turned round. Her face, puffed up, red, with swollen eyes and swollen lips, looked terrible. She seemed as though she couldn't understand why Laura was there. What did it mean? Why was this

171

stranger standing in the kitchen with a basket? What was it all about? And the poor face puckered up again.

'All right, my dear,' said the other. 'I'll thenk the young lady.'

And again she began, 'You'll excuse her, miss, I'm sure,' and her face, swollen too, tried an oily smile.

Laura only wanted to get out, to get away. She was back in the passage. The door opened. She walked straight through into the bedroom where the dead man was lying.

'You'd like a look at 'im, wouldn't you?' said Em's sister, and she brushed past Laura over to the bed. 'Don't be afraid, my lass' – and now her voice sounded fond and sly, and fondly she drew down the sheet – ''e looks a picture. There's nothing to show. Come along, my dear.'

Laura came.

There lay a young man, fast asleep – sleeping so soundly, so deeply, that he was far, far away from them both. Oh, so remote, so peaceful. He was dreaming. Never wake him up again. His head was sunk in the pillow, his eyes were closed; they were blind under the closed eyelids. He was given up to his dream. What did garden-parties and baskets and lace frocks matter to him? He was far from all those things. He was wonderful, beautiful. While they were laughing and while the band was playing, this marvel had come to the lane. Happy . . . happy . . . All is well, said that sleeping face. This is just as it should be. I am content.

But all the same you had to cry, and she couldn't go out of the room without saying something to him. Laura gave a loud childish sob.

'Forgive my hat,' she said.

And this time she didn't wait for Em's sister. She found her way out of the door, down the path, past all those dark people. At the corner of the lane she met Laurie.

He stepped out of the shadow. 'Is that you, Laura?'

'Yes.'

'Mother was getting anxious. Was it all right?'

'Yes, quite. Oh, Laurie!' She took his arm, she pressed up against him.

'I say, you're not crying, are you?' asked her brother.

Laura shook her head. She was.

Laurie put his arm round her shoulder. 'Don't cry,' he said in his warm, loving voice. 'Was it awful?'

'No,' sobbed Laura. 'It was simply marvellous. But, Laurie –' She stopped, she looked at her brother. 'Isn't life,' she stammered, 'isn't life –' But what life was she couldn't explain. No matter. He quite understood.

'*Isn't* it, darling?' said Laurie.

THE DOLL'S HOUSE

When dear old Mrs. Hay went back to town after staying with the Burnells she sent the children a doll's house. It was so big that the carter and Pat carried it into the courtyard, and there it stayed, propped up on two wooden boxes beside the feed-room door. No harm could come to it; it was summer. And perhaps the smell of paint would have gone off by the time it had to be taken in. For, really, the smell of paint coming from that doll's house ('Sweet of old Mrs. Hay, of course; most sweet and generous!') – but the smell of paint was quite enough to make anyone seriously ill, in Aunt Beryl's opinion. Even before the sacking was taken off. And when it was . . .

There stood the doll's house, a dark, oily, spinach green, picked out with bright yellow. Its two solid little chimneys, glued on to the roof, were painted red and white, and the door, gleaming with yellow varnish, was like a little slab of toffee. Four windows, real windows, were divided into panes by a broad streak of green. There was actually a tiny porch, too, painted yellow, with big lumps of congealed paint hanging along the edge.

But perfect, perfect little house! Who could possibly mind the smell. It was part of the joy, part of the newness.

'Open it quickly, someone!'

The hook at the side was stuck fast. Pat prised it open with his penknife, and the whole house front swung back, and – there you were, gazing at one and the same moment into the drawing-room and dining-room, the kitchen and two bedrooms. That is the way for a house to open! Why don't all houses open like that? How much more exciting than peering through the slit of a door into a mean little hall with a hat-stand and two umbrellas! That is – isn't it? – what you long to know about a house when you put your hand on the knocker. Perhaps it is the way God opens houses at the dead of night when He is taking a quiet turn with an angel. . . .

'O-oh!' The Burnell children sounded as though they were in despair. It was too marvellous; it was too much for them. They had never seen anything like it in their lives. All the rooms were papered. There were pictures on the walls, painted on the paper, with gold frames complete. Red carpet covered all the floors except the kitchen; red plush chairs in the drawing-room, green in the dining-room; tables, beds with real bedclothes, a cradle, a stove, a dresser with tiny plates and one big jug. But what Kezia liked more than anything, what she liked frightfully, was the lamp. It stood in the middle of the dining-room table, an exquisite little amber lamp with a white globe. It was even filled all ready for lighting, though, of course, you couldn't light it. But there was something inside that looked like oil and moved when you shook it.

The father and mother dolls, who sprawled very stiff as though they had fainted in the drawing-room, and their two little children asleep upstairs, were really too big for the doll's house. They didn't look as though they belonged. But the lamp was perfect. It seemed to smile at Kezia, to say, 'I live here.' The lamp was real.

The Burnell children could hardly walk to school fast enough the next morning. They burned to tell everybody, to describe, to – well – to boast about their doll's house before the school-bell rang.

'I'm to tell,' said Isabel, 'because I'm the eldest. And you two can join in after. But I'm to tell first.'

There was nothing to answer. Isabel was bossy, but she was always right, and Lottie and Kezia knew too well the powers that went with being eldest. They brushed through the thick buttercups at the road edge and said nothing.

'And I'm to choose who's to come and see it first. Mother said I might.'

For it had been arranged that while the doll's house stood in the courtyard they might ask the girls at school, two at a time, to come and look. Not to stay to tea, of course, or to come traipsing through the house. But just to stand quietly in the courtyard while Isabel pointed out the beauties, and Lottie and Kezia looked pleased. . . .

But hurry as they might, by the time they had reached the tarred palings of the boys' playground the bell had begun to jangle. They only just had time to whip off their hats and fall into line before the roll was called. Never mind. Isabel tried to make up for it by looking very important and mysterious and by whispering behind her hand to the girls near her, 'Got something to tell you at playtime.'

Playtime came and Isabel was surrounded. The girls of her class nearly fought to put their arms round her, to walk away with her, to beam flatteringly, to be her special friend. She held quite a court under the huge pine trees at the side of the playground. Nudging, giggling together, the little girls pressed up close. And the only two who stayed outside the ring were the two who were always outside, the little Kelveys. They knew better than to come anywhere near the Burnells.

For the fact was, the school the Burnell children went to was not at all the kind of place their parents would have chosen if there had been any choice. But there was none. It was the only school for miles. And the consequence was all the children of the neighbourhood, the Judge's little girls, the doctor's daughters, the store-keeper's children, the milkman's, were forced to mix together. Not to speak of there being an equal number of rude, rough little boys as well. But the line had to be drawn somewhere. It was drawn at the Kelveys. Many of the children, including the Burnells, were not allowed even to speak to them. They walked past the Kelveys with their heads in the air, and as they set the fashion in all matters of behaviour, the Kelveys were shunned by everybody. Even the teacher had a special voice for them, and a special smile for the other children when Lil Kelvey came up to her desk with a bunch of dreadfully common-looking flowers.

They were the daughters of a spry, hard-working little washerwoman, who went about from house to house by the day. This was awful enough. But where was Mr. Kelvey? Nobody knew for certain. But everybody said he was in prison. So they were the daughters of a washerwoman and a gaolbird. Very nice company for other people's children! And they looked it. Why Mrs. Kelvey made them so conspicuous was hard to understand. The truth was they were dressed in 'bits' given to her by the people for whom she worked. Lil, for instance, who was a stout, plain child, with big freckles, came to school in a dress made from a green art-serge table-cloth of the Burnells', with red plush sleeves from the Logans' curtains. Her hat, perched on top of her high forehead, was a grown-up woman's hat, once the property of Miss Lecky, the postmistress. It was turned up at the back and trimmed with a large scarlet quill. What a little guy she looked! It was impossible not to laugh. And her little sister, our Else, wore a long white dress, rather like a nightgown, and a pair of little boy's boots. But whatever our Else wore she would have looked strange. She was a tiny wishbone of a child, with cropped hair and enormous solemn eyes – a little white owl. Nobody had ever seen her smile; she scarcely ever spoke. She went through life holding on to Lil, with a piece of Lil's skirt screwed up in her hand. Where Lil went, our Else followed. In the playground, on the road going to and from school, there was Lil marching in front and our Else holding on behind. Only when she wanted anything, or when she was out of breath, our Else gave Lil a tug, a twitch, and Lil stopped and turned round. The Kelveys never failed to understand each other.

Now they hovered at the edge; you couldn't stop them listening. When the little girls turned round and sneered, Lil, as usual, gave her silly, shamefaced smile, but our Else only looked.

And Isabel's voice, so very proud, went on telling. The carpet made a great sensation, but so did the beds with real bedclothes, and the stove with an oven door.

When she finished Kezia broke in. 'You've forgotten the lamp, Isabel.'

'Oh yes,' said Isabel, 'and there's a teeny little lamp, all made of yellow glass, with a white globe that stands on the dining-room table. You couldn't tell it from a real one.'

'The lamp's best of all,' cried Kezia. She thought Isabel wasn't making half enough of the little lamp. But nobody paid any attention. Isabel was choosing the two who were to come back with them that afternoon and see it. She chose Emmie Cole and Lena Logan. But when the others knew they were all to have a chance, they couldn't be nice enough to Isabel. One by one they put their arms round Isabel's waist and walked her off. They had something to whisper to her, a secret. 'Isabel's *my* friend.'

Only the little Kelveys moved away forgotten; there was nothing more for them to hear.

Days passed, and as more children saw the doll's house, the fame of it spread. It became the one subject, the rage. The one question was, 'Have you seen Burnells' doll's house? Oh, ain't it lovely!' 'Haven't you seen it? Oh, I say!'

Even the dinner hour was given up to talking about it. The little girls sat under the pines eating their thick mutton sandwiches and big slabs of johnny cake spread with butter. While always, as near as they could get, sat the Kelveys, our Else holding on to Lil, listening too, while they chewed their jam sandwiches out of a newspaper soaked with large red blobs.

'Mother,' said Kezia, 'can't I ask the Kelveys just once?'

'Certainly not, Kezia.'

'But why not?'

'Run away, Kezia; you know quite well why not.'

At last everybody had seen it except them. On that day the subject rather flagged. It was the dinner hour. The children stood together under the pine trees, and suddenly, as they looked at the Kelveys eating out of their paper, always by themselves, always listening, they wanted to be horrid to them. Emmie Cole started the whisper.

'Lil Kelvey's going to be a servant when she grows up.'

'O-oh, how awful!' said Isabel Burnell, and she made eyes at Emmie.

Emmie swallowed in a very meaning way and nodded to Isabel as she'd seen her mother do on those occasions.

'It's true – it's true – it's true,' she said.

Then Lena Logan's little eyes snapped. 'Shall I ask her?' she whispered.

'Bet you don't,' said Jessie May.

'Pooh, I'm not frightened,' said Lena. Suddenly she gave a little squeal and danced in front of the other girls. 'Watch! Watch me! Watch me now!' said Lena. And sliding, gliding, dragging one foot, giggling behind her hand, Lena went over to the Kelveys.

Lil looked up from her dinner. She wrapped the rest quickly away. Our Else stopped chewing. What was coming now?

'Is it true you're going to be a servant when you grow up, Lil Kelvey?' shrilled Lena.

Dead silence. But instead of answering, Lil only gave her silly, shamefaced smile. She didn't seem to mind the question at all. What a sell for Lena! The girls began to titter.

Lena couldn't stand that. She put her hands on her hips; she shot forward. 'Yah, yer father's in prison!' she hissed spitefully.

This was such a marvellous thing to have said that the little girls rushed away in a body, deeply, deeply excited, wild with joy. Someone found a long rope, and they began skipping. And never did they skip so high, run in and out so fast, or do such daring things as on that morning.

In the afternoon Pat called for the Burnell children with the buggy and they drove home. There were visitors. Isabel and Lottie, who liked visitors, went upstairs to change their pinafores. But Kezia thieved out at the back. Nobody was about; she began to swing on the big white gates of the courtyard. Presently, looking along the road, she saw two little dots. They grew bigger, they were coming towards her. Now she could see that one was in front and one close behind. Now she could see that they were the Kelveys. Kezia stopped swinging. She slipped off the gate as if she was going to run away. Then she hesitated. The Kelveys came nearer, and beside them walked their shadows, very long, stretching right across the road with their heads in the buttercups. Kezia clambered back on the gate; she had made up her mind; she swung out.

'Hullo,' she said to the passing Kelveys.

They were so astounded that they stopped. Lil gave her silly smile. Our Else stared.

'You can come and see our doll's house if you want to,' said Kezia, and she dragged one toe on the ground. But at that Lil turned red and shook her head quickly.

'Why not?' asked Kezia.

Lil gasped, then she said, 'Your ma told our ma you wasn't to speak to us.'

'Oh, well,' said Kezia. She didn't know what to reply. 'It doesn't matter. You can come and see our doll's house all the same. Come on. Nobody's looking.'

But Lil shook her head still harder.

'Don't you want to?' asked Kezia.

Suddenly there was a twitch, a tug at Lil's skirt. She turned round. Our Else was looking at her with big, imploring eyes; she was frowning; she wanted to go. For a moment Lil looked at our Else very doubtfully. But then our Else twitched her skirt again. She started forward. Kezia led the way. Like two little stray cats they followed across the courtyard to where the doll's house stood.

'There it is,' said Kezia.

There was a pause. Lil breathed loudly, almost snorted; our Else was still as stone.

'I'll open it for you,' said Kezia kindly. She undid the hook and they looked inside.

'There's the drawing-room and the dining-room, and that's the –'

'Kezia!'

Oh, what a start they gave!

'Kezia!'

It was Aunt Beryl's voice. They turned round. At the back door stood Aunt Beryl, staring as if she couldn't believe what she saw.

'How dare you ask the little Kelveys into the courtyard?' said her cold, furious voice. 'You know as well as I do, you're not allowed to talk to them. Run away, children, run away at once. And don't come back again,' said Aunt Beryl. And she stepped into the yard and shooed them out as if they were chickens.

'Off you go immediately!' she called, cold and proud.

They did not need telling twice. Burning with shame, shrinking together, Lil huddling along like her mother, our Else dazed, somehow they crossed the big courtyard and squeezed through the white gate.

'Wicked, disobedient little girl!' said Aunt Beryl bitterly to Kezia, and she slammed the doll's house to.

The afternoon had been awful. A letter had come from Willie Brent, a terrifying, threatening letter, saying if she did not meet him that evening in Pulman's Bush, he'd come to the front door and ask the reason why! But now that she had frightened those little rats of Kelveys and given Kezia a good scolding, her heart felt lighter. That ghastly pressure was gone. She went back to the house humming.

When the Kelveys were well out of sight of Burnells', they sat down to rest on a big red drainpipe by the side of the road. Lil's cheeks were still burning; she took off the hat with the quill and held it on her knee. Dreamily they looked over the hay paddocks, past the creek, to the group of wattles where

Logan's cows stood waiting to be milked. What were their thoughts?

Presently our Else nudged up close to her sister. But now she had forgotten the cross lady. She put out a finger and stroked her sister's quill; she smiled her rare smile.

'I seen the little lamp,' she said, softly.

Then both were silent once more.

SIX YEARS AFTER

It was not the afternoon to be on deck – on the contrary. It was exactly the afternoon when there is no snugger place than a warm cabin, a warm bunk. Tucked up with a rug, a hot-water bottle and a piping hot cup of tea she would not have minded the weather in the least. But he – hated cabins, hated to be inside anywhere more than was absolutely necessary. He had a passion for keeping, as he called it, above board, especially when he was travelling. And it wasn't surprising, considering the enormous amount of time he spent cooped up in the office. So, when he rushed away from her as soon as they got on board and came back five minutes later to say he had secured two deck chairs on the lee side and the steward was undoing the rugs, her voice through the high sealskin collar murmured 'Good'; and because he was looking at her, she smiled with bright eyes and blinked quickly, as if to say, 'Yes, perfectly all right – absolutely.' And she meant it.

'Then we'd better –' said he, and he tucked her hand inside his arm and began to rush her off to where their chairs stood. But she just had time to breathe, 'Not so fast, Daddy, please,' when he remembered too and slowed down.

Strange! They had been married twenty-eight years, and

it was still an effort to him, each time, to adapt his pace to hers.

'Not cold, are you?' he asked, glancing sideways at her. Her little nose, geranium pink above the dark fur, was answer enough. But she thrust her free hand into the velvet pocket of her jacket and murmured gaily, 'I shall be glad of my rug.'

He pressed her tighter to his side – a quick, nervous pressure. He knew, of course, that she ought to be down in the cabin; he knew that it was no afternoon for her to be sitting on deck, in this cold and raw mist, lee side or no lee side, rugs or no rugs, and he realised how she must be hating it. But he had come to believe that it really was easier for her to make these sacrifices than it was for him. Take their present case, for instance. If he had gone down to the cabin with her, he would have been miserable the whole time, and he couldn't have helped showing it. At any rate, she would have found him out. Whereas, having made up her mind to fall in with his ideas, he would have betted anybody she would even go so far as to enjoy the experience. Not because she was without person-ality of her own. Good Lord! She was absolutely brimming with it. But because . . . but here his thoughts always stopped. Here they always felt the need of a cigar, as it were. And, looking at the cigar-tip, his fine blue eyes narrowed. It was a law of marriage, he supposed. . . . All the same, he always felt guilty when he asked these sacrifices of her. That was what the quick pressure meant. His being said to her being: 'You do understand, don't you?' and there was an answering tremor of her fingers, 'I *understand*.'

Certainly the steward – good little chap – had done all in his power to make them comfortable. He had put up their chairs in whatever warmth there was and out of the smell. She did hope he would be tipped adequately. It was on occasions like these (and her life seemed to be full of such occasions) that she wished it was the woman who controlled the purse.

'Thank you, steward. That will do beautifully.'

'Why are stewards so often delicate-looking?' she wondered, as her feet were tucked under. 'This poor little chap looks as though he'd got a chest, and yet one would have thought . . . the sea air . . .'

The button of the pigskin purse was undone. The tray was tilted. She saw sixpences, shillings, half-crowns.

'I should give him five shillings,' she decided, 'and tell him to buy himself a good nourishing –'

He was given a shilling, and he touched his cap and seemed genuinely grateful.

Well, it might have been worse. It might have been sixpence. It might, indeed. For at that moment Father turned towards her and said, half apologetically, stuffing the purse back, 'I gave him a shilling. I think it was worth it, don't you?'

'Oh, quite! Every bit!' said she.

It is extraordinary how peaceful it feels on a little steamer once the bustle of leaving port is over. In a quarter of an hour one might have been at sea for days. There is something almost touching, childish, in the way people submit themselves to the new conditions. They go to bed in the early afternoon, they shut their eyes and 'it's night' like little children who turn the table upside down and cover themselves with the tablecloth. And those who remain on deck – they seem to be always the same, those few hardened men travellers – pause, light their pipes, stamp softly, gaze out to sea, and their voices are subdued as they walk up and down. The long-legged little girl chases after the red-cheeked boy, but soon both are captured; and the old sailor, swinging an unlighted lantern, passes and disappears. . . .

He lay back, the rug up to his chin and she saw he was breathing deeply. Sea air! If anyone believed in sea air it was he. He had the strongest faith in its tonic qualities. But the great thing was, according to him, to fill the lungs with it the moment you came on board. Otherwise, the sheer strength of it was enough to give you a chill. . . .

She gave a small chuckle, and he turned to her quickly. 'What is it?'

'It's your cap,' she said. 'I never can get used to you in a cap. You look such a thorough burglar.'

'Well, what the deuce am I to wear?' He shot up one grey eyebrow and wrinkled his nose. 'It's a very good cap, too. Very fine specimen of its kind. It's got a very rich white satin lining.' He paused. He declaimed, as he had hundreds of times before at this stage, 'Rich and rare were the gems she wore.'

But she was thinking he really was childishly proud of the white satin lining. He would like to have taken off his cap and made her feel it. 'Feel the quality!' How often had she rubbed between finger and thumb his coat, his shirt cuff, tie, sock, linen handkerchief, while he said that.

She slipped down more deeply into her chair.

And the little steamer pressed on, pitching gently, over the grey, unbroken, gently moving water, that was veiled with slanting rain.

Far out, as though idly, listlessly, gulls were flying. Now they settled on the waves, now they beat up into the rainy air and shone against the pale sky like the lights within a pearl. They looked cold and lonely. How lonely it will be when we have passed by, she thought. There will be nothing but the waves and those birds and rain falling.

She gazed through the rust-spotted railing along which big drops trembled, until suddenly she shut her lids. It was as if a warning voice inside her had said, 'Don't look!'

'No, I won't,' she decided. 'It's too depressing, much too depressing.'

But, immediately, she opened her eyes and looked again. Lonely birds, water lifting, white pale sky – how were they changed?

And it seemed to her there was a presence far out there, between the sky and the water; someone very desolate and longing watched them pass and cried as if to stop them – but cried to her alone.

'Mother!'

'Don't leave me,' sounded in the cry. 'Don't forget me! You are forgetting me, you know you are!' And it was as though from her own breast there came the sound of childish weeping.

'My son – my precious child – it isn't true!'

Sh! How was it possible that she was sitting there on that quiet steamer beside Father and at the same time she was hushing and holding a little slender boy – so pale – who had just waked out of a dreadful dream?

191

'I dreamed I was in a wood – somewhere far away from everybody – and I was lying down and a great blackberry vine grew over me. And I called and called to you – and you wouldn't come – you wouldn't come – so I had to lie there for ever.'

What a terrible dream! He had always had terrible dreams. How often, years ago, when he was small, she had made some excuse and escaped from their friends in the dining-room or the drawing-room to come to the foot of the stairs and listen. 'Mother!' And when he was asleep, his dream had journeyed with her back into the circle of lamplight; it had taken its place there like a ghost. And now –

Far more often – at all times – in all places – like now, for instance – she never settled down, she was never off her guard for a moment but she heard him. He wanted her. 'I am coming as fast as I can! As fast as I can!' But the dark stairs have no ending, and the worst dream of all – the one that is always the same – goes for ever and ever uncomforted.

This is anguish! How is it to be borne? Still, it is not the idea of her suffering which is unbearable – it is his. Can one do nothing for the dead? And for a long time the answer had been – Nothing!

. . . But softly without a sound the dark curtain has rolled down. There is no more to come. That is the end of the play.

But it can't end like that – so suddenly. There must be more. No, it's cold, it's still. There is nothing to be gained by waiting.

But – did he go back again? Or, when the war was over, did

he come home for good? Surely, he will marry – later on – not for several years. Surely, one day I shall remember his wedding and my first grandchild – a beautiful dark-haired boy born in the early morning – a lovely morning – spring!

'Oh, Mother, it's not fair to me to put these ideas into my head! Stop, Mother, stop! When I think of all I have missed, I can't bear it.'

'I can't bear it!' She sits up breathing the words and tosses the dark rug away. It is colder than ever, and now the dusk is falling, falling like ash upon the pallid water.

And the little steamer, growing determined, throbbed on, pressed on, as if at the end of the journey there waited . . .

unfinished

WIDOWED

They came down to breakfast next morning absolutely their own selves. Rosy, fresh, and just chilled enough by the cold air blowing through the bedroom windows to be very ready for hot coffee.

'Nippy.' That was Geraldine's word as she buttoned on her orange coat with pink-washed fingers. 'Don't you find it decidedly nippy?' And her voice, so matter-of-fact, so natural, sounded as though they had been married for years.

Parting his hair with two brushes (marvellous feat for a woman to watch) in the little round mirror, he had replied, lightly clapping the brushes together, 'My dear, have you got enough *on*?' and he, too, sounded as though well he knew from the experience of years her habit of clothing herself underneath in wisps of chiffon and two satin bows. . . . Then they ran down to breakfast, laughing together and terribly startling the shy parlour-maid who, after talking it over with Cook, had decided to be invisible until she was rung for.

'Good morning, Nellie, I think we shall want more toast than *that*,' said the smiling Geraldine as she hung over the breakfast table. She deliberated – 'Ask Cook to make us four more pieces, please.'

Marvellous, the parlour-maid thought it was. And as she closed the door she heard the voice say, 'I do so hate to be short of toast, don't you?'

He was standing in the sunny window. Geraldine went up to him. She put her hand on his arm and gave it a gentle squeeze. How pleasant it was to feel that rough man's tweed again. Ah, how pleasant! She rubbed her hand against it, touched it with her cheek, sniffed the smell.

The window looked out on to flower beds, a tangle of Michaelmas daisies, late dahlias, hanging heavy, and shaggy little asters. Then there came a lawn strewn with yellow leaves with a broad path beyond and a row of gold-fluttering trees. An old gardener, in woollen mitts, was sweeping the path, brushing the leaves into a neat little heap. Now, the broom tucked in his arm, he fumbled in his coat pocket, brought out some matches, and scooping a hole in the leaves he set fire to them.

Such lovely blue smoke came breathing into the air through those dry leaves; there was something so calm and orderly in the way the pile burned that it was a pleasure to watch. The old gardener stumped away and came back with a handful of withered twigs. He flung them on and stood by, and little light flames began to flicker.

'I do think,' said Geraldine, 'I do think there is nothing nicer than a real satisfactory fire.'

'Jolly, isn't it,' he murmured back, and they went to their first breakfast.

Just over a year ago, thirteen months, to be exact, she had been standing before the dining-room window of the little house in Sloane Street. It looked over the railed gardens. Breakfast was over, cleared away and done with . . . she had a fat bunch of letters in her hand that she meant to answer, snugly, over the fire. But before settling down, the autumn sun, the freshness had drawn her to the window. Such a perfect morning for the Row. Jimmie had gone riding.

'Good-bye, dear thing.'

'Good-bye, Gerry mine.' And then the morning kiss, quick and firm. He looked so handsome in his riding kit. She imagined him as she stood there . . . riding. Geraldine was not very good at imagining things. But there was mist, a thud of hooves and Jimmie's moustache was damp. From the garden there sounded the creak of a gardener's barrow. An old man came into sight with a load of leaves and a broom lying across.

He stopped; he began to sweep. 'What enormous tufts of irises grow in London gardens,' mused Geraldine. 'Why?' And now the smoke of a real fire ascended.

'There is nothing nicer,' she thought, 'than a really satisfactory fire.'

Just at that moment the telephone bell rang. Geraldine sat down at Jimmie's desk to answer it. It was Major Hunter.

'Good morning, Major. You're a very early bird!'

'Good morning, Mrs. Howard. Yes. I am.' (Geraldine made a little surprised face at herself. How odd he sounded!) 'Mrs. Howard, I'm coming round to see you . . . now. . . . I'm taking a taxi. . . . Please don't go out. And – and –' the voice stammered, 'p-please don't let the servants go out.'

'*Par*-don?' This last was so very peculiar, though the whole thing had been peculiar enough, that Geraldine couldn't believe what she heard. But he was gone. He had rung off. What on earth – and putting down the receiver, she took up a pencil and drew what she always drew when she sat down before a piece of blotting-paper – the behind of a little cat with whiskers and tail complete. Geraldine must have drawn that little cat hundreds of times, all over the world, in hotels, in clubs, at steamer desks, waiting at the bank. The little cat was her sign, her mark. She had copied it from a little girl at school when she thought it most wonderful. And she never tried anything else. She was . . . not very good at drawing. This particular cat was drawn with an extra firm pen and even its whiskers looked surprised.

'Not to let the servants go out!' But she had never heard anything so peculiar in her life. She must have made a mistake. Geraldine couldn't help a little giggle of amusement. And why should he tell her he was taking a taxi? And why – above all – should he be coming to see her at that hour of the morning?

Then – it came over her – like a flash she remembered Major Hunter's mania for old furniture. They had been discussing it at the Carlton the last time they lunched together. And he had said something to Jimmie about some – Jacobean or Queen Anne – Geraldine knew nothing about these things – something or other. Could he possibly be bringing it round? But of course. He must be. And that explained the remark about the servants. He wanted them to help getting it into the house. What a bore! Geraldine did hope it would tone in. And really, she must say she thought Major Hunter was taking a good deal for granted to produce a thing that size at that hour of the day without a word of warning. They hardly knew him well enough for that. Why make such a mystery of it too? Geraldine hated mysteries. But she had heard his head was rather troublesome at times ever since the Somme affair. Perhaps this was one of his bad days. In that case, a pity Jimmie was not back. She rang. Mullins answered.

'Oh, Mullins, I'm expecting Major Hunter in a few moments. He's bringing something rather heavy. He may want you to help with it. And Cook had better be ready too.'

Geraldine's manner was slightly lofty with her servants. She enjoyed carrying things off with a high hand. All the same, Mullins did look surprised. She seemed to hover for a moment before she went out. It annoyed Geraldine greatly. What was there to be surprised at? What could have been simpler? she thought, sitting down to her batch of letters, and the fire, and the clock and her pen began to whisper together.

There was the taxi – making an enormous noise at the door. She thought she heard the driver's voice too, arguing. It took her a long moment to clasp her writing-case and to get up out of the low chair. The bell rang. She went straight to the dining-room door –

And there was Major Hunter in his riding kit, coming quickly towards her, and behind him, through the open door at the bottom of the steps, she saw something big, something grey. It was an ambulance.

'There's been an accident,' cried Geraldine sharply.

'Mrs. Howard.' Major Hunter ran forward. He put out his

icy cold hand and wrung hers. 'You'll be brave, won't you?' he said, he pleaded.

But of course she would be brave.

'Is it serious?'

Major Hunter nodded gravely. He said the one word 'Yes.'

'Very serious?'

Now he raised his head. He looked her full in the eyes. She'd never realised until that moment that he was extraordinarily handsome though in a melodrama kind of way. 'It's as bad as it can be, Mrs. Howard,' said Major Hunter simply. 'But – go in there,' he said hastily, and he almost pushed her into her own dining-room. 'We must bring him in – where can we –'

'Can he be taken upstairs?' asked Geraldine.

'Yes, yes, of course.' Major Hunter looked at her so strangely – so painfully.

'There's his dressing-room,' said Geraldine. 'It's on the first floor. I'll lead the way,' and she put her hand on the Major's arm. 'It's quite all right, Major,' she said, 'I'm not going to break down –' and she actually smiled, a confident brilliant smile.

To her amazement, as Major Hunter turned away he burst out with, 'Ah, my God! I'm so sorry.'

Poor man. He was quite overcome. 'Brandy afterwards,' thought Geraldine. 'Not now, of course.'

It was a painful moment when she heard those measured deliberate steps in the hall. But Geraldine, realising this was not the moment, and there was nothing to be gained by it, refrained from looking.

'This way, Major.' She skimmed on in front, up the stairs, along the passage; she flung open the door of Jimmie's gay, living, breathing dressing-room and stood to one side – for Major Hunter, for the two stretcher-bearers. Only then she realised that it must be a scalp wound – some injury to the head. For there was nothing to be seen of Jimmie; the sheet was pulled right over. . . .

unfinished

SECOND VIOLIN

A February morning, windy, cold, with chill-looking clouds hurrying over a pale sky and chill snowdrops for sale in the grey streets. People look small and shrunken as they flit by; they look scared as if they were trying to hide inside their coats from something big and brutal. The shop doors are closed, the awnings are furled, and the policemen at the crossings are lead policemen. Huge empty vans shake past with a hollow sound; and there is a smell of soot and wet stone staircases, a raw, grimy smell. . . .

Flinging her small scarf over her shoulder again, clasping her violin, Miss Bray darts along to orchestra practice. She is conscious of her cold hands, her cold nose and her colder feet. She can't feel her toes at all. Her feet are just little slabs of cold, all of a piece, like the feet of china dolls. Winter is a terrible time for thin people – terrible! Why should it hound them down, fasten on them, worry them so? Why not, for a change, take a nip, take a snap at the fat ones who wouldn't notice? But no! It is sleek, warm, cat-like summer that makes the fat one's life a misery. Winter is all for bones. . . .

Threading her way, like a needle, in and out and along, went Miss Bray, and she thought of nothing but the cold. She had just come out of her kitchen, which was pleasantly snug in the morning, with her gas-fire going for her breakfast and the window closed. She had just drunk three large cups of really boiling tea. Surely, they ought to have warmed her. One always read in books of people going on their way warmed and invigorated by even one cup. And she had had three! How she loved her tea! She was getting fonder and fonder of it. Stirring the cup, Miss Bray looked down. A little fond smile parted her lips, and she breathed tenderly, 'I love my tea.'

But all the same, in spite of the books, it didn't keep her warm. Cold! Cold! And now as she turned the corner she took such a gulp of damp, cold air that her eyes filled. *Yi-yi-yi*, a little dog yelped; he looked as though he'd been hurt. She hadn't time to look round, but that high, sharp yelping soothed her, was a comfort even. She could have made just that sound herself.

And here was the Academy. Miss Bray pressed with all her might against the stiff, sulky door, squeezed through into the vestibule hung with pallid notices and concert pro- grammes, and stumbled up the dusty stairs and along the passage to the dressing-room. Through the open door there came such shrill loud laughter, such high, indifferent voices that it sounded like a play going on in there. It was hard to believe people were not laughing and talking like that . . . on purpose. 'Excuse me – pardon – sorry,' said Miss Bray, nudging her way in and looking quickly round the dingy little room. Her two friends had not yet come.

The First Violins were there; a dreamy, broad-faced girl leaned against her 'cello; two Violas sat on a bench, bent over a music book, and the Harp, a small grey little person, who only came occasionally, leaned against a bench and looked for her pocket in her underskirt. . . .

'I've a run of three twice, ducky,' said Ma, 'a pair of queens make eight, and one for his nob makes nine.'

With an awful hollow groan Alexander, curling his little finger high, pegged nine for Ma. And 'Wait now, wait now,' said she, and her quick short little hands snatched at the other cards. 'My crib, young man!' She spread them out, leaned back, twitched her shawl, put her head on one side. 'H'm, not so bad! A flush of four and a pair!'

'Betrayed! Betrayed!' moaned Alexander, bowing his dark head over the cribbage board, 'and by a woo-man.' He sighed deeply, shuffled the cards and said to Ma, 'Cut for me, my love!'

Although, of course, he was only having his joke like all professional young gentlemen, something in the tone in which he said 'my love!' gave Ma quite a turn. Her lips trembled as she cut the cards, she felt a sudden pang as she watched those long slim fingers dealing.

Ma and Alexander were playing cribbage in the basement kitchen of number 9 Bolton Street. It was late, it was on eleven, and Sunday night, too – shocking! They sat at the kitchen table that was covered with a worn art serge cloth spotted with candle grease. On one corner of it stood three glasses, three spoons, a saucer of sugar lumps and a bottle of gin. The stove was still alight and the lid of the kettle had just begun to lift, cautiously, stealthily, as though there was someone inside who wanted to have a peep and pop back again. On the horse-hair sofa against the wall by the door the owner of the third glass lay asleep, gently snoring. Perhaps because he had his back to them, perhaps because his feet poked out from the short overcoat covering him, he looked forlorn, pathetic and the long, fair hair covering his collar looked forlorn and pathetic, too.

'Well, well,' said Ma, sighing as she put out two cards and arranged the others in a fan, 'such is life. I little thought when I saw the last of you this morning that we'd be playing a game together to-night.'

'The caprice of destiny,' murmured Alexander. But, as a matter of fact, it was no joking matter. By some infernal mischance that morning he and Rinaldo had missed the train that all the company travelled by. That was bad enough. But being Sunday, there was no other train until midnight, and as they had a full rehearsal at 10 o'clock on Monday it meant going by that, or getting what the company called the beetroot. But God! what a day it had been. They had left the luggage at the station and come back to Ma's, back to Alexander's frowsy bedroom with the bed unmade and water standing about. Rinaldo had spent the whole day sitting on the side of the bed swinging his leg, dropping ash on the floor and saying, 'I wonder what made us lose that train. Strange we should have lost it. I bet the others are wondering what made us lose it, too.' And Alexander had stayed by the window gazing into the small garden that was so black with grime even the old lean cat who came and scraped seemed revolted by it, too. It was only after Ma had seen the last of her Sunday visitors . . .

unfinished

HONESTY

There was an expression Rupert Henderson was very fond of using: 'If you want my *honest* opinion. . . .' He had an honest opinion on every subject under the sun, and nothing short of a passion for delivering it. But Archie Cullen's pet phrase was 'I cannot *honestly* say. . . .' Which meant that he had not really made up his mind. He had not really made up his mind on any subject whatsoever. Why? Because he could not. He was unlike other men. He was minus something – or was it plus? No matter. He was not in the least proud of the fact. It depressed him – one might go so far as to say – terribly at times.

Rupert and Archie lived together. That is to say, Archie lived in Rupert's rooms. Oh, he paid his share, his half in everything; the arrangement was a purely, strictly business arrangement. But perhaps it was because Rupert had invited Archie that Archie remained always – his guest. They each had a bedroom – there was a common sitting-room and a largish bathroom which Rupert used as a dressing-room as well. The first morning after his arrival Archie had left his sponge in the bathroom, and a moment after there was a knock at his door and Rupert said, kindly but firmly, 'Your sponge, I fancy.' The first evening Archie had brought his tobacco jar into the

sitting-room and placed it on a corner of the mantelpiece.
Rupert was reading the newspaper. It was a round china jar,
the surface painted and roughened to represent a sea-urchin.
On the lid was a spray of china seaweed with two berries for a
knob. Archie was excessively fond of it. But after dinner, when
Rupert took out his pipe and pouch, he suddenly fixed his
eyes on this object, blew through his moustaches, gasped, and
said in a wondering, astonished voice, 'I say! Is that yours or
Mrs. Head's?' Mrs. Head was their landlady.

'It's mine,' said Archie, and he blushed and smiled just a
trifle timidly.

'I *say*!' said Rupert again – this time very meaningly.

'Would you rather I . . .' said Archie, and he moved in his
chair to get up.

'No, no! Certainly not! On no account!' answered Rupert,
and he actually raised his hand. 'But perhaps' – and here he
smiled at Archie and gazed about him – 'perhaps we might
find some spot for it that was a trifle less conspicuous.'

The spot was not decided on, however, and Archie nipped
his sole personal possession into his bedroom as soon as
Rupert was out of the way.

But it was chiefly at meals that the attitude of host and
guest was most marked. For instance, on each separate occasion, even before they sat down, Rupert said, 'Would you mind
cutting the bread, Archie?' Had he not made such a point
of it, it is possible that Archie in a moment of abstracted-
ness might have grasped the bread knife. . . . An unpleasant
thought! Again, Archie was never allowed to serve. Even at
breakfast, the hot dishes and the tea, both were dispensed

by Rupert. True, he had half apologised about the tea; he seemed to feel the necessity of some slight explanation, there.

'I'm rather a fad about my tea,' said he. 'Some people, females especially, pour in the milk first. Fatal habit, for more reasons than one. In my opinion, the cup should be filled just *so* and the tea then coloured. Sugar, Archie?'

'Oh, please,' said Archie, almost bowing over the table. Rupert was so very impressive.

'But I suppose,' said his friend, 'you don't notice any of these little things?'

And Archie answered vaguely, stirring: 'No, I don't suppose I do.'

Rupert sat down and unfolded his napkin.

'It would be very inconsistent with your character and disposition,' said he genially, 'if you did! Kidneys and bacon? Scrambled eggs? Either? Both? Which?'

Poor Archie hated scrambled eggs, but, alas! he was practically certain that scrambled eggs were expected of him too. This 'psychological awareness', as Rupert called it, which existed between them, might after a time make things a trifle difficult. He felt a little abject as he murmured, 'Eggs, please.' And he saw by Rupert's expression that he had chosen right. Rupert helped him to eggs largely.

Psychological awareness . . . perhaps it was that which explained their intimacy. One might have been tempted to say it was a case of mutual fascination. But whereas Archie's reply to the suggestion would have been a slow 'Poss-ibly!' Rupert would have flouted it at once.

'Fascination! The word's preposterous in this connection. What on earth would there be in Cullen to fascinate me even if I was in the habit of being fascinated by my fellow creatures; which I certainly am not. No, I'll own I am deeply interested. I confess my belief is, I understand him better than anybody else. And if you want my honest opinion, I am certain that my – my – h'm – influence over – sympathy for – him – call it what you like, is all to the good. There is a psychological awareness . . . . Moreover, as a companion, instinctively I find him extremely agreeable. He stimulates some part of my mind which is less active without him. But fascination – wide of the mark, my dear – wide!'

But supposing one remained unconvinced? Supposing one still played with the idea. Wasn't it possible to see Rupert and Archie as the python and the rabbit keeping house together? Rupert that handsome, well-fed python with his moustaches, his glare, his habit of uncoiling before the fire and swaying against the mantelpiece, pipe and pouch in hand. And Archie, soft, hunched, timid, sitting in the lesser arm-chair, there and not there, flicking back into the darkness at a word but emerging again at a look – with sudden wholly unexpected starts of playfulness (instantly suppressed by the python). Of course, there was no question of anything so crude and dreadful as the rabbit being eaten by his house-mate. Nevertheless, it was a strange fact, after a typical evening the one looked immensely swelled, benign and refreshed, and the other, pale, small and exhausted. . . . And more often than not Rupert's final comment was – ominous this – as he doused his whisky with soda:

'This has been very absorbing, Archie.' And Archie gasped out, 'Oh, *very*!'

Archie Cullen was a journalist and the son of a journalist. He had no private money, no influential connections, scarcely any friends. His father had been one of those weak, disappointed, unsuccessful men who see in their sons a weapon for themselves. He would get his own back on life through Archie. Archie would show them the stuff he – his father was made of. Just you wait till my son comes along! This, though highly consoling to Mr. Cullen *père*, was terribly poor fun for Archie. At two and a half his infant nose was put to the grindstone and even on Sundays it was not taken off. Then his father took him out walking and improved the occasion by making him spell the shop signs, count the yachts racing in the harbour, divide them by four and multiply the result by three.

But the experiment was an amazing success. Archie turned away from the distractions of life, shut his ears, folded his feet, sat over the table with his book, and when the holidays came he didn't like them; they made him uneasy; so he went on reading for himself. He was a model boy. On prize-giving days his father accompanied him to school, carried the great wad of stiff books home for him and, flinging them on the dining-room table, he surveyed them with an exultant smile. My prizes! The little sacrifice stared at them, too, through his spectacles as other little boys stared at puddings. He ought, of course, at this juncture to have been rescued by a doting mother who, though cowed herself, rose on the . . .

unfinished

ALL SERENE!

At breakfast that morning they were in wonderfully good spirits. Who was responsible – he or she? It was true she made a point of looking her best in the morning; she thought it part of her duty to him – to their love, even, to wear charming little caps, funny little coats, coloured mules at breakfast time, and to see that the table was perfect as he and she – fastidious pair! – understood the word. But he, too, so fresh, well-groomed and content, contributed his share. . . . She had been down first, sitting at her place when he came in. He leaned over the back of her chair, his hands on her shoulders; he bent down and lightly rubbed his cheek against hers, murmuring gently but with just enough pride of proprietorship to make her flush with delight, 'Give me my tea, love.' And she lifted the silver teapot that had a silver pear modelled on the lid and gave him his tea.

'Thanks. . . . You know you look awfully well this morning!'

'Do I?'

'Yes. Do that again. Look at me again. It's your eyes. They're like a child's. I've never known anyone have such shining eyes as you.'

'Oh, dear!' She sighed for joy. 'I do love having sweet things said to me!'

'Yes, you do – spoilt child! Shall I give you some of this?'

'No, thank you. . . . Darling!' Her hand flew across the table and clasped his hand.

'Yes?'

But she said nothing, only 'Darling!' again. There was the look on his face she loved – a kind of sweet jesting. He was pretending he didn't know what she meant, and yet of course he did know. He was pretending to be feeling 'Here she is – trust a woman – all ready for a passionate love scene over the breakfast table at nine o'clock in the morning.' But she wasn't deceived. She knew he felt just the same as she did. That amused tolerance, that mock despair was part of the ways of men – no more.

'May I be allowed to *use* this knife please, or to put it down?'

Really! Mona had never yet got accustomed to her husband's smile. They had been married for three years. She was in love with him for countless reasons, but apart from them all, a special reason all to itself, was because of his smile. If it hadn't sounded nonsense she would have said she fell in love at first sight over and over again when he smiled. Other people felt the charm of it, too. Other women, she was certain. Sometimes she thought that even the servants watched for it. . . .

'Don't forget we're going to the theatre to-night.'

'Oh, good egg! I had forgotten. It's ages since we went to a show.'

'Yes, isn't it? I feel quite thrilled.'

'Don't you think we might have a tiny small celebration at

dinner?' ('Tiny small' was one of her expressions. But why did it sound so sweet when he used it?)

'Yes, let's. You mean champagne?' And she looked into the distance, and said in a far-away voice: 'Then I must revise the sweet.'

At that moment the maid came in with the letters. There were four for him, three for her. No, one of hers belonged to him, too, rather a grimy little envelope with a dab of sealing-wax on the back.

'Why do you get all the letters?' she wailed, handing it across. 'It's awfully unfair. I love letters and I never get any.'

'Well, I do like that!' said he. 'How can you sit there and tell such awful bangers? It's the rarest thing on earth for me to get a letter in the morning. It's always you who get those mysterious epistles from girls you were at college with or faded aunts. Here, have half my pear – it's a beauty.' She held out her plate.

The Rutherfords never shared their letters. It was her idea that they should not. He had been violently opposed to it at first. She couldn't help laughing; he had so absolutely misunderstood her reason.

'Good God! my dear. You're perfectly welcome to open any letters of mine that come to the house – or to read any letters of mine that may be lying about. I think I can promise you . . .'

'Oh no, no, darling, that's not what I mean. I don't suspect you.' And she put her hands on his cheeks and kissed him quickly. He looked like an offended boy. 'But so many of Mother's old friends write to me – confide in me – don't you know? – tell me things they wouldn't for the world tell a man. I feel it wouldn't be fair to them. Don't you see?'

He gave way at last. But 'I'm old-fashioned,' he said, and his smile was a little rueful. 'I like to feel my wife reads my letters.'

'My precious dear! I've made you unhappy.' She felt so repentant; she didn't know quite about what. 'Of course I'd love to read . . .'

'No, no! That's all right. It's understood. We'll keep the bond.' And they had kept it.

He slit open the grimy envelope. He began to read. 'Damn!' he said and thrust out his under lip.

'Why, what is it? Something horrid?'

'No – annoying. I shall be late this evening. A man wants to meet me at the office at six o'clock.'

'Was that a business letter?' She sounded surprised.

'Yes, why?'

'It looked so awfully unbusinesslike. The sealing-wax and the funny writing – much more like a woman's than a man's.'

He laughed. He folded the letter, put it in his pocket and picked up the envelope. 'Yes,' he said, 'it is queer, isn't it. I shouldn't have noticed. How quick you are! But it does look exactly like a woman's hand. That capital R, for instance' – he flipped the envelope across to her.

'Yes, and that squiggle underneath. I should have said a rather uneducated female . . .'

'As a matter of fact,' said Hugh, 'he's a mining engineer.' And he got up, began to stretch and then stopped. 'I say, what a glorious morning! Why do I have to go to the office instead of staying at home and playing with you?' And he came over to her and locked his arms round her neck. 'Tell me that, little lovely one.'

'Oh,' she leaned against him, 'I wish you could. Life's arranged badly for people like you and me. And now you're going to be late this evening.'

'Never mind,' said he. 'All the rest of the time's ours. Every single bit of it. We shan't come back from the theatre to find –'

'Our porch black with mining engineers.' She laughed. Did other people – could other people – was it possible that anyone before had ever loved as they loved? She squeezed her head against him – she heard his watch ticking – precious watch!

'What are those purple floppy flowers in my bedroom?' he murmured.

'Petunias.'

'You smell exactly like a petunia.'

And he raised her up. She drew towards him. 'Kiss me,' said he.

It was her habit to sit on the bottom stair and watch his final preparations. Strange it should be so fascinating to see someone brush his hat, choose a pair of gloves and give a last quick look in the round mirror. But it was the same when he was shaving. Then she loved to curl up on the hard little couch in his dressing-room; she was as absorbed, as intent as he. How fantastic he looked, like a pierrot, like a mask, with those dark eyebrows, liquid eyes and the brush of fresh colour on his cheek-bones above the lather! But that was not her chief feeling. No, it was what she felt on the stairs, too. It was,

'So this is my husband, so this is the man I've married, this is the stranger who walked across the lawn that afternoon swinging his tennis racket and bowed, rolling up his shirt-sleeves. This is not only my lover and my husband but my brother, my dearest friend, my playmate, even at times a kind of very perfect father too. And here is where we live. Here is his room – and here is our hall.' She seemed to be showing their house and him to her other self, the self she had been before she had met him. Deeply admiring, almost awed by so much happiness, that other self looked on. . . .

'Will I do?' He stood there smiling, stroking on his gloves. But although he wouldn't like her to say the things she often longed to say about his appearance, she did think she detected that morning just the very faintest boyish showing-off. Children who know they are admired look like that at their mother.

'Yes, you'll do. . . .' Perhaps at that moment she was proud of him as a mother is proud; she could have blessed him before he went his way. Instead she stood in the porch thinking, 'There he goes. The man I've married. The stranger who came across the lawn.' The fact was never less wonderful. . . .

It was never less wonderful, never. It was even more wonderful if anything, and the reason was – Mona ran back into the house, into the drawing-room and sat down to the piano. Oh, why bother about reasons – She began to sing,

> 'See, love, I bring thee flowers
> To charm thy pain!'

But joy – joy breathless and exulting thrilled in her voice, on the word 'pain' her lips parted in such a happy – dreadfully unsympathetic smile that she felt quite ashamed. She stopped playing, she turned round on the piano stool facing the room. How different it looked in the morning, how severe and remote. The grey chairs with the fuchsia-coloured cushions, the black and gold carpet, the bright green silk curtains might have belonged to anybody. It was like a stage setting with the curtain still down. She had no right to be there, and as she thought that a queer little chill caught her; it seemed so extraordinary that anything, even a chair, should turn away from, should not respond to her happiness.

'I don't like this room in the morning, I don't like it at all,' she decided, and she ran upstairs to finish dressing. Ran into their big, shadowy bedroom . . . and leaned over the starry petunias. . . .

unfinished

WEAK HEART

Although it sounded all the year round, although it rang out sometimes as early as half-past six in the morning, sometimes as late as half-past ten at night, it was in the spring, when Bengel's violet patch just inside the gate was blue with flowers, that that piano . . . made the passers-by not only stop talking, but slow down, pause, look suddenly – if they were men – grave, even stern, and if they were women – dreamy, even sorrowful.

Tarana Street was beautiful in the spring; there was not a single house without its garden and trees and a plot of grass big enough to be called 'the lawn'. Over the low painted fences, you could see, as you ran by, whose daffys were out, whose wild snowdrop border was over and who had the biggest hyacinths, so pink and white, the colour of cocoanut ice. But nobody had violets that grew, that smelled in the spring sun like Bengel's. Did they really smell like that? Or did you shut your eyes and lean over the fence because of Edie Bengel's piano?

A little wind ruffles among the leaves like a joyful hand looking for the finest flowers; and the piano sounds gay, tender, laughing. Now a cloud, like a swan, flies across the sun, the violets shine cold, like water, and a sudden questioning cry rings from Edie Bengel's piano.

. . . Ah, if life must pass so quickly, why is the breath of these flowers so sweet? What is the meaning of this feeling of longing, of sweet trouble – of flying joy? Good-bye! Farewell! The young bees lie half awake on the slender dandelions, silver are the pink-tipped arrowy petals of the daisies; the new grass shakes in the light. Everything is beginning again, marvellous as ever, heavenly fair. 'Let me stay! Let me stay!' pleads Edie Bengel's piano.

It is the afternoon, sunny and still. The blinds are down in the front to save the carpets, but upstairs the slats are open and in the golden light little Mrs. Bengel is feeling under her bed for the square bonnet box. She is flushed. She feels timid, excited, like a girl. And now the tissue paper is parted, her best bonnet, the one trimmed with a jet butterfly, which reposes on top, is lifted out and solemnly blown upon.

Dipping down to the glass she tries it with fingers that tremble. She twitches her dolman round her slender shoulders, clasps her purse and before leaving the bedroom kneels down a moment to ask God's blessing on her 'goings out'. And as she kneels there quivering, she is rather like a butterfly herself, fanning her wings before her Lord. When the door is open the sound of the piano coming up through the silent house is almost frightening, so bold, so defiant, so reckless it rolls under Edie's fingers. And just for a moment the thought comes to Mrs. Bengel and is gone again, that there is a stranger with Edie in the drawing-room, but a fantastic person, out of a book, a – a – villain. It's very absurd. She flits across the hall, turns the door handle and confronts her flushed daughter. Edie's hands drop from the keys. She squeezes them between her knees, her head is bent, her curls are fallen forward. She gazes at her mother with brilliant eyes. There is something painful in that glance, something very strange. It is dusky in the drawing-room, the top of the piano is open. Edie has been playing from memory; it's as though the air still tingles.

'I'm going, dear,' said Mrs. Bengel softly, so softly it is like a sigh.

'Yes, Mother,' came from Edie.

'I don't expect I shall be long.'

Mrs. Bengel lingers. She would very much like just a word, of sympathy, of understanding, even from Edie, to cheer her on her way.

But Edie murmurs, 'I'll put the kettle on in half an hour.'

'Do, dear!' Mrs. Bengel grasped at that even. A nervous little smile touched her lips. 'I expect I shall want my tea.'

But to that Edie makes no reply; she frowns, she stretches out a hand, quickly unscrews one of the piano candlesticks, lifts off a pink china ring and screws all tight again. The ring has been rattling. As the front door bangs softly after her mother Edie and the piano seem to plunge together into deep dark water, into waves that flow over both, relentless. She plays on desperately until her nose is white and her heart beats. It is her way of getting over her nervousness and her way too of praying. Would they accept her? Would she be allowed to go? Was it possible that in a week's time she would be one of Miss Farmer's girls, wearing a red and blue hat band, running up the broad steps leading to the big grey painted house that buzzed, that hummed as you went by? Their pew in Church faced Miss

Farmer's boarders. Would she at last know the names of the girls she had looked at so often? The pretty pale one with red hair, the dark one with a fringe, the fair one who held Miss Farmer's hand during the sermon? . . . But after all . . .

It was Edie's fourteenth birthday. Her father gave her a silver brooch with a bar of music, two crotchets, two quavers and a minim headed by a very twisted treble clef. Her mother gave her blue satin gloves and two boxes for gloves and hand-kerchiefs, hand-painted the glove box with a sprig of gold roses tying up the capital G. and the handkerchief box with a marvellously life-like butterfly quivering on the capital H. From the aunts in . . .

There was a tree at the corner of Tarana Street and May Street. It grew so close to the pavement that the heavy boughs stretched over, and on that part of the pavement there was always a fine sifting of minute twigs.

But in the dusk, lovers parading came into its shade as into a tent. There, however long they had been together, they greeted each other again with long kisses, with embraces that were sweet torture, agony to bear, agony to end.

Edie never knew that Roddie 'loved' it, Roddie never knew that it meant anything to Edie.

Roddie, spruce, sleek with water, bumped his new bike down the wooden steps, through the gate. He was off for a spin, and looking at that tree, dark in the glow of evening, he felt the tree was watching him. He wanted to do marvels, to astonish, to shock, to amaze it.

Roddie had a complete new outfit for the occasion. A black serge suit, a black tie, a straw hat so white it was almost silver, a dazzling white straw hat with a broad black band. Attached to the hat there was a thick guard that somehow reminded one of a fishing line and the little clasp on the brim was like a fly. . . . He stood at the graveside, his legs apart, his hands loosely clasped, and watched Edie being lowered into the grave – as a half-grown boy watches anything, a man at work, or a bicycle accident, or a chap cleaning a spring-carriage wheel – but suddenly as the men drew back he gave a violent start, turned, muttered something to his father and dashed away, so fast that people looked positively frightened, through the cemetery, down the avenue of dripping clay banks into Tarana Road, and started pelting for home. His suit was very tight and hot. It was like a dream. He kept his head down and his fists clenched, he couldn't look up, nothing could have made him look higher than the tops of the fences – What was he thinking of as he pressed along? On, on until the gate was reached, up the steps, in at the front door, through the hall, up to the drawing-room.

'Edie!' called Roddie. 'Edie, old girl!'

And he gave a low strange squawk and cried 'Edie!' and stared across at Edie's piano.

But cold, solemn, as if frozen, heavily the piano stared back at Roddie. Then it answered, but on its own behalf, on behalf of the house and the violet patch, the garden, the velvet tree at the corner of May Street, and all that was delightful: 'There is nobody here of that name, young man!'

unfinished

DAPHNE

I had been in Port Willin six months when I decided to give a one-man show. Not that I was particularly keen, but little Field, the picture-shop man, had just started a gallery and he wanted me – begged me, rather – to kick off for him. He was a decent little chap; I hadn't the heart to refuse. And besides, as it happened, I had a good deal of stuff that I felt it would be rather fun to palm off on any one who was fool enough to buy it. So with these high aims I had the cards printed, the pictures framed in plain white frames, and God knows how many cups and saucers ordered for the Private View.

What was I doing in Port Willin? Oh well – why not? I'll own it does sound an unlikely spot, but when you are an impermanent movable, as I am, it's just those unlikely spots that have a trick of holding you. I arrived, intending to stay a week and go on to Fiji. But I had letters to one or two people, and the morning of my arrival, hanging over the side of the ship while we were waiting in the stream, with nothing on earth to do but stare, I took an extraordinary fancy to the shape – to the look of the place.

It's a small town, you know, planted at the edge of a fine deep harbour like a lake. Behind it, on either side, there are

hills. The houses are built of light painted wood. They have
iron roofs coloured red. And there are big dark plumy trees
massed together, breaking up those light shapes, giving a
depth – warmth – making a composition of it well worth
looking at. . . . Well, we needn't go into that – But it had me
that fine morning. And the first days after my arrival, walking,
or driving out in one of the big swinging, rocking cabs, I took
an equal fancy to the people.

Not to quite all of them. The men left me cold. Yes, I must
say, colonial men are not the brightest specimens. But I never
struck a place where the average of female attractiveness
was so high. You can't help noticing it, for a peculiarity of Port
Willin is the number of its teashops and the vast quantity of
tea absorbed by its inhabitants. Not tea only – sandwiches,
cream cakes, ices, fruit salad with fresh pineapples. From
eleven o'clock in the morning you meet with couples and
groups of girls and young married women hurrying off to
their first tea. It was a real eleven o'clock function. Even the
business men knocked off and went to a café. And the same
thing happened in the afternoon. From four until half-past
six the streets were gay as a garden. Which reminds me, it was
early spring when I arrived and the town smelled of moist
earth and the first flowers. In fact, wherever one went one got
a strong whiff, like the whiff of violets in a wood, which was
enough in itself to make one feel like lingering. . . .

There was a theatre too, a big bare building plastered
over with red and blue bills which gave it an oriental look in
that blue air, and a touring company was playing 'San Toy',
I went my first evening. I found it, for some reason, fearfully

exciting. The inside smelled of gas, of glue and burnt paper. Whistling draughts cut along the corridors – a strong wind among the orchestra kept the palms trembling, and now and again the curtain blew out and there was a glimpse of a pair of large feet walking rapidly away. But what women! What girls in muslin dresses with velvet sashes and little caps edged with swansdown! In the intervals long ripples of laughter sounded from the stalls, from the dress-circle. And I leaned against a pillar that looked as though it was made of wedding-cake icing – and fell in love with whole rows at a time. . . .

Then I presented my letters, I was asked out to dine, and I met these charmers in their own homes. That decided it. They were something I had never known before – so gay, so friendly, so impressed with the idea of one's being an artist! It was rather like finding oneself in the playground of an extremely attractive girls' school.

I painted the Premier's daughter, a dark beauty, against a tree hung with long, bell-like flowers as white as wax. I painted a girl with a pigtail curled up on a white sofa playing with a pale-red fan . . . and a little blonde in a black jacket with pearl grey gloves. . . . I painted like fury.

I'm fond of women. As a matter of fact I'm a great deal more at my ease with women than I am with men. Because I've cultivated them, I suppose. You see, it's like this with me. I've always had enough money to live on, and the consequence is I have never had to mix with people more than I wished. And I've equally always had – well, I suppose you might call it a passion – for painting. Painting is far and away the most important thing in life – as I see it. But – my work's my own affair. It's the separate compartment which is me. No strangers allowed in. I haven't the smallest desire to explain what it is I'm after – or to hear other men. If people like my work I'm pleased. If they don't – well, if I was a shrugging person, I'd shrug. This sounds arrogant. It isn't; I know my limitations. But the truth about oneself always sounds arrogant, as no doubt you've observed.

But women – well, I can only speak for myself – I find the presence of women, the consciousness of women, an absolute necessity. I know they are considered a distraction, that the very Big Pots seal themselves in their hives to keep away. All I can say is work without women would be to me like dancing without music or food without wine or a sailing boat without a breeze. They just give me that . . . what is it? Stimulus is not enough; inspiration is far too much. That – well, if I knew what it is, I should have solved a bigger problem than my own! And problems aren't in my line.

I expected a mob at my Private View, and I got it, too. . . . What I hadn't reckoned on was that there would be no men. It was one thing to ask a painter fellow to knock you up something to the tune of fifty guineas or so, but it was quite another to make an ass of yourself staring. The Port Willin men would as soon have gazed into shops. True, when you came to Europe, you visited the galleries, but then you shop-gazed too. It didn't matter what you did in Europe. You could walk about for a week without being recognised.

So there were little Field and I absolutely alone among all that loveliness; it frightened him out of his life, but I didn't mind, I thought it rather fun, especially as the sightseers didn't hesitate to find my pictures amusing. I'm by no means an out-and-out modern, as they say; people, like violins and landscapes of telegraph poles, leave me cold. But Port Willin is still trying to swallow Rossetti, and Hope by Watts is looked upon as very advanced. It was natural my pictures should surprise them. The fat old Lady Mayoress became quite hysterical. She drew me over to one drawing; she patted my arm with her fan.

'I don't wonder you drew her slipping out,' she gurgled. 'And how depressed she looks! The poor dear never could have sat down in it. It's much too small. There ought to be a little cake of Pear's Soap on the floor.' And overcome by her own joke, she flopped on the little double bench that ran down the middle of the room, and even her fan seemed to laugh.

At that moment two girls passed in front of us. One I knew, a big fair girl called May Pollock, who pulled her companion by the sleeve. 'Daphne!' she said. 'Daphne!' And the other turned towards her, then towards us, smiled and was born, christened part of my world from that moment.

'Daphne!' Her quick, beautiful smile answered. . . .

Saturday morning was gloriously fine. When I woke up and saw the sun streaming over the polished floor I felt like a little boy who has been promised a picnic. It was all I could do not to telephone Daphne. Was she feeling the same? It seemed somehow such a terrific lark that we should be going off together like this, just with a couple of rucksacks and our bathing suits. I thought of other week-ends, the preparation, the emotional tension, the amount of managing they'd needed. But I couldn't really think of them; I couldn't be bothered, they belonged to another life. . . .

It seemed to me suddenly so preposterous that two people should be as happy as we were and not be happier. Here we were, alone, miles away from everybody, free as air, and in love with each other. I looked again at Daphne, at her slender shoulders, her throat, her bosom, and, passionately in love, I decided, with fervour: wouldn't it be rather absurd, then, to behave like a couple of children? Wouldn't she even, in spite of all she had said, be disappointed if we did? . . .

And I went off at a tremendous pace, not because I thought she'd run after me, but I did think she might call, or I might look round. . . .

It was one of those still, hushed days when the sea and the sky seem to melt into one another, and it is long before the moisture dries on the leaves and grasses. One of those days when the sea smells strong and there are gulls standing in a row on the sand. The smoke from our wood fire hung in the air and the smoke of my pipe mingled with it. I caught myself staring at nothing. I felt dull and angry. I couldn't get over the ridiculous affair. You see, my *amour propre* was wounded.

Monday morning was grey, cloudy, one of those mornings peculiar to the seaside when everything, the sea most of all, seems exhausted and sullen. There had been a very high tide, the road was wet – on the beach there stood a long line of sickly-looking gulls. . . .

When we got on board she sat down on one of the green benches and, muttering something about a pipe, I walked quickly away. It was intolerable that we should still be together after what had happened. It was indecent. I only asked – I only longed for one thing – to be free of this still, unsmiling and pitiful – that was the worst of it – creature who had been my playful Daphne.

For answer I telephoned her at once and asked if I might come and see her that evening. Her voice sounded grave, unlike the voice I remembered, and she seemed to deliberate. There was a long pause before she said, 'Yes – perhaps that would be best.'

'Then I shall come at half-past six.'

'Very well.'

And we went into a room full of flowers and very large art photographs of The Harbour by Night, A Misty Day, Moonrise over the Water, and I know I wondered if she admired them.

'Why did you send me that letter?'

'Oh, but I had to,' said Daphne. 'I meant every word of it. I only let you come to-night to . . . No, I know I shall disappoint you. I'm wiser than you are for all your experience. I shan't be able to live up to it. I'm not the person for you. Really I'm not!' . . .

unfinished

.

THE DOVES' NEST

After lunch Milly and her mother were sitting as usual on the balcony beyond the salon, admiring for the five-hundredth time the stocks, the roses, the small, bright grass beneath the palms, and the oranges against a wavy line of blue, when a card was brought them by Marie. Visitors at the Villa Martin were very rare. True, the English clergyman, Mr. Sandiman, had called, and he had come a second time with his wife to tea. But an awful thing had happened on that second occasion. Mother had made a mistake. She had said 'More tea, Mr. Sandybags?' Oh, what a frightful thing to have happened! How could she have done it? Milly still flamed at the thought. And he had evidently not forgiven them; he'd never come again. So this card put them both into quite a flutter.

Mr. Walter Prodger, they read. And then an American address, so very much abbreviated that neither of them understood it. Walter Prodger? But they'd never heard of him. Mother looked from the card to Milly.

'Prodger, dear?' she asked mildly, as though helping Milly to a slice of a never-before-tasted pudding.

And Milly seemed to be holding her plate back in the way she answered 'I – don't – know, Mother.'

'These are the occasions,' said Mother, becoming a little flustered, 'when one does so feel the need of our dear English servants. Now if I could just say, "What is he like, Annie?" I should know whether to see him or not. But he may be some common man, selling something – one of those American inventions for peeling things, you know, dear. Or he may even be some kind of foreign sharper.' Mother winced at the hard, bright little word as though she had given herself a dig with her embroidery scissors.

But here Marie smiled at Milly and murmured, 'C'est un très beau Monsieur.'

'What does she say, dear?'

'She says he looks very nice, Mother.'

'Well, we'd better –' began Mother. 'Where is he now, I wonder.'

Marie answered 'In the vestibule, Madame.'

In the hall! Mother jumped up, seriously alarmed. In the hall, with all those valuable little foreign things that didn't belong to them scattered over the tables.

'Show him in, Marie. Come, Milly, come dear. We will see him in the salon. Oh, why isn't Miss Anderson here?' almost wailed Mother.

But Miss Anderson, Mother's new companion, never was on the spot when she was wanted. She had been engaged to be a comfort, a support to them both. Fond of travelling, a cheerful disposition, a good packer and so on. And then, when they had come all this way and taken the Villa Martin and moved in, she had turned out to be a Roman Catholic. Half her time, more than half, was spent wearing

236

out the knees of her skirts in cold churches. It was really
too . . .

The door opened. A middle-aged, clean-shaven, very well
dressed stranger stood bowing before them. His bow was
stately. Milly saw it pleased Mother very much; she bowed her
Queen Alexandra bow back. As for Milly, she never could bow.
She smiled, feeling shy, but deeply interested.

'Have I the pleasure,' said the stranger very courteously,
with a strong American accent, 'of speaking with Mrs.
Wyndham Fawcett?'

'I am Mrs. Fawcett,' said Mother graciously, 'and this is my
daughter, Mildred.'

'Pleased to meet you, Miss Fawcett.' And the stranger
shot a fresh, chill hand at Milly, who grasped it just in time
before it was gone again.

'Won't you sit down?' said Mother, and she waved faintly at
all the gilt chairs.

'Thank you, I will,' said the stranger.

Down he sat, still solemn, crossing his legs and, most
surprisingly, his arms as well. His face looked at them over his
dark arms as over a gate.

'Milly, sit down, dear.'

So Milly sat down, too, on the Madame Récamier couch,
and traced a filet lace flower with her finger. There was a little
pause. She saw the stranger swallow; Mother's fan opened
and shut.

Then he said, 'I took the liberty of calling, Mrs. Fawcett,
because I had the pleasure of your husband's acquaintance
in the States when he was lecturing there some years ago. I

should like very much to renoo our – well – I venture to hope we might call it friendship. Is he with you at present? Are you expecting him out? I noticed his name was not mentioned in the local paper. But I put that down to a foreign custom, perhaps – giving precedence to the lady.'

And here the stranger looked as though he might be going to smile.

But as a matter of fact it was extremely awkward. Mother's mouth shook. Milly squeezed her hands between her knees, but she watched hard from under her eyebrows. Good, noble little Mummy! How Milly admired her as she heard her say, gently and quite simply, 'I am sorry to say my husband died two years ago.'

Mr. Prodger gave a great start. 'Did he?' He thrust out his under lip, frowned, pondered. 'I am truly sorry to hear that, Mrs. Fawcett. I hope you'll believe me when I say I had no idea your husband had . . . passed over.'

'Of course.' Mother softly stroked her skirt.

'I do trust,' said Mr. Prodger, more seriously still, 'that my inquiry didn't give you too much pain.'

'No, no. It's quite all right,' said the gentle voice.

But Mr. Prodger insisted. 'You're sure? You're positive?'

At that Mother raised her head and gave him one of her still, bright, exalted glances that Milly knew so well. 'I'm not in the least hurt,' she said, as one might say it from the midst of the fiery furnace.

Mr. Prodger looked relieved. He changed his attitude and continued. 'I hope this regrettable circumstance will not deprive me of your –'

'Oh, certainly not. We shall be delighted. We are always so pleased to know anyone who –' Mother gave a little bound, a little flutter. She flew from her shadowy branch on to a sunny one. 'Is this your first visit to the Riviera?'

'It is,' said Mr. Prodger. 'The fact is I was in Florence until recently. But I took a heavy cold there –'

'Florence so damp,' cooed Mother.

'And the doctor recommended I should come here for the sunshine before I started for home.'

'The sun is so very lovely here,' agreed Mother, enthusiastically.

'Well, I don't think we get too much of it,' said Mr. Prodger dubiously, and two lines showed at his lips. 'I seem to have been sitting around in my hotel more days than I care to count.'

'Ah, hotels are so very trying,' said Mother, and she drooped sympathetically at the thought of a lonely man in an hotel. . . . 'You are alone here?' she asked, gently, just in case . . . one never knew . . . it was better to be on the safe, the tactful side.

But her fears were groundless.

'Oh yes, I'm alone,' cried Mr. Prodger, more heartily than he had spoken yet, and he took a speck of thread off his immaculate trouser leg. Something in his voice puzzled Milly. What was it?

'Still, the scenery is so very beautiful,' said Mother, 'that one really does not feel the need of friends. I was only saying to my daughter yesterday I could live here for years without going outside the garden gate. It is all so beautiful.'

239

'Is that so?' said Mr. Prodger, soberly. He added, 'You have a very charming villa.' And he glanced round the salon. 'Is all this antique furniture genuine, may I ask?'

'I believe so,' said Mother. 'I was certainly given to understand it was. Yes, we love our villa. But, of course, it is very large for two, that is to say three, ladies. My companion, Miss Anderson, is with us. But unfortunately she is a Roman Catholic, and so she is out most of the time.'

Mr. Prodger bowed as one who agreed that Roman Catholics were very seldom in.

'But I am so fond of space,' continued Mother, 'and so is my daughter. We both love large rooms and plenty of them – don't we, Milly?'

This time Mr. Prodger looked at Milly quite cordially and remarked, 'Yes, young people like plenty of room to run about.'

He got up, put one hand behind his back, slapped the other upon it and went over to the balcony.

'You've a view of the sea from here,' he observed.

The ladies might well have noticed it; the whole Mediterranean swung before the windows.

'We are so fond of the sea,' said Mother, getting up, too.

Mr. Prodger looked towards Milly. 'Do you see those yachts, Miss Fawcett?'

Milly saw them.

'Do you happen to know what they're doing?' asked Mr. Prodger.

What they were doing? What a funny question! Milly stared and bit her lip.

'They're racing!' said Mr. Prodger, and this time he did actually smile at her.

'Oh yes, of course,' stammered Milly. 'Of course they are.' She knew that.

'Well, they're not always at it,' said Mr. Prodger, good-humouredly. And he turned to Mother and began to take a ceremonious farewell.

'I wonder,' hesitated Mother, folding her little hands and eyeing him, 'if you would care to lunch with us – if you would not be too dull with two ladies. We should be so very pleased.'

Mr. Prodger became intensely serious again. He seemed to brace himself to meet the luncheon invitation. 'Thank you very much, Mrs. Fawcett. I should be delighted.'

'That will be very nice,' said Mother warmly. 'Let me see. To-day is Monday – isn't it, Milly? Would Wednesday suit you?'

Mr. Prodger replied, 'It would suit me excellently to lunch with you on Wednesday, Mrs. Fawcett. At *mee-dee*, I presume, as they call it here.'

'Oh no! We keep our English times. At one o'clock,' said Mother.

And that being arranged, Mr. Prodger became more and more ceremonious and bowed himself out of the room.

Mother rang for Marie to look after him, and a moment later the big, glass hall-door shut.

'Well!' said Mother. She was all smiles. Little smiles like butterflies, alighting on her lips and gone again. 'That was an adventure, Milly, wasn't it, dear? And I thought he was such a very charming man, didn't you?'

Milly made a little face at Mother and rubbed her eye.

'Of course you did. You must have, dear. And his appearance was so satisfactory – wasn't it?' Mother was obviously
enraptured. 'I mean he looked so very well kept. Did you
notice his hands? Every nail shone like a diamond. I must say
I do like to see . . .'

She broke off. She came over to Milly and patted her big
collar straight.

'You do think it was right of me to ask him to lunch – don't
you, dear?' said Mother pathetically.

Mother made her feel so big, so tall. But she was tall. She
could pick Mother up in her arms. Sometimes, rare moods
came when she did. Swooped on Mother who squeaked like a
mouse and even kicked. But not lately. Very seldom now. . . .

'It was so strange,' said Mother. There was the still, bright,
exalted glance again. 'I suddenly seemed to hear Father
say to me "Ask him to lunch." And then there was some –
warning. . . . I think it was about the wine. But that I didn't
catch – very unfortunately,' she added, mournfully. She put
her hand on her breast; she bowed her head. 'Father is still so
near,' she whispered.

Milly looked out of the window. She hated Mother going
on like this. But of course she couldn't say anything. Out
of the window there was the sea and the sunlight silver on
the palms, like water dripping from silver oars. Milly felt a
yearning – what was it? – it was like a yearning to fly.

But Mother's voice brought her back to the salon, to the
gilt chairs, the gilt couches, sconces, cabinets, the tables with
the heavy-sweet flowers, the faded brocade, the pink-spotted

Chinese dragons on the mantelpiece and the two Turks' heads in the fireplace that supported the broad logs.

'I think a leg of lamb would be nice, don't you, dear?' said Mother. 'The lamb is so very small and delicate just now. And men like nothing so much as plain roast meat. Yvonne prepares it so nicely, too, with that little frill of paper lace round the top of the leg. It always reminds me of something – I can't think what. But it certainly makes it look very attractive indeed.'

Wednesday came. And the flutter that Mother and Milly had felt over the visiting card extended to the whole villa. Yes, it was not too much to say that the whole villa thrilled and fluttered at the idea of having a man to lunch. Old, flat-footed Yvonne came waddling back from market with a piece of gorgonzola in so perfect a condition that when she found Marie in the kitchen she flung down her great basket, snatched the morsel up and held it, rustling in its paper, to her quivering bosom.

'J'ai trouvé un morceau de gorgonzola,' she panted, rolling up her eyes as though she invited the heavens themselves to look down upon it. 'J'ai un morceau de gorgonzola ici pour un prr-ince, ma fille.' And hissing the word 'prr-ince' like light-ning, she thrust the morsel under Marie's nose. Marie, who was a delicate creature, almost swooned at the shock.

'Do you think,' cried Yvonne scornfully, 'that I would ever buy such cheese *pour ces dames*? Never. Never. *Jamais de ma vie*.' Her sausage finger wagged before her nose, and she minced in a dreadful imitation of Mother's French, 'We have none of us large appetites, Yvonne. We are very fond of boiled eggs and mashed potatoes and a nice, plain salad. Ah-Bah!' With a snort of contempt she flung away her shawl, rolled up her sleeves, and began unpacking the basket. At the bottom there was a flat bottle which, sighing, she laid aside.

'De quoi pour mes cors,' said she.

And Marie, seizing a bottle of Sauterne and bearing it off to the dining-room murmured, as she shut the kitchen door behind her, 'Et voilà pour les cors de Monsieur!'

The dining-room was a large room panelled in dark wood. It had a massive mantelpiece and carved chairs covered in crimson damask. On the heavy, polished table stood an oval glass dish decorated with little gilt swags. This dish, which it was Marie's duty to keep filled with fresh flowers, fascinated her. The sight of it gave her a *frisson*. It reminded her always, as it lay solitary on the dark expanse, of a little tomb. And one day, passing through the long windows on to the stone terrace and down the steps into the garden, she had the happy thought of so arranging the flowers that they would be appropriate to one of the ladies on a future tragic occasion. Her first creation had been terrible. *Tomb of Mademoiselle Anderson* in black pansies, lily-of-the-valley, and a frill of heliotrope. It gave her a most intense, curious pleasure to hand Miss Anderson the potatoes at lunch and at the same time to gaze beyond her at her triumph. It was like (*O ciel!*) – it was like handing potatoes to a corpse.

The *Tomb of Madame* was, on the contrary, almost gay. Foolish little flowers, half yellow, half blue, hung over the edge, wisps of green trailed across, and in the middle there was a large scarlet rose. *Cœur saignant*, Marie had called it. But it did not look in the least like a *cœur saignant*. It looked flushed and cheerful, like Mother emerging from the luxury of a warm bath.

Milly's, of course, was all white. White stocks, little white rose-buds, with a sprig or two of dark box edging. It was Mother's favourite.

Poor innocent! Marie, at the sideboard, had to turn her back when she heard Mother exclaim, 'Isn't it pretty, Milly? Isn't it sweetly pretty? Most artistic. So original.' And she had said to Marie, 'C'est très joli, Marie. Très original.'

Marie's smile was so remarkable that Milly, peeling a tangerine, remarked to Mother, 'I don't think she likes you to admire them. It makes her uncomfortable.'

But to-day – the glory of her opportunity made Marie feel quite faint as she seized her flower scissors. *Tombeau d'un beau Monsieur*. She was forbidden to cut the orchids that grew round the fountain basin. But what were orchids for if not for such an occasion? Her fingers trembled as the scissors snipped away. They were enough; Marie added two small sprays of palm. And back in the dining-room she had the happy idea of binding the palm together with a twist of gold thread deftly torn off the fringe of the dining-room curtains. The effect was superb. Marie almost seemed to see her *beau Monsieur*, very small, very small, at the bottom of the bowl, in full evening dress with a ribbon across his chest and his ears white as wax.

What surprised Milly, however, was that Miss Anderson should pay any attention to Mr. Prodger's coming. She rustled

245

to breakfast in her best black silk blouse, her Sunday blouse, with the large, painful-looking crucifix dangling over the front. Milly was alone when Miss Anderson entered the dining-room. This was unfortunate, for she always tried to avoid being left alone with Miss Anderson. She could not say exactly why; it was a feeling. She had the feeling that Miss Anderson might say something about God, or something fearfully intimate. Oh, she would sink through the floor if such a thing happened; she would expire. Supposing she were to say 'Milly, do you believe in our Lord?' Heavens! It simply didn't bear thinking about.

'Good morning, my dear,' said Miss Anderson, and her fingers, cold, pale, like church candles, touched Milly's cheeks.

'Good morning, Miss Anderson. May I give you some coffee?' said Milly, trying to be natural.

'Thank you, dear child,' said Miss Anderson, and laughing her light, nervous laugh, she hooked on her eyeglasses and stared at the basket of rolls. 'And is it to-day that you expect your guest?' she asked.

Now why did she ask that? Why pretend when she knew perfectly well? That was all part of her strangeness. Or was it because she wanted to be friendly? Miss Anderson was more than friendly; she was genial. But there was always this something. Was she spying? People said at school that Roman Catholics spied. . . . Miss Anderson rustled, rustled about the house like a dead leaf. Now she was on the stairs, now in the upstairs passage. Sometimes, at night, when Milly was feverish, she woke up and heard that rustle outside her door. Was Miss Anderson looking through the keyhole? And one night she actually had the idea that Miss Anderson had bored two holes in the wall above her head and was watching her from there. The feeling was so strong that next time she went into Miss Anderson's room her eyes flew to the spot. To her horror a large picture hung there. Had it been there before? . . .

'Guest?' The crisp breakfast roll broke in half at the word.

'Yes, I think it is,' said Milly vaguely, and her blue, flower-like eyes were raised to Miss Anderson in a vague stare.

'It will make quite a change in our little party,' said the much-too-pleasant voice. 'I confess I miss very much the society of men. I have had such a great deal of it in my life. I think that ladies by themselves are apt to get a little – h'm – h'm . . .' And helping herself to cherry jam, she spilt it on the cloth.

Milly took a large, childish bite out of her roll. There was nothing to reply to this. But how young Miss Anderson made her feel! She made her want to be naughty, to pour milk over her head or make a noise with a spoon.

'Ladies by themselves,' went on Miss Anderson, who realised none of this, 'are very apt to find their interests limited.'

'Why?' said Milly, goaded to reply. People always said that; it sounded most unfair.

'I think,' said Miss Anderson, taking off her eyeglasses and looking a little dim, 'it is the absence of political discussion.'

'Oh, politics!' cried Milly, airily. 'I hate politics. Father always said –' But here she pulled up short. She crimsoned. She didn't want to talk about Father to Miss Anderson.

'Oh! Look! Look! A butterfly!' cried Miss Anderson, softly and hastily. 'Look, what a darling!' Her own cheeks flushed a slow red at the sight of the darling butterfly fluttering so softly over the glittering table.

That was very nice of Miss Anderson – fearfully nice of her. She must have realised that Milly didn't want to talk about Father and so she had mentioned the butterfly on purpose. Milly smiled at Miss Anderson as she never had smiled at her before. And she said in her warm, youthful voice, 'He is a duck, isn't he? I love butterflies. I think they are great lambs.'

The morning whisked away as foreign mornings do. Mother had half decided to wear her hat at lunch.

'What do you think, Milly? Do you think as head of the house it might be appropriate? On the other hand, one does not want to do anything at all extreme.'

'Which do you mean, Mother? Your mushroom or the jampot?'

'Oh, not the jampot, dear.' Mother was quite used to Milly's name for it. 'I somehow don't feel myself in a hat without a brim. And to tell you the truth, I am still not quite certain whether I was wise in buying the jampot. I cannot help feeling that if I were to meet Father in it he would be a little too surprised. More than once lately,' went on Mother quickly, 'I have thought of taking off the trimming, turning it upside down and making it into a nice little workbag. What do you think, dear? But we must not go into it now, Milly. This is not the moment for such schemes. Come on to the balcony. I have told Marie we shall have coffee there. What about bringing out that big chair with the nice, substantial legs for Mr. Prodger? Men are so fond of nice, substantial . . . No, not by yourself, love! Let me help you.'

When the chair was carried out Milly thought it looked exactly like Mr. Prodger. It *was* Mr. Prodger admiring the view.

'No, don't sit down on it. You mustn't,' she cried hastily, as Mother began to subside. She put her arm through Mother's and drew her back into the salon.

Happily, at that moment there was a rustle and Miss Anderson was upon them. In excellent time, for once. She carried a copy of the *Morning Post*.

'I have been trying to find out from this,' said she, lightly tapping the newspaper with her eyeglasses, 'whether Congress is sitting at present. But unfortunately, after reading my copy right through, I happened to glance at the heading and discovered it was five weeks' old.'

Congress! Would Mr. Prodger expect them to talk about Congress? The idea terrified Mother. Congress! The American parliament, of course, composed of senators – grey-bearded old men in frock coats and turn-down collars, rather like missionaries. But she did not feel at all competent to discuss them.

'I think we had better not be too intellectual,' she suggested timidly, fearful of disappointing Miss Anderson, but more fearful still of the alternative.

'Still, one likes to be prepared,' said Miss Anderson. And after a pause she added softly, 'One never knows.'

Ah, how true that is! One never does. Miss Anderson and Mother seemed both to ponder this truth. They sat silent, with head bent, as though listening to the whisper of the words.

'One never knows,' said the pink-spotted dragons on the mantelpiece and the Turks' heads pondered. Nothing is known – nothing. Everybody just waits for things to happen as they were waiting there for the stranger who came walking towards them through the sun and shadow under the budding plane trees, or driving, perhaps, in one of the small, cotton-covered cabs. . . . An angel passed over the Villa Martin. In that moment of hovering silence something timid, something beseeching seemed to lift, seemed to offer itself, as the flowers in the salon, uplifted, gave themselves to the light.

Then Mother said, 'I hope Mr. Prodger will not find the scent of the mimosa too powerful. Men are not fond of flowers in a room as a rule. I have heard it causes actual hay-fever in some cases. What do you think, Milly? Ought we perhaps –' But there was no time to do anything. A long, firm trill sounded from the hall door. It was a trill so calm and composed and unlike the tentative little push they gave the bell that it brought them back to the seriousness of the moment. They heard a man's voice; the door clicked shut again. He was inside. A stick rattled on the table. There was a pause, and then the door handle of the salon turned and Marie, in frilled muslin cuffs and an apron shaped like a heart, ushered in Mr. Prodger.

Only Mr. Prodger, after all? But whom had Milly expected to see? The feeling was there and gone again that she would not have been surprised to see somebody quite different, before she realised this wasn't quite the same Mr. Prodger as before. He was smarter than ever; all brushed, combed, shining. The ears that Marie had seen white as wax flashed as if they had been pink enamelled. Mother fluttered up in her pretty little way, so hoping he had not found the heat of the day too trying to be out in . . . but happily it was a little early in the year for dust. Then Miss Anderson was introduced. Milly was ready this time for that fresh hand, but she almost gasped; it was so very chill. It was like a hand stretched out to you from the water. Then together they all sat down.

'Is this your first visit to the Riviera?' asked Miss Anderson, graciously, dropping her handkerchief.

'It is,' answered Mr. Prodger composedly, and he folded his arms as before. 'I was in Florence until recently, but I caught a heavy cold –'

'Florence is so –' began Mother, when the beautiful brass gong, that burned like a fallen sun in the shadows of the hall, began to throb. First it was a low muttering, then it swelled, it quickened, it burst into a clash of triumph under Marie's sympathetic fingers. Never had they been treated to such a performance before. Mr. Prodger was all attention.

'That's a very fine gong,' he remarked approvingly.

'We think it is so very oriental,' said Mother. 'It gives our little meals quite an Eastern flavour. Shall we . . .'

Their guest was at the door bowing.

'So many gentlemen and only one lady,' fluttered Mother. 'What I mean is the boot is on the other shoe. That is to say – come, Milly, come, dear.' And she led the way to the dining-room.

Well, there they were. The cold, fresh napkins were shaken out of their charming shapes and Marie handed the omelette. Mr. Prodger sat on Mother's right, facing Milly, and Miss Anderson had her back to the long windows. But after all – why should the fact of their having a man with them make such a difference? It did; it made all the difference. Why should they feel so stirred at the sight of that large hand outspread, moving among the wine glasses? Why should the sound of that loud, confident 'Ah-hm!' change the very look of the dining-room? It was not a favourite room of theirs as a rule; it was overpowering. They bobbed uncertainly at the pale table with a curious feeling of exposure. They were like those meek guests who arrive unexpectedly at the fashionable hotel, and are served with whatever may be ready, while the real luncheon, the real guests lurk important and contemptuous in the background. And although it was impossible for Marie to be other than deft, nimble and silent, what heart could she have in ministering to that most uninspiring of spectacles – three ladies dining alone?

Now all was changed. Marie filled their glasses to the brim as if to reward them for some marvellous feat of courage. These timid English ladies had captured a live lion, a real one, smelling faintly of eau de cologne, and with a tip of handkerchief showing, white as a flake of snow.

'He is worthy of it,' decided Marie, eyeing her orchids and palms.

Mr. Prodger touched his hot plate with appreciative fingers.

'You'll hardly believe it, Mrs. Fawcett,' he remarked, turning to Mother, 'but this is the first hot plate I've happened on since I left the States. I had begun to believe there were two things that just weren't to be had in Europe. One was a hot plate and the other was a glass of cold water. Well, the cold water one can do without; but a hot plate is more difficult. I'd got so discouraged with the cold wet ones I encountered everywhere that when I was arranging with Cook's Agency about my room here I explained to them "I don't mind where I go to. I don't care what the expense may be. But for mercy's sake find me an hotel where I can get a hot plate by ringing for it."'

Mother, though outwardly all sympathy, found this a little bewildering. She had a momentary vision of Mr. Prodger ringing for hot plates to be brought to him at all hours. Such strange things to want in any numbers.

'I have always heard the American hotels are so very well equipped,' said Miss Anderson. 'Telephones in all the rooms and even tape machines.'

Milly could see Miss Anderson reading that tape machine.

'I should like to go to America awfully,' she cried, as Marie brought in the lamb and set it before Mother.

'There's certainly nothing wrong with America,' said Mr. Prodger, soberly. 'America's a great country. What are they? Peas? Well, I'll just take a few. I don't eat peas as a rule. No, no salad, thank you. Not with the hot meat.'

'But what makes you want to go to America?' Miss Anderson ducked forward, smiling at Milly, and her eyeglasses fell into her plate, just escaping the gravy.

Because one wants to go everywhere, was the real answer.

But Milly's flower-blue gaze rested thoughtfully on Miss Anderson as she said, 'The ice-cream. I adore ice-cream.'

'Do you?' said Mr. Prodger, and he put down his fork; he seemed moved. 'So you're fond of ice-cream, are you, Miss Fawcett?'

Milly transferred her dazzling gaze to him. It said she was.

'Well,' said Mr. Prodger quite playfully, and he began eating again, 'I'd like to see you get it. I'm sorry we can't manage to ship some across. I like to see young people have just what they want. It seems right, somehow.'

Kind man! Would he have any more lamb?

Lunch passed so pleasantly, so quickly, that the famous piece of gorgonzola was on the table in all its fatness and richness before there had been an awkward moment. The truth was that Mr. Prodger proved most easy to entertain, most ready to chat. As a rule men were not fond of chat as Mother understood it. They did not seem to understand that it does not matter very much what one says; the important thing is not to let the conversation drop. Strange! Even the best of men ignored that simple rule. They refused to realise that conversation is like a dear little baby that is brought in to be handed round. You must rock it, nurse it, keep it on the move if you want it to keep on smiling. What could be simpler? But even Father . . . Mother winced away from memories that were not as sweet as memories ought to be.

All the same, she could not help hoping that Father saw what a successful little lunch party it was. He did so love to see Milly happy, and the child looked more animated than she had done for weeks. She had lost that dreamy expression, which, though very sweet, did not seem natural at her age. Perhaps what she wanted was not so much Easton's Syrup as taking out of herself.

'I have been very selfish,' thought Mother, blaming herself as usual. She put her hand on Milly's arm; she pressed it gently as they rose from the table. And Marie held the door open for the white and the grey figure; for Miss Anderson, who peered shortsightedly, as though looking for something; for Mr. Prodger, who brought up the rear, walking stately, with the benign air of a Monsieur who had eaten well.

Beyond the balcony, the garden, the palms and the sea lay bathed in quivering brightness. Not a leaf moved; the oranges were little worlds of burning light. There was the sound of grasshoppers ringing their tiny tambourines, and the hum of bees as they hovered, as though to taste their joy in advance, before burrowing close into the warm wide-open stocks and roses. The sound of the sea was like a breath, was like a sigh.

Did the little group on the balcony hear it? Mother's fingers moved among the black and gold coffee-cups; Miss Anderson brought the most uncomfortable chair out of the salon and sat down. Mr. Prodger put his large hand on to the yellow stone ledge of the balcony and remarked gravely, 'This balcony rail is just as hot as it can be.'

'They say,' said Mother, 'that the greatest heat of the day is at about half-past two. We have certainly noticed it is very hot then.'

'Yes, it's lovely then,' murmured Milly, and she stretched out her hand to the sun. 'It's simply baking!'

'Then you're not afraid of the sunshine?' said Mr. Prodger, taking his coffee from Mother. 'No, thank you. I won't take any cream. Just one lump of sugar.' And he sat down balancing the little, chattering cup on his broad knee.

'No, I adore it,' answered Milly, and she began to nibble the lump of sugar. . . .

unfinished

A CUP OF TEA

Rosemary Fell was not exactly beautiful. No, you couldn't have called her beautiful. Pretty? Well, if you took her to pieces. . . . But why be so cruel as to take anyone to pieces? She was young, brilliant, extremely modern, exquisitely well dressed, amazingly well read in the newest of the new books, and her parties were the most delicious mixture of the really important people and . . . artists – quaint creatures, discoveries of hers, some of them too terrifying for words, but others quite presentable and amusing.

Rosemary had been married two years. She had a duck of a boy. No, not Peter – Michael. And her husband absolutely adored her. They were rich, really rich, not just comfortably well off, which is odious and stuffy and sounds like one's grandparents. But if Rosemary wanted to shop she would go to Paris as you and I would go to Bond Street. If she wanted to buy flowers, the car pulled up at that perfect shop in Regent Street, and Rosemary inside the shop just gazed in her dazzled, rather exotic way, and said: 'I want those and those and those. Give me four bunches of those. And that jar of roses. Yes, I'll have all the roses in the jar. No, no lilac. I hate lilac. It's got no shape.' The attendant bowed and put the lilac out of sight, as though this was only too true; lilac was dreadfully shapeless. 'Give me those stumpy little tulips. Those red and white ones.' And she was followed to the car by a thin shop-girl staggering under an immense white paper armful that looked like a baby in long clothes. . . .

One winter afternoon she had been buying something in a little antique shop in Curzon Street. It was a shop she liked. For one thing, one usually had it to oneself. And then the man who kept it was ridiculously fond of serving her. He beamed whenever she came in. He clasped his hands; he was so gratified he could scarcely speak. Flattery, of course. All the same, there was something . . .

'You see, madam,' he would explain in his low respectful tones, 'I love my things. I would rather not part with them than sell them to someone who does not appreciate them, who has not that fine feeling which is so rare. . . .' And, breathing deeply, he unrolled a tiny square of blue velvet and pressed it on the glass counter with his pale finger-tips.

To-day it was a little box. He had been keeping it for her. He had shown it to nobody as yet. An exquisite little enamel box with a glaze so fine it looked as though it had been baked in cream. On the lid a minute creature stood under a flowery tree, and a more minute creature still had her arms round his neck. Her hat, really no bigger than a geranium petal, hung from a branch; it had green ribbons. And there was a pink cloud like a watchful cherub floating above their heads. Rosemary took her hands out of her long gloves. She always took off her gloves to examine such things. Yes, she liked it very much. She loved it; it was a great duck. She must have it.

And, turning the creamy box, opening and shutting it, she couldn't help noticing how charming her hands were against the blue velvet. The shopman, in some dim cavern of his mind, may have dared to think so too. For he took a pencil, leant over the counter, and his pale bloodless fingers crept timidly towards those rosy, flashing ones, as he murmured gently: 'If I may venture to point out to madam, the flowers on the little lady's bodice.'

'Charming!' Rosemary admired the flowers. But what was the price? For a moment the shopman did not seem to hear. Then a murmur reached her. 'Twenty-eight guineas, madam.'

'Twenty-eight guineas.' Rosemary gave no sign. She laid the little box down; she buttoned her gloves again. Twenty-eight guineas. Even if one is rich . . . She looked vague. She stared at a plump tea-kettle like a plump hen above the shopman's head, and her voice was dreamy as she answered: 'Well, keep it for me – will you? I'll . . .'

But the shopman had already bowed as though keeping it for her was all any human being could ask. He would be willing, of course, to keep it for her for ever.

The discreet door shut with a click. She was outside on the step, gazing at the winter afternoon. Rain was falling, and with the rain it seemed the dark came too, spinning down like ashes. There was a cold bitter taste in the air, and the new-lighted lamps looked sad. Sad were the lights in the houses opposite. Dimly they burned as if regretting something. And people hurried by, hidden under their hateful umbrellas. Rosemary felt a strange pang. She pressed her muff against her breast; she wished she had the little box, too, to cling to. Of course, the car was there. She'd only to cross the pavement. But still she waited. There are moments, horrible moments in life, when one emerges from shelter and looks out, and it's awful. One oughtn't to give way to them. One ought to go home and have an extra-special tea. But at the very instant of thinking that, a young girl, thin, dark, shadowy – where had she come from? – was standing at Rosemary's elbow and a voice like a sigh, almost like a sob, breathed: 'Madam, may I speak to you a moment?'

'Speak to me?' Rosemary turned. She saw a little battered creature with enormous eyes, someone quite young, no older than herself, who clutched at her coat-collar with reddened hands, and shivered as though she had just come out of the water.

'M-madam,' stammered the voice. 'Would you let me have the price of a cup of tea?'

'A cup of tea?' There was something simple, sincere in that voice; it wasn't in the least the voice of a beggar. 'Then have you no money at all?' asked Rosemary.

'None, madam,' came the answer.

'How extraordinary!' Rosemary peered through the dusk, and the girl gazed back at her. How more than extraordinary! And suddenly it seemed to Rosemary such an adventure. It was like something out of a novel by Dostoevsky, this meeting in the dusk. Supposing she took the girl home? Supposing she did do one of those things she was always reading about or seeing on the stage, what would happen? It would be thrilling. And she heard herself saying afterwards to the amazement of her friends: 'I simply took her home with me', as she stepped forward and said to that dim person beside her: 'Come home to tea with me.'

The girl drew back startled. She even stopped shivering for a moment. Rosemary put out a hand and touched her arm. 'I mean it,' she said, smiling. And she felt how simple and kind her smile was. 'Why won't you? Do. Come home with me now in my car and have tea.'

'You – you don't mean it, madam,' said the girl, and there was pain in her voice.

'But I do,' cried Rosemary. 'I want you to. To please me. Come along.'

The girl put her fingers to her lips and her eyes devoured Rosemary. 'You're – you're not taking me to the police station?' she stammered.

'The police station!' Rosemary laughed out. 'Why should I be so cruel? No, I only want to make you warm and to hear – anything you care to tell me.'

Hungry people are easily led. The footman held the door of the car open, and a moment later they were skimming through the dusk.

'There!' said Rosemary. She had a feeling of triumph as she slipped her hand through the velvet strap. She could have said, 'Now I've got you,' as she gazed at the little captive she had netted. But of course she meant it kindly. Oh, more than kindly. She was going to prove to this girl that – wonderful things did happen in life, that – fairy godmothers were real, that – rich people had hearts, and that women *were* sisters. She turned impulsively, saying: 'Don't be frightened. After all, why shouldn't you come back with me? We're both women. If I'm the more fortunate, you ought to expect . . .'

But happily at that moment, for she didn't know how the sentence was going to end, the car stopped. The bell was rung, the door opened, and with a charming, protecting, almost embracing movement, Rosemary drew the other into the hall. Warmth, softness, light, a sweet scent, all those things so familiar to her she never even thought about them, she watched that other receive. It was fascinating. She was like the rich little girl in her nursery with all the cupboards to open, all the boxes to unpack.

'Come, come upstairs,' said Rosemary, longing to begin to be generous. 'Come up to my room.' And, besides, she wanted to spare this poor little thing from being stared at by the servants; she decided as they mounted the stairs she would not even ring for Jeanne, but take off her things by herself. The great thing was to be natural!

And 'There!' cried Rosemary again, as they reached her beautiful big bedroom with the curtains drawn, the fire leaping on her wonderful lacquer furniture, her gold cushions and the primrose and blue rugs.

The girl stood just inside the door; she seemed dazed. But Rosemary didn't mind that.

'Come and sit down,' she cried, dragging her big chair up to the fire, 'in this comfy chair. Come and get warm. You look so dreadfully cold.'

'I daren't, madam,' said the girl, and she edged backwards.

'Oh, please,' – Rosemary ran forward – 'you mustn't be frightened, you mustn't, really. Sit down, and when I've taken off my things we shall go into the next room and have tea and be cosy. Why are you afraid?' And gently she half pushed the thin figure into its deep cradle.

But there was no answer. The girl stayed just as she had been put, with her hands by her sides and her mouth slightly open. To be quite sincere, she looked rather stupid. But Rosemary wouldn't acknowledge it. She leant over her, saying: 'Won't you take off your hat? Your pretty hair is all wet. And one is so much more comfortable without a hat, isn't one?'

There was a whisper that sounded like 'Very good, madam,' and the crushed hat was taken off.

'And let me help you off with your coat, too,' said Rosemary.

The girl stood up. But she held on to the chair with one hand and let Rosemary pull. It was quite an effort. The other scarcely helped her at all. She seemed to stagger like a child, and the thought came and went through Rosemary's mind, that if people wanted helping they must respond a little, just a little, otherwise it became very difficult indeed. And what was she to do with the coat now? She left it on the floor, and the hat too. She was just going to take a cigarette off the mantel-piece when the girl said quickly, but so lightly and strangely: 'I'm very sorry, madam, but I'm going to faint. I shall go off, madam, if I don't have something.'

'Good heavens, how thoughtless I am!' Rosemary rushed to the bell.

'Tea! Tea at once! And some brandy immediately!'

The maid was gone again, but the girl almost cried out: 'No, I don't want no brandy. I never drink brandy. It's a cup of tea I want, madam.' And she burst into tears.

It was a terrible and fascinating moment. Rosemary knelt beside her chair.

'Don't cry, poor little thing,' she said. 'Don't cry.' And she gave the other her lace handkerchief. She really was touched beyond words. She put her arm round those thin, bird-like shoulders.

Now at last the other forgot to be shy, forgot everything except that they were both women, and gasped out: 'I can't go on no longer like this. I can't bear it. I can't bear it. I shall do away with myself. I can't bear no more.'

'You shan't have to. I'll look after you. Don't cry any more. Don't you see what a good thing it was that you met me? We'll have tea and you'll tell me everything. And I shall arrange something. I promise. *Do* stop crying. It's so exhausting. Please!'

The other did stop just in time for Rosemary to get up before the tea came. She had the table placed between them. She plied the poor little creature with everything, all the sandwiches, all the bread and butter, and every time her cup was empty she filled it with tea, cream and sugar. People always said sugar was so nourishing. As for herself she didn't eat; she smoked and looked away tactfully so that the other should not be shy.

And really the effect of that slight meal was marvellous. When the tea-table was carried away a new being, a light, frail creature with tangled hair, dark lips, deep, lighted eyes, lay back in the big chair in a kind of sweet languor, looking at the blaze. Rosemary lit a fresh cigarette; it was time to begin.

'And when did you have your last meal?' she asked softly.

But at that moment the door-handle turned.

'Rosemary, may I come in?' It was Philip.

'Of course.'

He came in. 'Oh, I'm so sorry,' he said, and stopped and stared.

'It's quite all right,' said Rosemary, smiling. 'This is my friend, Miss –'

'Smith, madam,' said the languid figure, who was strangely still and unafraid.

'Smith,' said Rosemary. 'We are going to have a little talk.'

'Oh yes,' said Philip. 'Quite,' and his eye caught sight of the coat and hat on the floor. He came over to the fire and turned his back to it. 'It's a beastly afternoon,' he said curiously, still looking at that listless figure, looking at its hands and boots, and then at Rosemary again.

'Yes, isn't it?' said Rosemary enthusiastically. 'Vile.'

Philip smiled his charming smile. 'As a matter of fact,' said he, 'I wanted you to come into the library for a moment. Would you? Will Miss Smith excuse us?'

The big eyes were raised to him, but Rosemary answered for her: 'Of course she will.' And they went out of the room together.

'I say,' said Philip, when they were alone. 'Explain. Who is she? What does it all mean?'

Rosemary, laughing, leaned against the door and said: 'I picked her up in Curzon Street. Really. She's a real pick-up. She asked me for the price of a cup of tea, and I brought her home with me.'

'But what on earth are you going to do with her?' cried Philip.

'Be nice to her,' said Rosemary quickly. 'Be frightfully nice to her. Look after her. I don't know how. We haven't talked yet. But show her – treat her – make her feel –'

'My darling girl,' said Philip, 'you're quite mad, you know. It simply can't be done.'

'I knew you'd say that,' retorted Rosemary. 'Why not? I want to. Isn't that a reason? And besides, one's always reading about these things. I decided –'

'But,' said Philip slowly, and he cut the end of a cigar, 'she's so astonishingly pretty.'

'Pretty?' Rosemary was so surprised that she blushed. 'Do you think so? I – I hadn't thought about it.'

'Good Lord!' Philip struck a match. 'She's absolutely lovely. Look again, my child. I was bowled over when I came into your room just now. However . . . I think you're making a ghastly mistake. Sorry, darling, if I'm crude and all that. But let me know if Miss Smith is going to dine with us in time for me to look up *The Milliner's Gazette*.'

'You absurd creature!' said Rosemary, and she went out of the library, but not back to her bedroom. She went to her writing-room and sat down at her desk. Pretty! Absolutely lovely! Bowled over! Her heart beat like a heavy bell. Pretty! Lovely! She drew her cheque-book towards her. But no, cheques would be no use, of course. She opened a drawer and took out five pound notes, looked at them, put two back, and holding the three squeezed in her hand, she went back to her bedroom.

Half an hour later Philip was still in the library, when Rosemary came in.

'I only wanted to tell you,' said she, and she leaned against the door again and looked at him with her dazzled exotic gaze, 'Miss Smith won't dine with us to-night.'

Philip put down the paper. 'Oh, what's happened? Previous engagement?'

Rosemary came over and sat down on his knee. 'She insisted on going,' said she, 'so I gave the poor little thing a present of money. I couldn't keep her against her will, could I?' she added softly.

Rosemary had just done her hair, darkened her eyes a little, and put on her pearls. She put up her hands and touched Philip's cheeks.

'Do you like me?' said she, and her tone, sweet, husky, troubled him.

'I like you awfully,' he said, and he held her tighter. 'Kiss me.'

There was a pause.

Then Rosemary said dreamily: 'I saw a fascinating little box to-day. It cost twenty-eight guineas. May I have it?'

Philip jumped her on his knee. 'You may, little wasteful one,' said he.

But that was not really what Rosemary wanted to say.

'Philip,' she whispered, and she pressed his head against her bosom, 'am I *pretty*?'

HONEYMOON

And when they came out of the lace shop there was their own driver and the cab they called their own cab waiting for them under a plane tree. What luck! Wasn't it luck? Fanny pressed her husband's arm. These things seemed always to be happening to them ever since they – came abroad. Didn't he think so too? But George stood on the pavement edge, lifted his stick, and gave a loud 'Hi!' Fanny sometimes felt a little uncomfortable about the way George summoned cabs, but the drivers didn't seem to mind, so it must have been all right. Fat, good-natured, and smiling, they stuffed away the little newspaper they were reading, whipped the cotton cover off the horse, and were ready to obey.

'I say,' George said as he helped Fanny in, 'suppose we go and have tea at the place where the lobsters grow. Would you like to?'

'Most awfully,' said Fanny fervently, as she leaned back wondering why the way George put things made them sound so very nice.

'R-right, *bien*.' He was beside her. '*Allay*,' he cried gaily, and off they went.

Off they went, spanking along lightly, under the green and gold shade of the plane trees, through the small streets that smelled of lemons and fresh coffee, past the fountain square where women, with water-pots lifted, stopped talking to gaze after them, round the corner past the café, with its pink and white umbrellas, green tables, and blue siphons, and so to the sea front. There a wind, light, warm, came flowing over the boundless sea. It touched George, and Fanny it seemed to linger over while they gazed at the dazzling water. And George said, 'Jolly, isn't it?' And Fanny, looking dreamy, said, as she said at least twenty times a day since they – came abroad: 'Isn't it extraordinary to think that here we are quite alone, away from everybody, with nobody to tell us to go home, or to – to order us about except ourselves?'

George had long since given up answering 'Extraordinary!' As a rule he merely kissed her. But now he caught hold of her hand, stuffed it into his pocket, pressed her fingers, and said, 'I used to keep a white mouse in my pocket when I was a kid.'

'Did you?' said Fanny, who was intensely interested in everything George had ever done. 'Were you very fond of white mice?'

'Fairly,' said George, without conviction. He was looking at something, bobbing out there beyond the bathing steps. Suddenly he almost jumped in his seat. 'Fanny!' he cried. 'There's a chap out there bathing. Do you see? I'd no idea people had begun. I've been missing it all these days.' George glared at the reddened face, the reddened arm, as though he could not look away. 'At any rate,' he muttered, 'wild horses won't keep me from going in to-morrow morning.'

Fanny's heart sank. She had heard for years of the frightful dangers of the Mediterranean. It was an absolute death-trap.

Beautiful, treacherous Mediterranean. There it lay curled before them, its white, silky paws touching the stones and gone again. . . . But she'd made up her mind long before she was married that never would she be the kind of woman who interfered with her husband's pleasures, so all she said was, airily, 'I suppose one has to be very up in the currents, doesn't one?'

'Oh, I don't know,' said George. 'People talk an awful lot of rot about the danger.'

But now they were passing a high wall on the land side, covered with flowering heliotrope, and Fanny's little nose lifted. 'Oh, George,' she breathed. 'The smell! The most divine . . .'

'Topping villa,' said George. 'Look, you can see it through the palms.'

'Isn't it rather large?' said Fanny, who somehow could not look at any villa except as a possible habitation for herself and George.

'Well, you'd need a crowd of people if you stayed there long,' replied George. 'Deadly, otherwise. I say, it is ripping. I wonder who it belongs to.' And he prodded the driver in the back.

The lazy, smiling driver, who had no idea, replied, as he always did on these occasions, that it was the property of a wealthy Spanish family.

'Masses of Spaniards on this coast,' commented George, leaning back again, and they were silent until, as they rounded a bend, the big, bone-white hotel-restaurant came into view. Before it there was a small terrace built up against the sea, planted with umbrella palms, set out with tables, and at their approach, from the terrace, from the hotel, waiters came running to receive, to welcome Fanny and George, to cut them off from any possible kind of escape.

'Outside?'

Oh, but of course they would sit outside. The sleek manager, who was marvellously like a fish in a frock-coat, skimmed forward.

'Dis way, sir. Dis way, sir. I have a very nice little table,' he gasped. 'Just the little table for you, sir, over in de corner. Dis way.'

So George, looking most dreadfully bored, and Fanny, trying to look as though she'd spent years of life threading her way through strangers, followed after.

'Here you are, sir. Here you will be very nice,' coaxed the manager, taking the vase off the table, and putting it down again as if it were a fresh little bouquet out of the air. But George refused to sit down immediately. He saw through these fellows; he wasn't going to be done. These chaps were always out to rush you. So he put his hands in his pockets, and said to Fanny, very calmly, 'This all right for you? Anywhere else you'd prefer? How about over there?' And he nodded to a table right over the other side.

What it was to be a man of the world! Fanny admired him deeply, but all she wanted to do was to sit down and look like everybody else.

'I – I like this,' said she.

'Right,' said George hastily, and he sat down almost before Fanny, and said quickly, 'Tea for two and chocolate éclairs.'

'Very good, sir,' said the manager, and his mouth opened and shut as though he was ready for another dive under the water. 'You will not 'ave toasts to start with? We 'ave very nice toasts, sir.'

'No,' said George shortly. 'You don't want toast, do you, Fanny?'

'Oh, no, thank you, George,' said Fanny, praying the manager would go.

'Or perhaps de lady might like to look at de live lobsters in de tank while de tea is coming?' And he grimaced and smirked and flicked his serviette like a fin.

George's face grew stony. He said 'No' again, and Fanny bent over the table, unbuttoning her gloves. When she looked up the man was gone. George took off his hat, tossed it on to a chair, and pressed back his hair.

'Thank God,' said he, 'that chap's gone. These foreign fellows bore me stiff. The only way to get rid of them is simply to shut up as you saw I did. Thank Heaven!' sighed George again, with so much emotion that if it hadn't been ridiculous Fanny might have imagined that he had been as frightened of the manager as she. As it was she felt a rush of love for George. His hands were on the table, brown, large hands that she knew so well. She longed to take one of them and squeeze it hard. But, to her astonishment, George did just that thing. Leaning across the table, he put his hand over hers, and said, without looking at her, 'Fanny, darling Fanny!'

'Oh, George!' It was in that heavenly moment that Fanny heard a *twing-twing-tootle-tootle*, and a light strumming. There's going to be music, she thought, but the music didn't matter just then. Nothing mattered except love. Faintly smiling she gazed into that faintly smiling face, and the feeling was so blissful that she felt inclined to say to George, 'Let us stay here – where we are – at this little table. It's perfect, and the sea is perfect. Let us stay.' But instead her eyes grew serious.

'Darling,' said Fanny. 'I want to ask you something fearfully important. Promise me you'll answer. Promise.'

'I promise,' said George, too solemn to be quite as serious as she.

'It's this.' Fanny paused a moment, looked down, looked up again. 'Do you feel,' she said softly, 'that you really know me now? But really, really know *me*?'

It was too much for George. Know his Fanny? He gave a broad, childish grin. 'I should jolly well think I do,' he said emphatically. 'Why, what's up?'

Fanny felt he hadn't quite understood. She went on quickly: 'What I mean is this. So often people, even when they love each other, don't seem to – to – it's so hard to say – know each other perfectly. They don't seem to want to. And I think that's awful. They misunderstand each other about the most important things of all.' Fanny looked horrified. 'George, we couldn't do that, could we? We never could.'

'Couldn't be done,' laughed George, and he was just going to tell her how much he liked her little nose, when the waiter arrived with the tea and the band struck up. It was a flute, a guitar, and a violin, and it played so gaily that Fanny felt if she wasn't careful even the cups and saucers might grow little wings and fly away. George absorbed three chocolate éclairs,

Fanny two. The funny-tasting tea – 'Lobster in the kettle,' shouted George above the music – was nice all the same, and when the tray was pushed aside and George was smoking, Fanny felt bold enough to look at the other people. But it was the band grouped under one of the dark trees that fascinated her most. The fat man stroking the guitar was like a picture. The dark man playing the flute kept raising his eyebrows as though he was astonished at the sounds that came from it. The fiddler was in shadow.

The music stopped as suddenly as it had begun. It was then she noticed a tall old man with white hair standing beside the musicians. Strange she hadn't noticed him before. He wore a very high, glazed collar, a coat green at the seams, and shamefully shabby button boots. Was he another manager? He did not look like a manager, and yet he stood there gazing over the tables as though thinking of something different and far away from all this. Who could he be?

Presently, as Fanny watched him, he touched the points of his collar with his fingers, coughed slightly, and half-turned to the band. It began to play again. Something boisterous, reckless, full of fire, full of passion, was tossed into the air, was tossed to that quiet figure, which clasped its hands, and still with that far-away look, began to sing.

'Good Lord!' said George. It seemed that everybody was equally astonished. Even the little children eating ices stared, with their spoons in the air. . . . Nothing was heard except a thin, faint voice, the memory of a voice singing something in Spanish. It wavered, beat on, touched the high notes, fell again, seemed to implore, to entreat, to beg for something, and then the tune changed, and it was resigned, it bowed down, it knew it was denied.

Almost before the end a little child gave a squeak of laughter, but everybody was smiling – except Fanny and George. Is life like this too? thought Fanny. There are people like this. There is suffering. And she looked at that gorgeous sea, lapping the land as though it loved it, and the sky, bright with the brightness before evening. Had she and George the right to be so happy? Wasn't it cruel? There must be something else in life which made all these things possible. What was it? She turned to George.

But George had been feeling differently from Fanny. The poor old boy's voice was funny in a way, but, God, how it made you realise what a terrific thing it was to be at the beginning of everything, as they were, he and Fanny! George, too, gazed at the bright, breathing water, and his lips opened as if he could drink it. How fine it was! There was nothing like the sea for making a chap feel fit. And there sat Fanny, his Fanny, leaning forward, breathing so gently.

'Fanny!' George called to her.

As she turned to him something in her soft, wondering look made George feel that for two pins he would jump over the table and carry her off.

'I say,' said George, rapidly, 'let's go, shall we? Let's go back to the hotel. Come. Do, Fanny darling. Let's go now.'

The band began to play. 'Oh, God!' almost groaned George. 'Let's go before the old codger begins squawking again.'

And a moment later they were gone.

TAKING THE VEIL

It seemed impossible that anyone should be unhappy on such a beautiful morning. Nobody was, decided Edna, except herself. The windows were flung wide in the houses. From within there came the sound of pianos, little hands chased after each other and ran away from each other, practising scales. The trees fluttered in the sunny gardens, all bright with spring flowers. Street boys whistled, a little dog barked; people passed by, walking so lightly, so swiftly, they looked as though they wanted to break into a run. Now she actually saw in the distance a parasol, peach-coloured, the first parasol of the year.

Perhaps even Edna did not look quite as unhappy as she felt. It is not easy to look tragic at eighteen, when you are extremely pretty, with the cheeks and lips and shining eyes of perfect health. Above all, when you are wearing a French blue frock and your new spring hat trimmed with cornflowers. True, she carried under her arm a book bound in horrid black leather. Perhaps the book provided a gloomy note, but only by accident; it was the ordinary Library binding. For Edna had made going to the Library an excuse for getting out of the house to think, to realise what had happened, to decide somehow what was to be done now.

An awful thing had happened. Quite suddenly, at the
theatre last night, when she and Jimmy were seated side by
side in the dress-circle, without a moment's warning – in fact,
she had just finished a chocolate almond and passed the box
to him again – she had fallen in love with an actor. But – fallen
– in – love. . .

The feeling was unlike anything she had ever imagined
before. It wasn't in the least pleasant. It was hardly thrilling.
Unless you can call the most dreadful sensation of hopeless
misery, despair, agony and wretchedness, thrilling. Combined
with the certainty that if that actor met her on the pavement
after, while Jimmy was fetching their cab, she would follow
him to the ends of the earth, at a nod, at a sign, without giving
another thought to Jimmy or her father and mother or her
happy home and countless friends again. . . .

The play had begun fairly cheerfully. That was at the
chocolate almond stage. Then the hero had gone blind.
Terrible moment! Edna had cried so much she had to borrow
Jimmy's folded, smooth-feeling handkerchief as well. Not
that crying mattered. Whole rows were in tears. Even the
men blew their noses with a loud trumpeting noise and tried
to peer at the programme instead of looking at the stage.
Jimmy, most mercifully dry-eyed – for what would she have
done without his handkerchief? – squeezed her free hand,
and whispered 'Cheer up, darling girl!' And it was then she
had taken a last chocolate almond to please him and passed
the box again. Then there had been that ghastly scene with
the hero alone on the stage in a deserted room at twilight,
with a band playing outside and the sound of cheering

coming from the street. He had tried – ah! how painfully, how pitifully! – to grope his way to the window. He had succeeded at last. There he stood holding the curtain while one beam of light, just one beam, shone full on his raised sightless face, and the band faded away into the distance. . . .

It was – really, it was absolutely – oh, the most – it was simply – in fact, from that moment Edna knew that life could never be the same. She drew her hand away from Jimmy's, leaned back, and shut the chocolate box for ever. This at last was love!

Edna and Jimmy were engaged. She had had her hair up for a year and a half; they had been publicly engaged for a year. But they had known they were going to marry each other ever since they walked in the Botanical Gardens with their nurses, and sat on the grass with a wine biscuit and a piece of barley-sugar each for their tea. It was so much an accepted thing that Edna had worn a wonderfully good imitation of an engagement-ring out of a cracker all the time she was at school. And up till now they had been devoted to each other.

But now it was over. It was so completely over that Edna found it difficult to believe that Jimmy did not realise it too. She smiled wisely, sadly, as she turned into the gardens of the Convent of the Sacred Heart and mounted the path that led through them to Hill Street. How much better to know it now than to wait until after they were married! Now it was possible that Jimmy would get over it. No, it was no use deceiving herself; he would never get over it! His life was wrecked, was ruined; that was inevitable. But he was young . . . Time, people always said, Time might make a little, just a little difference. In forty years when he was an old man, he might be able to think of her calmly – perhaps. But she – what did the future hold for her?

Edna had reached the top of the path. There under a new-leafed tree, hung with little bunches of white flowers, she sat down on a green bench and looked over the Convent flower-beds. In the one nearest to her there grew tender stocks, with a border of blue, shell-like pansies, with at one corner a clump of creamy freesias, their light spears of green criss-crossed over the flowers. The Convent pigeons were tumbling high in the air, and she could hear the voice of Sister Agnes who was giving a singing lesson. *Ah-me*, sounded the deep tones of the nun, and *Ah-me*, they were echoed. . . .

If she did not marry Jimmy, of course she would marry nobody. The man she was in love with, the famous actor – Edna had far too much common-sense not to realise that would never be. It was very odd. She didn't even want it to be. Her love was too intense for that. It had to be endured, silently; it had to torment her. It was, she supposed, simply that kind of love.

'But, Edna!' cried Jimmy. 'Can you never change? Can I never hope again?'

Oh, what sorrow to have to say it, but it must be said. 'No, Jimmy, I will never change.'

Edna bowed her head; and a little flower fell on her lap, and the voice of Sister Agnes cried suddenly *Ah-no*, and the echo came, *Ah-no*. . . .

At that moment the future was revealed. Edna saw it all. She was astonished; it took her breath away at first. But, after all, what could be more natural? She would go into a convent . . . . Her father and mother do everything to dissuade her, in vain. As for Jimmy, his state of mind hardly bears thinking about. Why can't they understand? How can they add to her suffering like this? The world is cruel, terribly cruel! After a last scene when she gives away her jewellery and so on to her best friends – she so calm, they so broken-hearted – into a convent she goes. No, one moment. The very evening of her going is the actor's last evening at Port Willin. He receives by a strange messenger a box. It is full of white flowers. But there is no name, no card. Nothing? Yes, under the roses, wrapped in a white handkerchief, Edna's last photograph with, written underneath,

The world forgetting, by the world forgot.

Edna sat very still under the trees; she clasped the black book in her fingers as though it were her missal. She takes the name of Sister Angela. Snip! Snip! All her lovely hair is cut off. Will she be allowed to send one curl to Jimmy? It is contrived somehow. And in a blue gown with a white head-band Sister Angela goes from the convent to the chapel, from the chapel to the convent with something unearthly in her look, in her sorrowful eyes, and in the gentle smile with which she greets the little children who run to her. A saint! She hears it whispered as she paces the chill, wax-smelling corridors. A saint! And visitors to the chapel are told of the nun whose voice is heard above the other voices, of her youth, her beauty, of her tragic, tragic love. 'There is a man in this town whose life is ruined. . . .'

A big bee, a golden furry fellow, crept into a freesia, and the delicate flower leaned over, swung, shook; and when the bee flew away it fluttered still as though it were laughing. Happy, careless flower!

Sister Angela looked at it and said, 'Now it is winter.' One night, lying in her icy cell, she hears a cry. Some stray animal is out there in the garden, a kitten or a lamb or – well, whatever little animal might be there. Up rises the sleepless nun. All in white, shivering but fearless, she goes and brings it in. But next morning, when the bell rings for matins, she is found tossing in high fever . . . in delirium . . . and she never recovers. In three days all is over. The service has been said in the chapel, and she is buried in the corner of the cemetery reserved for the nuns, where there are plain little crosses of wood. Rest in Peace, Sister Angela. . . .

Now it is evening. Two old people leaning on each other come slowly to the grave and kneel down sobbing, 'Our daughter! Our only daughter!' Now there comes another. He is all in black; he comes slowly. But when he is there and lifts his black hat, Edna sees to her horror his hair is snow-white. Jimmy! Too late, too late! The tears are running down his face; he is crying *now*. Too late, too late! The wind shakes the leafless trees in the churchyard. He gives one awful bitter cry.

Edna's black book fell with a thud to the garden path. She jumped up, her heart beating. My darling! No, it's not too late. It's all been a mistake, a terrible dream. Oh, that white hair! How could she have done it? She has not done it. Oh, heavens! Oh, what happiness! She is free, young, and nobody knows her secret. Everything is still possible for her and

Jimmy. The house they have planned may still be built, the little solemn boy with his hands behind his back watching them plant the standard roses may still be born. His baby sister . . . But when Edna got as far as his baby sister, she stretched out her arms as though the little love came flying through the air to her, and gazing at the garden, at the white sprays on the tree, at those darling pigeons blue against the blue, and the Convent with its narrow windows, she realised that now at last for the first time in her life – she had never imagined any feeling like it before – she knew what it was to be in love, but – in – love!

THE FLY

'Y'are very snug in here,' piped old Mr. Woodifield, and he peered out of the great, green leather armchair by his friend the boss's desk as a baby peers out of its pram. His talk was over; it was time for him to be off. But he did not want to go. Since he had retired, since his . . . stroke, the wife and the girls kept him boxed up in the house every day of the week except Tuesday. On Tuesday he was dressed and brushed and allowed to cut back to the City for the day. Though what he did there the wife and girls couldn't imagine. Made a nuisance of himself to his friends, they supposed. . . . Well, perhaps so. All the same, we cling to our last pleasures as the tree clings to its last leaves. So there sat old Woodifield, smoking a cigar and staring almost greedily at the boss, who rolled in his office chair, stout, rosy, five years older than he, and still going strong, still at the helm. It did one good to see him.

Wistfully, admiringly, the old voice added, 'It's snug in here, upon my word!'

'Yes, it's comfortable enough,' agreed the boss, and he flipped the *Financial Times* with a paper-knife. As a matter of fact he was proud of his room; he liked to have it admired, especially by old Woodifield. It gave him a feeling of deep, solid satisfaction to be planted there in the midst of it in full view of that frail old figure in the muffler.

'I've had it done up lately,' he explained, as he had explained for the past – how many? – weeks. 'New carpet,' and he pointed to the bright red carpet with a pattern of large white rings. 'New furniture,' and he nodded towards the massive bookcase and the table with legs like twisted treacle. 'Electric heating!' He waved almost exultantly towards the five transparent, pearly sausages glowing so softly in the tilted copper pan.

But he did not draw old Woodifield's attention to the photograph over the table of a grave-looking boy in uniform standing in one of those spectral photographers' parks with photographers' storm-clouds behind him. It was not new. It had been there for over six years.

'There was something I wanted to tell you,' said old Woodifield, and his eyes grew dim remembering. 'Now what was it? I had it in my mind when I started out this morning.' His hands began to tremble, and patches of red showed above his beard.

Poor old chap, he's on his last pins, thought the boss. And, feeling kindly, he winked at the old man, and said jokingly, 'I tell you what. I've got a little drop of something here that'll do you good before you go out into the cold again. It's beautiful stuff. It wouldn't hurt a child.' He took a key off his watch-chain, unlocked a cupboard below his desk, and drew forth a dark, squat bottle. 'That's the medicine,' said he. 'And the man from whom I got it told me on the strict Q.T. it came from the cellars at Windsor Castle.'

Old Woodifield's mouth fell open at the sight. He couldn't have looked more surprised if the boss had produced a rabbit.

'It's whisky, ain't it?' he piped, feebly.

The boss turned the bottle and lovingly showed him the label. Whisky it was.

'D'you know,' said he, peering up at the boss wonderingly, 'they won't let me touch it at home.' And he looked as though he was going to cry.

'Ah, that's where we know a bit more than the ladies,' cried the boss, swooping across for two tumblers that stood on the table with the water-bottle, and pouring a generous finger into each. 'Drink it down. It'll do you good. And don't put any water with it. It's sacrilege to tamper with stuff like this. Ah!' He tossed off his, pulled out his handkerchief, hastily wiped his moustaches, and cocked an eye at old Woodifield, who was rolling his in his chaps.

The old man swallowed, was silent a moment, and then said faintly, 'It's nutty!'

But it warmed him; it crept into his chill old brain – he remembered.

'That was it,' he said, heaving himself out of his chair. 'I thought you'd like to know. The girls were in Belgium last week having a look at poor Reggie's grave, and they happened to come across your boy's. They're quite near each other, it seems.'

Old Woodifield paused, but the boss made no reply. Only a quiver in his eyelids showed that he heard.

'The girls were delighted with the way the place is kept,' piped the old voice. 'Beautifully looked after. Couldn't be better if they were at home. You've not been across, have yer?'

'No, no!' For various reasons the boss had not been across.

'There's miles of it,' quavered old Woodifield, 'and it's all as neat as a garden. Flowers growing on all the graves. Nice broad paths.' It was plain from his voice how much he liked a nice broad path.

The pause came again. Then the old man brightened wonderfully.

'D'you know what the hotel made the girls pay for a pot of jam?' he piped. 'Ten francs! Robbery, I call it. It was a little pot, so Gertrude says, no bigger than a half-crown. And she hadn't taken more than a spoonful when they charged her ten francs. Gertrude brought the pot away with her to teach 'em a lesson. Quite right, too; it's trading on our feelings. They think because we're over there having a look round we're ready to pay anything. That's what it is.' And he turned towards the door.

'Quite right, quite right!' cried the boss, though what was quite right he hadn't the least idea. He came round by his desk, followed the shuffling footsteps to the door, and saw the old fellow out. Woodifield was gone.

For a long moment the boss stayed, staring at nothing, while the grey-haired office messenger, watching him, dodged in and out of his cubby hole like a dog that expects to be taken for a run. Then: 'I'll see nobody for half an hour, Macey,' said the boss. 'Understand? Nobody at all.'

'Very good, sir.'

The door shut, the firm heavy steps recrossed the bright

carpet, the fat body plumped down in the spring chair, and leaning forward, the boss covered his face with his hands. He wanted, he intended, he had arranged to weep. . . .

It had been a terrible shock to him when old Woodifield sprang that remark upon him about the boy's grave. It was exactly as though the earth had opened and he had seen the boy lying there with Woodifield's girls staring down at him. For it was strange. Although over six years had passed away, the boss never thought of the boy except as lying unchanged, unblemished in his uniform, asleep for ever. 'My son!' groaned the boss. But no tears came yet. In the past, in the first months and even years after the boy's death, he had only to say those words to be overcome by such grief that nothing short of a violent fit of weeping could relieve him. Time, he had declared then, he had told everybody, could make no difference. Other men perhaps might recover, might live their loss down, but not he. How was it possible? His boy was an only son. Ever since his birth the boss had worked at building up this business for him; it had no other meaning if it was not for the boy. Life itself had come to have no other meaning. How on earth could he have slaved, denied himself, kept going all those years without the promise for ever before him of the boy's stepping into his shoes and carrying on where he left off?

And that promise had been so near being fulfilled. The boy had been in the office learning the ropes for a year before the war. Every morning they had started off together; they had come back by the same train. And what congratulations he had received as the boy's father! No wonder; he had taken to it marvellously. As to his popularity with the staff, every man jack of them down to old Macey couldn't make enough of the boy. And he wasn't in the least spoilt. No, he was just his bright natural self, with the right word for everybody, with that boyish look and his habit of saying, 'Simply splendid!'

But all that was over and done with as though it never had been. The day had come when Macey had handed him the telegram that brought the whole place crashing about his head. 'Deeply regret to inform you . . .' And he had left the office a broken man, with his life in ruins.

Six years ago, six years. . . . How quickly time passed! It might have happened yesterday. The boss took his hands from his face; he was puzzled. Something seemed to be wrong with him. He wasn't feeling as he wanted to feel. He decided to get up and have a look at the boy's photograph. But it wasn't a favourite photograph of his; the expression was unnatural. It was cold, even stern-looking. The boy had never looked like that.

At that moment the boss noticed that a fly had fallen into his broad inkpot, and was trying feebly but desperately to clamber out again. Help! help! said those struggling legs. But the sides of the inkpot were wet and slippery; it fell back again and began to swim. The boss took up a pen, picked the fly out of the ink, and shook it on to a piece of blotting-paper. For a fraction of a second it lay still on the dark patch that oozed round it. Then the front legs waved, took hold, and, pulling its small, sodden body up, it began the immense task of cleaning the ink from its wings. Over and under, over and under, went a leg along a wing, as the stone goes over and under the scythe. Then there was a pause, while the fly, seeming to stand on the tips of its toes, tried to expand first one wing and then the other. It succeeded at last, and, sitting down, it began, like a minute cat, to clean its face. Now one could imagine that the little front legs rubbed against each other lightly, joyfully. The horrible danger was over; it had escaped; it was ready for life again.

But just then the boss had an idea. He plunged his pen back into the ink, leaned his thick wrist on the blotting-paper, and as the fly tried its wings down came a great heavy blot. What would it make of that? What indeed! The little beggar seemed absolutely cowed, stunned, and afraid to move because of what would happen next. But then, as if painfully, it dragged itself forward. The front legs waved, caught hold, and, more slowly this time, the task began from the beginning.

He's a plucky little devil, thought the boss, and he felt a real admiration for the fly's courage. That was the way to tackle things; that was the right spirit. Never say die; it was only a question of . . . But the fly had again finished its laborious task, and the boss had just time to refill his pen, to shake fair and square on the new-cleaned body yet another dark drop. What about it this time? A painful moment of suspense followed. But behold, the front legs were again waving; the boss felt a rush of relief. He leaned over the fly and said to it tenderly, 'You artful little b . . .' And he actually had the brilliant notion of breathing on it to help the drying process. All the same, there was something timid and weak about its efforts now, and the boss decided that this time should be the last, as he dipped the pen deep into the inkpot.

It was. The last blot fell on the soaked blotting-paper, and the draggled fly lay in it and did not stir. The back legs were stuck to the body; the front legs were not to be seen.

'Come on,' said the boss. 'Look sharp!' And he stirred it with his pen – in vain. Nothing happened or was likely to happen. The fly was dead.

The boss lifted the corpse on the end of the paper-knife and flung it into the waste-paper basket. But such a grinding feeling of wretchedness seized him that he felt positively frightened. He started forward and pressed the bell for Macey.

'Bring me some fresh blotting-paper,' he said sternly, 'and look sharp about it.' And while the old dog padded away he fell to wondering what it was he had been thinking about before. What was it? It was . . . He took out his handkerchief and passed it inside his collar. For the life of him he could not remember.

THE CANARY

. . . You see that big nail to the right of the front door? I can scarcely look at it even now and yet I could not bear to take it out. I should like to think it was there always even after my time. I sometimes hear the next people saying, 'There must have been a cage hanging from there.' And it comforts me; I feel he is not quite forgotten.

. . . You cannot imagine how wonderfully he sang. It was not like the singing of other canaries. And that isn't just my fancy. Often, from the window, I used to see people stop at the gate to listen, or they would lean over the fence by the mock-orange for quite a long time – carried away. I suppose it sounds absurd to you – it wouldn't if you had heard him – but it really seemed to me that he sang whole songs with a beginning and an end to them.

For instance, when I'd finished the house in the afternoon, and changed my blouse and brought my sewing on to the verandah here, he used to hop, hop, hop from one perch to another, tap against the bars as if to attract my attention, sip a little water just as a professional singer might, and then break into a song so exquisite that I had to put my needle down to listen to him. I can't describe it; I wish I could. But it was always the same, every afternoon, and I felt that I understood every note of it.

. . . I loved him. How I loved him! Perhaps it does not matter so very much what it is one loves in this world. But love something one must. Of course there was always my little house and the garden, but for some reason they were never enough. Flowers respond wonderfully, but they don't sympathise. Then I loved the evening star. Does that sound foolish? I used to go into the backyard, after sunset, and wait for it until it shone above the dark gum tree. I used to whisper, 'There you are, my darling.' And just in that first moment it seemed to be shining for me alone. It seemed to understand this . . . something which is like longing, and yet it is not longing. Or regret – it is more like regret. And yet regret for what? I have much to be thankful for.

. . . But after he came into my life I forgot the evening star; I did not need it any more. But it was strange. When the Chinaman who came to the door with birds to sell held him up in his tiny cage, and instead of fluttering, fluttering, like the poor little goldfinches, he gave a faint, small chirp, I found myself saying, just as I had said to the star over the gum tree, 'There you are, my darling.' From that moment he was mine.

. . . It surprises me even now to remember how he and I shared each other's lives. The moment I came down in the morning and took the cloth off his cage he greeted me with a drowsy little note. I knew it meant 'Missus! Missus!' Then I hung him on the nail outside while I got my three young men their breakfasts, and I never brought him in until we had the house to ourselves again. Then, when the washing-up was done, it was quite a little entertainment. I spread a newspaper over a corner of the table, and when I put the cage on it he used to beat with his wings despairingly, as if he didn't know what was coming. 'You're a regular little actor,' I used to scold him. I scraped the tray, dusted it with fresh sand, filled his seed and water tins, tucked a piece of chickweed and half a chilli between the bars. And I am perfectly certain he understood and appreciated every item of this little performance. You see by nature he was exquisitely neat. There was never a speck on his perch. And you'd only to see him enjoy his bath to realise he had a real small passion for cleanliness. His bath was put in last. And the moment it was in he positively leapt into it. First he fluttered one wing, then the other, then he ducked his head and dabbled his breast feathers. Drops of water were scattered all over the kitchen, but still he would not get out. I used to say to him, 'Now that's quite enough. You're only showing off.' And at last out he hopped and, standing on one leg, he began to peck himself dry. Finally he gave a shake, a flick, a twitter and he lifted his throat – Oh, I can hardly bear to recall it. I was always cleaning the knives at the time. And it almost seemed to me the knives sang too, as I rubbed them bright on the board.

. . . Company, you see – that was what he was. Perfect company. If you have lived alone you will realise how precious that is. Of course there were my three young men who came in to supper every evening, and sometimes they stayed in the dining-room afterwards reading the paper. But I could not expect them to be interested in the little things that made my day. Why should they be? I was nothing to them. In fact, I overheard them one evening talking about me on the stairs as 'the Scarecrow'. No matter. It doesn't matter. Not in the least. I quite understand. They are young. Why should I mind? But I remember feeling so especially thankful that I was not quite alone that evening. I told him, after they had gone out. I said, 'Do you know what they call Missus?' And he put his head on one side and looked at me with his little bright eye until I could not help laughing. It seemed to amuse him.

. . . Have you kept birds? If you haven't all this must sound, perhaps, exaggerated. People have the idea that birds are heartless, cold little creatures, not like dogs or cats. My washerwoman used to say on Mondays when she wondered why I didn't keep 'a nice fox-terrier', 'There's no comfort, Miss, in a canary.' Untrue. Dreadfully untrue. I remember one night. I had had a very awful dream – dreams can be dreadfully cruel – even after I had woken up I could not get over it. So I put on my dressing-gown and went down to the kitchen for a glass of water. It was a winter night and raining hard. I suppose I was still half asleep, but through the kitchen window, that hadn't a blind, it seemed to me the dark was staring in, spying. And suddenly I felt it was unbearable that I had no one to whom I could say 'I've had such a dreadful dream,' or 'Hide me from the dark.' I even covered my face for a minute. And then there came a little 'Sweet! Sweet!' His cage was on the table, and the cloth had slipped so that a chink of light shone through. 'Sweet, Sweet!' said the darling little fellow again, softly, as much as to say, 'I'm here, Missus!

I'm here!' That was so beautifully comforting that I nearly cried.

. . . And now he's gone. I shall never have another bird, another pet of any kind. How could I? When I found him, lying on his back, with his eye dim and his claws wrung, when I realised that never again should I hear my darling sing, something seemed to die in me. My heart felt hollow, as if it was his cage. I shall get over it. Of course. I must. One can get over anything in time. And people always say I have a cheerful disposition. They are quite right. I thank God I have.

. . . All the same, without being morbid, and giving way to – to memories and so on, I must confess that there does seem to me something sad in life. It is hard to say what it is. I don't mean the sorrow that we all know, like illness and poverty and death. No, it is something different. It is there, deep down, deep down, part of one, like one's breathing. However hard I work and tire myself I have only to stop to know it is there, waiting. I often wonder if everybody feels the same. One can never know. But isn't it extraordinary that under his sweet, joyful little singing it was just this – sadness? – Ah, what is it? – that I heard.

FATHER AND THE GIRLS

At midday, Ernestine, who had come down from the mountains with her mother to work in the vineyards belonging to the hotel, heard the faint, far-away *chuff-chuff* of the train from Italy. Trains were a novelty to Ernestine; they were fascinating, unknown, terrible. What were they like as they came tearing their way through the valley, plunging between the mountains as if not even the mountains could stop them? When she saw the dark, flat breast of the engine, so bare, so powerful, hurled as it were towards her, she felt a weakness – she could have sunk to the earth. And yet she must look. So she straightened up, stopped pulling at the blue-green leaves, tugging at the long, bright-green, curly suckers, and, with eyes like a bird, stared. The vines were very tall. There was nothing to be seen of Ernestine but her beautiful, youthful bosom buttoned into a blue cotton jacket and her small, dark head covered with a faded cherry-coloured handkerchief.

Chiff-chuff-chaff. Chiff-chuff-chaff, sounded the train. Now a wisp of white smoke shone and melted. Now there was another, and the monster itself came into sight and snorting horribly drew up at a little, toy-like station five minutes away. The railway ran at the bottom of the hotel garden which was perched high and surrounded by a stone wall. Steps cut in the stone led to the terraces where the vines were planted. Ernestine, looking out from the leaves like a bright bird, saw the terrible engine and looked beyond it at doors swinging open, at strangers stepping down. She would never know who they were or where they had come from. A moment ago they were not here; perhaps by to-morrow they would be gone again. And looking like a bird herself, she remembered how, at home, in the late autumn, she had sometimes seen strange birds in the fir tree that were there one day and gone the next. Where from? Where to? She felt an ache in her bosom. Wings were tight-folded there. Why could she not stretch them out and fly away and away? . . .

From the first-class carriage tall, thin Emily alighted and gave her hand to Father, whose brittle legs seemed to wave in the air as they felt for the iron step. Taller, thinner Edith followed, carrying Father's light overcoat, his field-glasses on a strap, and his new Baedeker. The blond hotel porter came forward. Wasn't that nice? He could speak as good English as you or me. So Edith had no trouble at all in explaining how, as they were going on by the morning train to-morrow, they would only need their suit-cases and what was left in the compartment. Was there a carriage outside? Yes, a carriage was there. But if they cared to walk there was a private entrance through the hotel gardens. . . No, they wouldn't walk.

'You wouldn't care to walk, would you, Father dear?'

'No, Edith, I won't walk. Do you girls wanna walk?'

'Why no, Father, not without you, dear.'

And the blond hotel porter leading, they passed through the little knot of sturdy peasants at the station gate to where the carriage waited under a group of limes.

'Did you ever see anything as big as that horse, Edith!' cried Emily. She was always the first to exclaim about things.

'It is a very big horse,' sang Edith, more sober. 'It's a farm horse, from the look of it, and it's been working. See how hot it is.' Edith had so much observation. The big, brown horse, his sides streaked with dark sweat, tossed his head and the bells on his collar set up a loud jangling.

'Hu-yup!' called the young peasant driver warningly, from his seat on the high box.

Father, who was just about to get in, drew back, a little scared.

'You don't think that horse will run away with us, do you, Edith?' he quavered.

'Why no, Father dear,' coaxed Edith. 'That horse is just as tame as you or me.' So in they got, the three of them. And as the horse bounded forward his ears seemed to twitch in surprise at his friend the driver. Call that a load? Father and the girls weighed nothing. They might have been three bones, three broomsticks, three umbrellas bouncing up and down on the hard seats of the carriage. It was a mercy the hotel was so close. Father could never have stood that for more than a minute, especially at the end of a journey. Even as it was his face was quite green when Emily helped him out, straightened him, and gave him a little pull.

'It's shaken you, dear, hasn't it?' she said tenderly.

But he refused her arm into the hotel. That would create a wrong impression.

'No, no, Emily. I'm all right. All right,' said Father, as staggering a little he followed them through big glass doors into a hall as dim as a church and as chill and as deserted.

My! Wasn't that hall cold! The cold seemed to come leaping at them from the floor. It clasped the peaked knees of Edith and Emily; it leapt high as the fluttering heart of Father. For a moment they hesitated, drew together, almost gasped. But then out from the Bureau a cheerful young person, her smiling face spotted with mosquito bites, ran to meet them, and welcomed them with such real enthusiasm (in English too) that the chill first moment was forgotten.

'Aw-yes. Aw-yes. I can let you ave very naice rooms on de firs floor wid a lif. Two rooms and bart and dressing-room for de chentleman. Beautiful rooms wid sun but nort too hot. Very naice. Till to-morrow. I taike you. If you please. It is dis way. You are tired wid the churney? Launch is at half-pas tvelf. Hort worter? Aw-yes. It is wid de bart. If you please.'

Father and the girls were drawn by her cheerful smiles and becks and nods along a cloister-like corridor, into the lift and up, until she flung open a heavy, dark door and stood aside for them to enter.

'It is a suite,' she explained. 'Wid a hall and tree doors.' Quickly she opened them. 'Now I gaw to see when your luggage is gum.'

And she went.

'Well!' cried Emily.

Edith stared.

Father craned his thin, old neck, looking, too.

'Did you – ever see the like, Edith?' cried Emily, in a little rush.

And Edith softly clasped her hands. Softly she sang 'No, I never did, Emily. I've never seen anything just like this before.'

'Sims to me a nice room,' quavered Father, still hovering. 'Do you girls wanna change it?'

Change it! 'Why, Father dear, it's just the loveliest thing we've ever set eyes on, isn't it, Emily? Sit down, Father dear, sit down in the arm-chair.'

Father's pale claws gripped the velvet arms. He lowered himself; he sank with an old man's quick sigh.

Edith still stood, as if bewitched, at the door. But Emily ran over to the window and leaned out, quite girlish. . . .

For a long time now – for how long? – for countless ages – Father and the girls had been on the wing. Nice, Montreux, Biarritz, Naples, Mentone, Lake Maggiore, they had seen them all and many, many more. And still they beat on, beat on, flying as if unwearied, never stopping anywhere for long. But the truth was – Oh, better not inquire what the truth was. Better not ask what it was that kept them going. Or why the only word that daunted Father was the word – home. . . .

Home! To sit around, doing nothing, listening to the clock, counting up the years, thinking back . . . thinking! To stay fixed in one place as if waiting for something or somebody. No! no! Better far to be blown over the earth like the husk, like the withered pod that the wind carries and drops and bears aloft again.

'Are you ready, girls?'

'Yes, Father dear.'

'Then we'd better be off if we're to make that train.'

But oh, it was a weariness, it was an unspeakable weariness. Father made no secret of his age; he was eighty-four. As for Edith and Emily – well, he looked now like their elder brother. An old, old brother and two ancient sisters, so the lovely room might have summed them up. But its shaded brightness, its beauty, the flutter of leaves at the creamy stone windows seemed only to whisper 'Rest! Stay!'

Edith looked at the pale, green-panelled walls, at the doors that had lozenges and squares of green picked out in gold. She made the amazing discovery that the floor had the same pattern in wood that was traced on the high, painted ceiling. But the colour of the shining floor was marvellous; it was like tortoiseshell. In one corner there was a huge, tiled stove, milky white and blue. The low wooden bed, with its cover of quilted yellow satin, had sheaves of corn carved on the bed-posts. It looked to fanciful, tired Edith – yes – that bed looked as if it were breathing, softly, gently breathing. Outside the narrow, deep-set windows, beyond their wreaths of green, she could see a whole, tiny landscape bright as a jewel in the summer heat.

'Rest! Stay!' Was it the sound of the leaves outside? No, it was in the air; it was the room itself that whispered joyfully, shyly. Edith felt so strange that she could keep quiet no longer.

'This is a very old room, Emily,' she warbled softly. 'I know what it is. This hotel has not always been a hotel. It's been an old château. I feel as sure of that as that I'm standing here.' Perhaps she wanted to convince herself that she was standing there. 'Do you see that stove?' She walked over to the stove. 'It's got figures on it. Emily,' she warbled faintly, 'it's 1623.'

'Isn't that too wonderful!' cried Emily.

Even Father was deeply moved.

'1623? Nearly three hundred years old.' And suddenly, in spite of his tiredness, he gave a thin, airy, old man's chuckle. 'Makes yer feel quite a chicken, don't it?' said Father.

Emily's breathless little laugh answered him; it, too, was gay.

'I'm going to see what's behind that door,' she cried. And half running to the door in the middle wall she lifted the slender steel catch. It led into a larger room, into Edith's and her bedroom. But the walls were the same and the floor, and there were the same deep-set windows. Only, two beds instead of one stood side by side, with blue silk quilts instead of yellow. And what a beautiful old chest there was under the windows!

'Oh,' cried Emily, in rapture. 'Isn't it all too perfectly historical for words, Edith! It makes me feel –' She stopped, she looked at Edith who had followed her and whose thin shadow lay on the sunny floor. 'Queer!' said Emily, trying to put all she felt into that one word. 'I don't know what it is.'

Perhaps if Edith, the discoverer, had had time she might have satisfied Emily. But a knock sounded at the outer door; it was the luggage boy. And while he brought in their suit-cases there came from downstairs the ringing of the luncheon bell. Father mustn't be kept waiting. Once a bell had gone he liked to follow it up right then. So without even a glance at the mirror – they had reached the age when it is as natural to avoid mirrors as it is to peer into them when one is young – Edith and Emily were ready.

'Are you ready, girls?'

'Yes, Father dear.'

And off they went again, to the left, to the right, down a stone staircase with a broad, worn balustrade, to the left again, finding their way as if by instinct – Edith first, then Father, and Emily close behind.

But when they reached the *salle à manger*, which was as big as a ball-room, it was still empty. All gay, all glittering, the long French windows opened on to the green and gold garden, the *salle à manger* stretched before them. And the fifty little tables with the fifty pots of dahlias looked as if they might begin dancing with . . .

unfinished

PUBLISHER'S COMMENTARY

When she moved in to the Chalet des Sapins Katherine was at first too ill and exhausted to write. *Journal* 13 July: 'Well, I must confess I have had an idle day. God knows why. All was to be written, but I just didn't write it. I thought I could, but I felt tired after tea and rested instead. Is it good or bad in me to behave so? I have a sense of guilt, but at the same time I know that to rest is the very best thing I can do. . . . Above all else I do still lack application. It's not right. There is so much to do, and I do so little. Life would be almost perfect here if only when I was *pretending* to work I always was working. But that is surely not too hard. Look at the stories that wait and wait just at the threshold. Why don't I let them in? And their place would be taken by others who are lurking beyond just out there – waiting for the chance.'

14 July: '. . . take this morning, for instance. I don't want to write anything. It's grey; it's heavy and dull. And short stories seem unreal and not worth doing. I don't want to write; I want to *live*. What does she mean by that? It's not easy to say. But there you are!'

'. . . And yet I love this quiet clouded day. A bell sounds from afar; the birds sing one after another as if they called across the tree-tops. I love this settled stillness, and this feeling that, at any moment, down may come the rain. Where the sky is not grey, it is silvery white, streaked with little clouds. The only disagreeable feature of the day is the flies. They are really maddening, and there is nothing really to be done for them: I feel that about hardly anything.'

'**Sixpence**' may have been written at Baugy, near Montreux, where Katherine had stayed before going to Sierre, but her companion Ida Baker, in her book about their friendship, remembered it as being written at Montana. The story appeared in *The Sphere* on 6 August, so would have to have been written by mid-July. It was to have appeared in *The Garden Party* but was 'pulled' by Katherine in November because she thought it was sentimental and did not fit in; but was published posthumously in *Something Childish and Other Stories* (1924).

Letter 24 July, to Lady Ottoline Morrell: '. . . I can't imagine anything lovelier than this end of Switzerland. Once one loses sight of that hideous Lac Leman and *Co.* everything is different. Sierre, a little warm sunripe town in the valley, was so perfect that I felt I would like to live there. It has all the flowers of the South and it's gay and "queynt" and full of nightingales. But since we have come up the mountains it seems lovelier still. We have taken a small – not very small – chalet here for two years. It is quite remote – in a forest clearing. . . . The air feels wonderful but smells more wonderful still. I have never lived *in* a forest before, one steps out of the house and in a moment one is hidden among the trees. And there are little glades and groves full of flowers – with small ice-cold streams twinkling through. It is my joy to sit there on a tree trunk; if only one could make some small grasshoppery sound of praise to *someone* – thanks to *someone*. But who?

'. . . One beaming servant who wears peasant "bodies" and full skirts striped with velvet looks after everything. And though the chalet is so arcadian it *has* got a bathroom with hot water and central heating for the winter and a piano and thick carpets and sunblinds. I am too old not to rejoice in these creature comforts as well.

'The only person whom we see is my Cousin Elizabeth [von Arnim] who lives half an hour's scramble away. We exchange Chateaubriand and baskets of apricots and have occasional lovely talks which are rather like what talks in the after-life will be like, I imagine . . . ruminative, and reminiscent – although dear knows what it is really all about. How strange talking is – what mists rise and fall – how one loses the other and then thinks to have found the other – then down comes another soft final curtain. . . . But it is incredible – don't you feel – how mysterious and isolated we each of us are – at the last. I suppose one ought to make this discovery once and for all, but I seem to be always making it again.

'It seems to me that writers don't acknowledge it half enough. They pretend to know all there is in the parcel. But how *is* one to do it without seeming vague?

'. . . I keep on with my short stories. I have been doing a series for *The Sphere*, because it pays better than any other paper I know [ten guineas a story]. But now they are done I don't believe they are much good. Too simple. It is always the next story which is going to contain everything, and that next story is always just out of reach. One seems to be saving up for it.'

'**Mr. and Mrs. Dove**' was written in July (on thirteen pages of a school exercise book), published in *The Sphere* on 13 August and in *The Garden Party* in February 1922. KM wrote in her *Journal*: 'I finished *Mr. and Mrs. Dove* yesterday. I am not altogether pleased with it. It's a little bit made up. It's not inevitable. I mean to imply that those two may not be happy together – that that is the kind of reason for which a young girl marries. But have I done so? I don't think so. Besides, it's not *strong* enough. I want to be nearer – far, far nearer than that. I want to use all my force even when I am taking a fine line. And I have a sneaking notion that I have, at the end, used the Doves *unwarrantably*. *Tu sais ce que je veux dire*. I used them to round off something – didn't I? Is that quite my game? No, it's not. It's not quite the kind of truth I'm after. Now for "Susannah". All must be *deeply felt*.'

'**Susannah**', a fragment, abandoned after three beginnings in July, was published posthumously in *The Doves' Nest*.

'**An Ideal Family**', finished on 22 July, was published in *The Sphere* on 20 August and in *The Garden Party*. From KM's *Journal*: 'Finished "An Ideal Family" yesterday. It seems to me better than "The Doves", but still it's not good enough. I worked at it hard enough, God knows, and yet I didn't get the deepest truth out of the idea, even once. What *is* this feeling? I feel again that this kind of knowledge is too easy for me; it's even a kind of trickery. I know so much more. This looks and smells like a story, but I wouldn't buy it. I don't want to possess it – to live with it. NO. Once I have written two more, I shall tackle something different – a long story: "At the Bay", with more difficult relationships. That's the whole problem.'

The story was originally called 'Goodbye, my Treasure', the words that come into old Mr. Neave's mind at the end and which are in part homage perhaps to the words unspokenly addressed by the professor to Katya, his adoptive daughter, at the end of Chekhov's 'A Dreary Story'. Katherine was professional enough, or enough in need of *The Sphere*'s ten guineas (about £500 in today's terms), to know that even glancing references to Chekhov would be rather unsuitable in its pages.

What she could not know was how cruelly some intellectuals would mock her for writing the *Sphere* stories, and how they would tarnish her reputation; so that when 1922 came to be recognised as a key year for Modernism – it was the year of *The Waste Land*, *Ulysses*, *Jacob's Room*, Proust's last work, Brecht's first play, Rilke's *Duino Elegies* – her work was for a long time left out of the equation. Yet her self-chastisement for not getting the deepest truth, for trickery, is evidence that she knew exactly what she was doing. But what choice did she have?

'**Her First Ball**' was written on 25 July and published in *The Sphere* on 28 November 1921 and in *The Garden Party*. In the *Journal* Murry wrote that the following note appeared in the middle of the (now lost) manuscript, dated 25 July: 'All this! All that I write – all that I am – is on the border of the sea. It's a kind of playing. I want to put *all* my force behind it, but somehow, I *cannot*!' Lorna Sage has commented that even in this outwardly charming story, 'death is more or less openly a theme'. She also pointed out that the Sheridan girls and their brother have names out of *Little Women* – Meg, Jo and Laurie.

'One seems to read a lot here. It's the kind of house in which you go into a room to comb your hair, find *Gulliver's Travels* on the shelf behind the door and are immediately lost to the world. The bedroom walls are of wood; there are thick white carpets on some of the floors – outside the windows wide balconies and thick striped cotton blinds shut out the midday glare . . .' (29 July to Dorothy Brett).

'**At the Bay**', conceived on 23 July (cf. previous page), was begun in early August and finished, after nine uninterrupted hours writing, on 10 September. Katherine's biographer Antony Alpers believes that it was in part written in response to Lawrence's *Women in Love*, sent that month for Murry to review and containing a couple, Gerald and Gudrun, with a marked similarity to Murry and Katherine; that Katherine wanted, in her story, to emphasise the importance of family love and 'that nothing will save the world but love. But

[Lawrence's] tortured, satanic, demon love I think is all wrong.' 'At the Bay' was published in the *London Mercury* in January 1922 and in *The Garden Party*. 'As in the earlier "Prelude",' wrote Claire Tomalin in 1983, 'the comedy here has an absolutely sure note, and the point of these stories, the longest she wrote, does not lie in any twist of plot. They are about memory and understanding, about things not being what they seem; about order and escape and the hatred which inhabits Alice, Beryl and Linda. Katherine Mansfield is not remembering her childhood . . . [about which] her memories are all tender. . . . But the stories are a different matter: gently, tenderly even, she strips the family, exposing alongside its cheerful absurdities the pretensions and cruelty of the household.'

The story is constructed 'as a sequence of twelve linked episodes, in each of which indirect free form is used to explore the consciousness of one or more of the central characters. . . . The controlling narrative framework . . . is the description of the passage of a single day from dawn to dusk, the same frame employed by Virginia Woolf in *The Waves* [in which] two characteristically Modernist assumptions are conflated: man's life is no more than a single day, a flickering brief candle in the wider context of historical time; but, conversely, the whole of a man's life can be revealed during the course of a single day, even in one epiphanic moment' (C. Hanson and A. Gurr, *Katherine Mansfield*, 1981).

Letter 8 August (to Dorothy Brett): 'I must stop this letter & get on with my new story. Its called "At the Bay" & its (I hope) full of sand and seaweed and bathing dresses hanging over verandahs & sandshoes on window sills, and little pink "sea" convolvulus, and rather gritty sandwiches and the tide coming. And it smells (oh I *do* hope it smells) a little bit fishy.'

And to Dorothy Brett 12 September: 'I've just finished my new book. Finished last night at 10.30. Laid down the pen after writing "Thanks be to God". I wish there was a God. I am longing to 1) praise him 2) thank him. The title is "At the Bay". That's the name of the very long story in it – a continuation of "Prelude". It's about 60 pages. I've been at it all last night. My precious children have sat in here, playing cards. I've wandered about all sorts of places – in and out – I hope it is good. It is as good as I can do, and all my heart and soul is in it . . . every single bit. Oh God, I hope it gives pleasure to someone. . . . It is so strange to bring the dead to life again. There's my Grandmother, back in her chair with her pink knitting, there stalks my uncle over the grass; I feel as I write, "You are not dead, my darlings. All is remembered. I bow down to you. I efface myself so that you may live again through me in your richness and beauty." And one feels *possessed*. And then the place where it all happens. I have tried to make it as familiar to "you" as it is to me. You know the marigolds? You know those pools in the rocks, you know the mouse trap on the wash-house window-sill? And too, one tries to go deep – to speak to the secret self we all have – to acknowledge that. I mustn't say any more about it.'

And 15 October to Dorothy Brett: '. . . the *Mercury* is bringing out that very long seaweedy story of mine "At the Bay". I feel inclined to suggest to them to give away a spade an' bucket with each copy. . . .'

'**Marriage à la Mode**' was written on 11 August and published in *The Sphere* on 31 December 1921 and in *The Garden Party*. It bears close – some have thought too close – comparison with Chekhov's 'Not Wanted'.

'**The Voyage**', tentatively called 'Going to stay with her Granma', was finished on 14 August, published in *The Sphere* on 24 December and in *The Garden Party*. KM's *Journal* 11 August: 'I don't know how I may write this next story. It's so difficult. But I suppose I shall. The trouble is I am so infernally cold. . . . '

Letter to William Gerhardi 13 March 1922: '. . . how strange, how delightful it is you should feel as you do about "The Voyage". No one has mentioned it to me but Middleton Murry. But when I wrote that little story I felt that I was on that very boat, going down those stairs, smelling the smell of the saloon. And when the stewardess came in and said, "We're rather empty, we may pitch a little," I can't believe that my sofa did not pitch. And one moment I had a little bun of silk-white hair and a bonnet and the next I was Fenella hugging the swan neck umbrella. . . .'

'**A Married Man's Story**', unfinished, published in *The Doves' Nest*, had possibly been begun in 1918 but was worked on at the end of August. KM's *Journal*: '"I have been writing a story about an old man." She [Ida Baker] looked vague. "But I don't think I like old men – do you?" said she. "They *exude* so." This horrified me. It seemed so infernally petty, and more than that . . . it was the saying of a vulgar little mind.

Later: I think it was shyness.' It is possible that the following remark, in a letter to Dorothy Brett dated 1 October 1921, also refers to 'A Married Man's Story', meaning that KM returned to it again after a few weeks. 'I've started and torn up two bad stories & now I am in the middle of the third. Its about a hypocrite. My flesh creeps as I write about him and my eyes pop at his iniquities. . . .'

Claire Tomalin wrote in 1983: 'It departs boldly and effectively from Katherine Mansfield's usual imaginative territories, with its mystery and its curious, muted male narrator. It is a fragment that feels very like the beginning of a full-length novel; and it is thoroughly absorbing with its confession of a hypocrite and wife-hater who gradually wins the sympathies of the reader with his reminiscences of his own starved childhood. There is a flavour of Dickens; and of all her unfinished stories it is one that most cries out for completion.' For 'A Married Man's Story' Katherine used nineteen pages of a small exercise book in which she had already written 'Marriage à la Mode' and 'The Voyage'.

Letter to Dorothy Brett 29 August: ' . . . the Furies have had me until to-day. Something quite new for a change – high fever, deadly sickness and weakness. I haven't been able to lift my head from the pillow. I think it has been a break-down from too much work. I have felt exhausted with all those stories lately and yet – couldn't stop. . . .

'My stories for the *Sphere* are all done – thank the Lord! I have had copies with ILLUSTRATIONS! [by W. Smithson Broadhead] Oh, Brett! such fearful horrors. All my dear people looking like – well – Harrod's 29/6 crêpe de chine blouses and young tailors' gents, and my old men – stuffy old woolly sheep. It's a sad trial. I am at present embedded in a terrific story, but it still frightens me' [this was probably 'A Married Man's Story' but could equally well have referred to 'At the Bay'].

In September KM wrote in her *Journal*: 'I am stuck beyond words, and again it seems to me that what I am doing has *no form*! I ought to finish my book of *stories first* and then, when it's gone, really get down to my novel . . .

'Why I should be so passionately determined to disguise this, I don't quite know. But here I lie, pretending, as Heaven knows how often I have before, to write. Supposing I were to give up this pretence and really did try? Supposing I only wrote half a page in a day – it would be half a page to the good; and I should at least be training my mind to get into the habit of regular performance. As it is, every day sees me further off my goal. *And*, once I had this book finished, I'm free to start the real one. *And* it's a question of money.

'But my idea, even of the short story, has changed rather, lately. . . .'

'**The Garden Party**' (the title was sometimes hyphenated, but not always) was begun on 9 October and finished on 14 October, on KM's 33rd birthday; it was written on nineteen loose sheets. Much cut, it was first published in the *Westminster Gazette* on 18 February 1922 and in *The Garden Party* in the same month. KM wrote at the end of the manuscript: 'This is a moderately successful story, and that's all. It's somehow, in the episode at the lane, scamped.' The story is based on the day in 1907, when Katherine was eighteen and living in New Zealand, when her mother gave a garden party at the family home at 75 Tinakori Road, Wellington. It again describes the Sheridans, who appeared in 'Her First Ball'.

Journal 16 October: 'Another radiant day. J is typing my last story, "The Garden Party", which I finished on my birthday. It took me nearly a month to "recover" from "At the Bay". I made at least three false starts. But I could not get away from the sound of the sea, and Beryl fanning her hair at the window. These things would not *die down*. But now I'm not at all sure about that story. It seems to me it's a little "wispy" – not what it might have been. "The Garden Party" is better. But that is not *good enough*, either . . .'

Letter to William Gerhardi 13 March 1922: '. . . that is what I tried to convey in "The Garden Party". The diversity of life and how we try to fit in everything, Death included. That is bewildering for a person of Laura's age. She feels things ought to happen differently. First one and then another. But life isn't like that. We haven't the ordering of it. Laura says, "But all these things must not happen at once." And Life answers, "Why not? How are they divided from each other." And they *do* all happen, it is inevitable. And it seems to me there is beauty in that inevitability.'

October, letter to Elizabeth von Arnim: 'I am just at the beginning of a new story, which I may turn into a serial. Clement Shorter [editor of *The Sphere*] wants one. But he stipulates for thirteen "curtains" and an adventure note! Thirteen curtains! And my stories haven't even a wisp of blind cord as a rule. I have never been able to manage curtains. I don't think I shall be able to see such a wholesale *hanging* through.'

Letter (to John Galsworthy) 25 October : 'I have just finished a new book which is to be published at the New Year. And now I am "thinking out" a long story about a woman which has been in my mind for years. But it is difficult. I want her whole life to be in it – a sense of time – and the feeling of "farewell". For by the time the story is told her life is over. One tells it in taking leave of her. . . . Not one of these modern women but one of those old-fashioned kind who seemed to have such a rich being, to live in such a living world. Is it fancy? Is it just that the harvest of the past is gathered? Who shall say?'

'**The Doll's House**' was written between 24 and 30 October and was published in the *Nation & the Athenaeum* on 4 February 1922 and in *The Doves' Nest*. Between draft versions (called first 'The Washerwoman's Children' and then 'At Karori', based on real people there) KM jotted down a list of ideas for her next collection of short stories. (L. = London, N.Z. = New Zealand.)

October 27: 'Stories for my new book.

N.Z. *Honesty*: The Doctor, Arnold Cullen, and his wife Lydia, and Archie the friend.

L. *Second Violin*: Alexander and his friend in the train. Spring – spouting rain. *Wet lilac.*

N.Z. *Six Years After*: A wife and husband on board a steamer. The cold buttons. They see someone who reminds them.

L. *Life like Logs of Driftwood*: This wants to be a long, very well-written story. The men are important, especially the lesser man. It wants a good deal of working . . . newspaper office.

N.Z. *A Weak Heart*: Ronnie on his bike in the evening, with his hands in his pockets, *doing marvels*, by that dark tree at the corner of May Street. Edie and Ronnie.

L. *Widowed*: Geraldine and Jimmie: a house overlooking Sloane Street and Square. Wearing those buds at her heart. 'Married or not married. . . .' From Autumn to Spring.

N.Z. *Our Maude*: Husband and wife play duets and ǎ ōne ǎ t̄wo ǎ thr̄ee ǎ ōne ǎ t̄wo thr̄ee ōne! His white waistcoats. Wifeling and Mahub! What a girl you are!

N.Z. *At Karori*: The little lamp. I seen it. And then they were silent. (*Finito*: October 30, 1921.)

I wish that *my* silence were only a two-minute one!'

Journal, October: 'I wonder why it should be so very difficult to be humble. I do not think I am a good writer; I realise my faults better than anyone else could realise them. I know exactly where I fail. And yet, when I have finished a story and before I have begun another, I catch myself *preening* my feathers. It is disheartening. There seems to be some bad old pride in my heart; a root of it that puts out a thick shoot on the slightest provocation. . . . This interferes very much with work. One can't be calm, clear, good as one must be, while it goes on. . . . One must learn, one must practise, to *forget* oneself. I can't tell the truth about Aunt Anne unless I am free to look into her life without self-consciousness. Oh God! I am divided still. I am bad, I fail in my personal life. I lapse into impatience, temper, vanity, and so I fail as thy priest. Perhaps poetry will help. . . .'

'**Six Years After**', unfinished fragment, begun in October (but thought by Murry also to have been worked on in November 1922, which would mean that it was in fact the last surviving page Katherine ever wrote), published in *The Doves' Nest*. The time-lapse referred to in the title links the story to the death of KM's brother in Flanders in October 1915.

'**Widowed**' – unfinished, published in *The Doves' Nest*, was probably written between KM finishing 'The Doll's House' on October 30 and a *Journal* entry for 21 November which says: 'I have begun two stories [the other was possibly '**Second Violin**', also unfinished, published in *The Doves' Nest*], but then told them and they [the stories] felt betrayed. It is absolutely fatal to give way to this temptation. . . .'

But it is possible that 'Widowed' was in fact started in August, just after 'Marriage à la Mode' was finished, and that 'Second Violin' was begun on 16 September.

Letter 21 November (to William Gerhardi): 'You know, if I may speak in confidence, I shall not be "fashionable" long. They will find me out; they will be disgusted; they will shiver in dismay. I like such awfully unfashionable things – and people. I like sitting on doorsteps, and talking to the old woman who brings quinces, and going for picnics in a jolting little waggon, and listening to the kind of music they play in public gardens on warm evenings, and talking to captains of shabby little steamers, and in fact, to all kinds of people in all kinds of places . . . you see I am not a high-brow. Sunday lunches and very intricate conversations on Sex and that "fatigue" which is so essential and that awful "brightness" which is even more essential – these things I flee from. I'm in love with life, terribly.'

'**Weak Heart**', unfinished fragments (apparently of the opening and closing passages, with some portions inbetween), published in *The Doves' Nest*, probably begun in September and abandoned in November. *Journal* 21 November: 'To-day I began to write, seriously, "The Weak Heart" – a story which fascinates me *deeply*. What I feel it needs so peculiarly is a very subtle variation of "tense" from the present to the past and back again – and softness, lightness, and the feeling that all is in bud, with a play of humour over the character of Ronnie. And the feeling of the Thorndon Baths, the wet, moist, oozy . . . no, I know how it must be done.'

Journal 24 November: 'These last days I have been awfully rebellious. Longing for something. I feel uprooted. I want things that J. can so easily do without, that aren't natural to him. I long for them. But then, stronger than all these desires, is the other, which is to *make good* before I do anything else. The sooner the books are written, the sooner I shall be well, the sooner my wishes will be in sight of fulfilment. That is sober truth, of course. . . . Why am I troubled every single day of my life by the nearness of death and its inevitability? I am really diseased on that point. And I can't speak of it. If I tell J. it makes him unhappy. If I don't tell him, it leaves me to fight it. I am tired of the battle. No one knows how tired.

To-night, when the evening-star shone through the side-window and the mountains were so lovely, I sat there thinking of death. Of all there was to do – of Life, which is so lovely – and of the fact that my body is a prison. But this state of mind is *evil*. It is only by acknowledging that I, being what I am, had to suffer *this* in order to do the work I am here to perform. It is only by acknowledging it, by being thankful that work was not taken away from me, that I shall recover. I am weak where I must be strong.

And today – Saturday – less than ever. But no matter. I have progressed . . . a little. I have realised *what* it is to be done – the strange barrier to be crossed from thinking it to writing it . . . Daphne.'

'**Daphne**', unfinished fragment, was published in *The Doves' Nest*, begun 26 November.

'**The Doves' Nest**', unfinished, published in *The Doves' Nest*, was begun in early 1922. *Journal* 1 January: 'Wrote "The Doves' Nest" this afternoon. I was in no mood to write; it seemed impossible. Yet when I had finished three pages, they were all right. This is a proof (never to be too often proved) that once one has thought out a story nothing remains but the *labour*.' 2 January: 'I have not done the work I should have done. I shirk the lunch party. This is very bad. In fact I am disgusted with myself. There must be a change from now on. What I chiefly admire in Jane Austen is that what she promises, she performs, ie. if Sir T is to arrive, we have his arrival at length, and it's excellent and exceeds our expectations. This is rare; it is also my very weakest point. Easy to see why. . . .' 5 January: 'I managed to work a little. Broke through. This is a great relief.' 7 January: 'I wrote at my story, but did not finish the lunch party as I ought to have done. How *very* bad this is!'

The title of 'The Doves' Nest' has overtones of Henry James and was to be about an American in Europe. It was unfinished partly because Katherine felt she had to turn to magazine stories again in order to pay for more medical treatment. To Dorothy Brett 9 January: 'I'm working at such a big story that I still can only just see the end in my imagination . . . the longest by far I've ever written. It's called 'The Doves' Nest' . . . . And to William Gerhardi 14 June: 'I am in the middle of a very long story written in the same style – horrible expression! – as "The Daughters of the Late Colonel". I enjoy writing it so much that even after I am asleep, I go on. The scene is the South of France in early spring. There is a real love story in it, too, and rain, buds, frogs, a thunderstorm, pink spotted Chinese dragons. There is no happiness greater than this leading a *double life*. But it's mysterious, too. How is it possible to be here in this remote, deserted hotel and at the same time to be leaning out of the window of the Villa Martin listening to the rain thrumming so gently on the leaves and smelling the night-scented stocks with Milly? (I shall be awfully disappointed if you don't like Milly.)'

'**A Cup of Tea**' 11 January 1922, published in the *Storyteller* in May 1922 (alongside a story by the popular writer Ethel M.Dell) and in *The Doves' Nest*, cf. *Journal* 11 January: 'Wrote and finished "A Cup of Tea". It took about 4–5 hours. . . . There is no feeling to be compared with the feeling of having written and finished a story. I did not go to sleep, but nothing mattered. There it was, *new* and complete.'

Journal 17 January: 'Chekhov made a mistake in thinking that if he had had more time he would have written more fully, described the rain, and the midwife and the doctor having tea. The truth is one can get only *so much* into a story; there is always a sacrifice. One has to leave out what one knows and longs to use. Why? I haven't any idea, but there it is. It's always a kind of race to get in as much as one can before it *disappears*.'

'**Honeymoon**' was published in the *Nation & the Athenaeum* on 29 April 1922 and in *The Doves' Nest*. This story is not mentioned anywhere by Katherine Mansfield, so accurate dating is impossible. However, in 1923 John Middleton Murry placed its writing between that of 'A Cup of Tea' and 'Taking the Veil'. Claire Tomalin also places it at this period and has written: 'It is difficult not to recall that it was written when Katherine Mansfield knew herself to be dying, when she was herself the spectre at any feast, a *memento mori* for all who saw her.

The light touch is the sign of artistry; it is also the sign of courage.'

'**Taking the Veil**' was written on 24 January, published in the *Sketch* on 22 February and in *The Doves' Nest*. 'It took me about 3 hours to write finally. But I had been thinking over the *decor* and so on for weeks – nay, months, I believe. I can't say how thankful I am to have been born in NZ, to know Wellington as I do, and to have it to range about in. Writing about the convent seemed so natural. I suppose I have not been in the grounds more than twice. But it is one of the places that remains as vivid as ever.'

Despite this period of intense creativity and relative calm, Katherine was becoming restless and, unfortunately encouraged by Ida, began to think about going to Paris for treatment. As Murry wrote, she turned to 'two alternative and in essence contradictory notions: one, that there was a physical or medical technique which would abolish her disease and annihilate her limitations; the other that there was a psychological or spiritual technique which would enable her to ignore them.'

Journal 29 January: 'Tidied all my papers. Tore up and ruthlessly destroyed much. This is always a great satisfaction. Whenever I prepare for a journey I prepare as though for death. Should I never return, all is in order. This is what life has taught me.'

On 30 January Katherine Mansfield left the Chalet des Sapins for Paris.

'**The Fly**' was written at the Victoria Palace Hotel in Montparnasse in February and published in the *Nation & the Athenaeum* on 18 March and in *The Doves' Nest*.

On 4 June Katherine and Murry returned to a hotel at Randogne-sur-Sierre.

'**The Canary**', the last short story she ever completed, was begun in Paris (where a woman opposite the hotel used to look after canaries in a cage) and finished on 7 July at a hotel in Sierre itself, to which she had moved without Murry. It was published in *The Doves' Nest*.

'**Father and the Girls**', a fragment that was typed, suggesting that it was originally part of something complete, was written in late July 1922 and published in *The Doves' Nest*; its setting is the hotel at Sierre.

On 14 August Katherine made her will. Two days later she left Sierre for London, where she spent six weeks before going to Paris; on 16 October she went on to Fontainebleau, to try and find the 'spiritual technique' referred to by Murry. Here she died on 9 January 1923.

Persephone Books publishes the following titles: